And The

Forecast

Called for Rain...

Novel By Kim Carter

Published by Raven South Publishing

Atlanta, Georgia 30324, USA

Copyright © 2016 by Kim Carter

Cover Design by www.mariondesigns.com

Editing by Antrina Franklin~Booked Right Editing

Interior Design by Lissha Sadler~Writing Royalty Promotions

Library of Congress Control Number: 2018933820

ISBN 978-1-947140-11-0 (paperback)

For speaking engagements, interviews, and book copies, please get in touch with Raven South Publishing:info@ravensouthpublishing.com.

Dedication

To Kelly Keylon, President of Raven South Publishing, and official *bestie*. I'm so grateful that God saw fit for our paths to cross. My life has never been the same since.

"I knew when I met you an adventure was going to happen."

-W.T.P.

Acknowledgments

At the completion of every book, I find myself mourning as I say good-bye to characters that I've grown to love, and at times, despise. As the last word is written, I reflect on all of the people that helped me along the way, either with research, ideas, friendship, or love. I can't allow them to go unrecognized, for their contributions made this novel possible.

Many thanks to the following: First and foremost, as always, my other half, my confidant, my shoulder to lean on… My husband Julius. It has been an honor to be your wife, and I love you more than mere words could ever manage to express.

To John Cross, of the Fulton County Medical Examiner's Office, many thanks for the years of help that you've given me with answered emails and phone calls. You've been invaluable in my writing.

To Keith Saunders, the best cover designer in the universe! You make my books come to life long before anyone opens them. You rock!!!

To Randy New, who went to bat for me when I was ready to give up. I'll never forget your adamant words, "I will NOT be a part of splitting the baby!" Thanks for making me be strong when I wanted to be weak. I'm still searching for an hourglass without any sand! Ha!

To Greg Headrick, thanks for the road trips, some that turned into road trips from hell, but we won't go there, and for being my friend. Where are our mint green bikes already?

To Lisa Mobley-Putnam who listened to me read my raw manuscripts on our many road trips. What a trooper and good friend you have been.

Lastly, to Raven South Publishing, what an unprecedented honor it is to represent your publishing house.

Note To Readers

I hope you enjoyed reading And The Forecast Called For Rain. I'd appreciate it if you would post a review on the site you purchased it from, as well as on Amazon and Goodreads. I'm grateful for every one I receive. Feel free to contact me on Facebook and my website if you have any questions or thoughts about the stories. I love hearing from readers.

Very best regards,

Kim

BOOK
EXCELLENCE
AWARDS
FINALIST

AND THE
FORECAST
CALLED FOR RAIN

AUTHOR OF *DEADLY ODDS*

KIM CARTER

Chapter 1

The wind whistled as the trees bent over, back and forth, touching their long, crooked fingers to the ground. Erin cringed as she leaned closer to the windshield to concentrate on her driving.

"Damn," she said aloud. "Why didn't I listen? I should've spent the night at the lodge." The margaritas had left a sour taste in her mouth, and her head ached as she rounded the next sharp curve.

There was far too much work waiting for her and deadlines didn't take thunderstorms into consideration. Her watch noted it was well after nine and Erin wondered just how much she expected to accomplish after the hour-long drive. Stubborn and determined, she'd said her good-byes and gotten into the old sputtering Mercedes.

The rain was unrelenting, inundating the windshield with swollen gushes of water. The wipers had long since lost their choice of how rapidly she needed them to perform, moving back and forth far too slowly to keep up with the demand. Grudgingly, Erin pulled

1

over, placed the gear into park, stretching her neck from side to side, then backward as far as her muscles would allow.

Her work kept her constantly stressed, making antidepressants a virtual necessity. Erin had been working for *The Seattle Times* for almost four years now, and loved her work, demanding as it always remained.

The job had been offered to her the year she'd graduated from Washington State, making her grateful she had struggled all the way through to remain at the top of her class. Erin's professors had insisted she had a knack for journalism and it'd been proven more than enough times for the paper to consider her a necessary part of their staff.

As the rain continued to pound the car, her mind filled with rambling thoughts. The latest column was about a murder in an affluent neighborhood. There'd been a *smoking gun* with the suspect immediately turning himself in to the police. It was an open and shut case and an easy one to write.

Erin appreciated those because they allowed more time for her independent research. With a serial killer on the loose in the small town of Sierra Hills, adjacent to the big city of Seattle, she was feeling the adrenaline rush that kept her investigations sharp and consistent. Her editor, although impressed with her past case-cracking skills, was adamant not to turn her loose on any wild goose chases. They relied too heavily on her daily column.

Erin used both hands to rub her eyes as violently as she could stand, and then massaged the stress knots forming in her neck. The loud strikes on the driver's side window shattered her thoughts. The rain was plummeting down, and she wondered how anyone could tolerate being out in the elements.

Contemplating whether to roll down her window or open the door, Erin felt the cold wind enter the car. Before her loud gasp could be completed, a large hand wrapped around her mouth and nose. All she could think about was getting air into her lungs but sleepiness engulfed her as the world turned black.

Chapter 2

Jennifer Hadley rambled through her junk drawers, searching for a candle. The smooth feel of wax soon rubbed across her palm as she pulled it quickly from the mass of other objects. With her lighter ready, the warming candlelight soon filtered throughout the room. She was grateful now for having taken her shower earlier. The lights had been out for over ten minutes and Jennifer had given up hope for their quick return.

Glancing at her watch, she was anxious for Ashley to return from the store. Jennifer's frustration over her leaving had turned into worry. The two young roommates were constantly barraged with safety tips, and it hadn't been a good time for her to leave the apartment alone. Beer and video rentals could've waited.

As her concerns grew, she heard the key turning in the lock. "Damn it, Ashley," Jennifer snapped. "I've been worried sick."

"The rain slowed me down," she answered, oblivious to the concerned anger in her friend's voice. The bag holding the beer was drenched and soggy. Jennifer took it out of her hands while Ashley pulled the movies from her jacket.

"The movies won't be necessary," Jennifer said, sarcasm still remaining in her voice.

"The electricity will be back on soon," Ashley said, taking time to roll her eyes at her friend. "Hand me a beer." The two twisted off their caps and settled back onto the plush sofa. It'd been one of their greatest thrift store finds. They sat silently for a few minutes until Ashley spoke. "At least it's Friday. We don't have to worry about work tomorrow."

"You're right. I thought the weekend would never come!" Jennifer said, sinking her teeth into a cold slice of pizza. Two beers later, the lights returned. They were well into the second film when they both drifted off to sleep. A light tapping on the apartment door startled them awake. Groggy, the girls looked at each other in confusion.

"What time is it?" Jennifer asked, looking down at her watch. It was well after midnight. Ashley went to the door and asked who was there.

"What is wrong with you?" Jennifer whispered.

A young man's voice on the other side of the door sounded quiet, almost afraid. "I broke down a couple of hours ago. The rain finally let up enough for me to get out. Could I use your phone? Actually, if you could just hand a phone out to me; I wouldn't expect you to let a stranger in."

Ashley looked through the small peephole but couldn't make out much about the man except that he was soaking wet. Although she was cautious, it didn't mean she was heartless.

"Just a minute," Ashley said. Cracking the door, she reached around to hand him the phone. The cheap metal door swung forcibly open, striking her in the collarbone and knocking her on her back. With her briefly debilitated, Jennifer was fair game. He swiftly wrapped the duct tape across her mouth and around both wrists.

Shoving her down next to her roommate, he unwrapped more tape, doing the same to Ashley. Her loud whimpering suggested her collarbone was broken. Jennifer closed her eyes tightly as she listened to Ashley's painful moans. He grunted and strained as he pulled them both up onto the couch.

"How quaint, you have candlelight waiting for me. You two ladies should be more careful. Haven't you ever been warned about strangers?"

He wasn't certain but thought he saw a flash of recognition in Jennifer's eyes before they rolled back in her head from the agony of the pain.

Chapter 3

The rain finally subsided around eight o'clock the next morning, leaving shiny prisms of oil leaking from passing vehicles. The late model gray Mercedes sat vacant along Interstate 82, looking like any other stalled vehicle along the deserted stretch of highway. It was four o'clock that afternoon before a state patrolman pulled up behind it.

Running the tags gave no indication it'd been stolen, but he decided to check it out anyway. The first things he'd noticed were the unlocked doors and the purse on the passenger's seat, making the hair on the back of his neck stand up. He'd seen this twice before and neither time had ended well. Speaking slowly and clearly into the radio, the trooper asked for crime scene investigators to be dispatched to the scene.

Canvassing the surrounding areas, Trooper Andrew Cohen searched for other evidence that might lead to a body. The rain hadn't helped to preserve any evidence. He followed a path, adjacent to the car, into the surrounding woods. Four feet into the dripping trees, Cohen saw her. He didn't see any blood, but it was painfully obvious she'd been brutalized. Bruises covered every visible part of her. Tugging at briars, it took him a several minutes to reach her. Her eyes were swollen shut, but he could see her chest lightly rising and falling.

"Ma'am, ma'am," he spoke quietly in her ear.

"Can you hear me?" Cohen waited patiently for a response that didn't come. Panic kicked in as he grabbed the radio, now slick from the dampness of the previous night's rain.

"I need an ambulance, ASAP!" he screamed into the mouthpiece. "I have a young, Caucasian woman, mid-twenties. Her breaths are shallow, pulse is faint, and she's incoherent."

The operator answered with the calmness with which she was trained. "Ten-four. We'll dispatch EMS."

Trooper Cohen didn't offer a response, instead concentrated on the young woman before him. He reached to cradle her head, then thought better of it. The possibilities of her having a spinal injury were high.

With a beating like the one she'd sustained, it'd be hard to assess the damage that'd been done. He pushed her wet hair off her face and studied her. It was impossible to estimate what she'd looked like before the attack.

She didn't appear to have on any jewelry but this situation wouldn't be considered a robbery. Any assailant would've taken her purse or its contents, and they certainly wouldn't have zipped it back up. It was obviously an intentional oversight by the perpetrator to let the police know he wasn't concerned about it appearing to be a robbery. Ballsy, really.

The wails of sirens could be heard in the distance as Trooper Cohen heaved a deep sigh of relief at the sounds of backup. Crime scene investigators arrived seconds before the ambulance, giving them just enough time to snap a couple of photos of the victim where she lay.

Trooper Cohen assisted the two paramedics as they moved her over to the backboard. She never moved or even whimpered. His shoulders slumped as he stood and watched the ambulance pull away.

Cohen wondered what her family would say when they were notified. He wondered if she had any children, a husband, or a boyfriend… and he wondered… who in the hell could do such a thing?

The investigators located her driver's license in her purse and dispatched a unit to her apartment. They'd wait to see if anyone was there. Trooper Cohen was no longer needed at the scene, so he slid behind the steering wheel, exhausted from witnessing such a tragedy. He pulled away, thankful he'd stopped. Maybe it'd made a difference.

Chapter 4

It was late Monday afternoon when Ashley Gregory's mother became concerned. Her job had phoned to inquire about her daughter's unexpected absence, and when she couldn't reach either her cell phone or home phone, she grew frantic. Ashley's apartment was only fourteen miles away, but she called the police department anyway. Maybe they could reach her quicker. Mrs. Gregory found comfort in the fact Jennifer hadn't called. Certainly, she would've if anything were wrong.

A unit from the Sierra Hills Police arrived within ten minutes, only to find the door of the apartment unlocked. They pulled their weapons, as was standard operating procedure for calls such as this. It only took a couple of steps inside the door to see the seriousness of the call.

The partners had joined the force together five years earlier. This was their first murder, and it stopped them both in their tracks. Several seconds passed before they thought to speak into their radio. Neither of them took a step toward to the victims. It wasn't necessary. They were obviously deceased.

The officers were startled by a wounded scream behind them. Mrs. Gregory ran to her daughter, and neither was able to stop her. She grabbed Ashley by her shoulders shaking her wildly. "Come on, Sweetheart!" she screamed. "Wake up for your mother. It's not too late. We can get you to the hospital."

Officer Martin Reynolds was the first to step toward her, his face crimson with disbelief.

"Ma'am," he said gently. "I need you to step away. We can't help her now."

The grief-stricken mother wasn't listening, just steadily rocking the young woman in her arms and whispering to her softly. A knot rose in Reynolds's throat as he slowly pried the woman's arms from her daughter, gently lifting her to her feet. She made it two steps before collapsing.

Time seemed to stand still. Neither officer was sure how much time had lapsed before several other police units arrived, along with the forensic team. The crime scene was sealed off, denying entrance to anyone inside except homicide and the department's photographers. It was a gruesome sight, and many of the more seasoned officers could hardly stomach it.

Two large butcher knives protruded like a bad horror flick from the girls' abdomens.

"Another classic from our serial killer," Homicide Detective Jose Ramirez commented. "Both of them suffered and bled to death. What a waste," he said harshly.

The seasoned detective coached the photography crew around the living room, pointing out areas he wanted them to focus on. He knew the pictures would be crucial evidence in a trial. That was if the case ever got that far.

Ken Malone, the medical examiner, arrived impatient and unscathed by the scene before him. He'd come from the crime-riddled city of Detroit, but it still seemed odd he didn't show any emotion for this type of brutality. It was disturbing to the detective, actually downright unsettling.

The ME looked both women over as if he were shopping for a used car. He roughly touched them, starting at the chin, followed by their elbows, then knees.

"Rigor Mortis has come and gone," he said flatly. "Ten to twelve hours before it sets at this room temperature, then twenty-four to thirty-six hours to dissipate. I'll have to do an autopsy, but it appears to have happened anywhere from Friday night to Saturday."

"Same scenario," Detective Ramirez said. "I hope we catch him soon. If not, we're going to be seeing more of this."

"Let me do my job," Ken Malone answered flatly. "Until I complete the autopsy, it's an unanswered question."

Detective Ramirez didn't bother to respond. Malone wasn't worth his sarcasm. Jose had turned forty the week before and hadn't taken it well. The homicide detective had been reflecting on his job, wondering if it was making him older before his time. After eleven years in the homicide division, he still wasn't accustomed to the crimes he witnessed.

They were senseless and unnecessary acts of violence that reminded him every day of what a crazy society he lived in. Surrounded by burned out cops who'd become unfazed by it all, Detective Jose Ramirez feared becoming one of them. *That* worried him most of all. Looking around the crime scene, he was struck with déjà vu. It was the fifth of the serial killer's hits.

Ramirez was unrelenting in his investigation, but a few things still bothered him. Although he wasn't a believer in profiling murderers, he couldn't turn his back on the rising body count of his predator. He wasn't following the profile.

He wasn't sexually assaulting his victims. His victims' manner of death wasn't strangulation, but slow bleeding wounds which caused a great deal of suffering and not a quick death. There weren't any noted personal items missing, which alleviated the stereotype that he was keeping trophies. The only thing that was consistent was the age of his victims, always young and pretty, most of them college students.

"Maybe he'll be white and stutter," Ramirez said.

"What?" one of the officers asked.

"Nothing," he answered. "Just thinking out loud."

Chapter 5

The state highway investigator entered Erin Sommers' apartment with the key given to him by the Superintendent of the building. It slid into the lock easily. He was relieved it was still daylight. It made him feel more comfortable. But his mind continued to play over the savage beating the young woman had incurred. It was one of those crimes that almost always ended up being personal.

The sun coming through the windows was bright and soothing, making it unnecessary for him to turn on any lights. It was an exclusive complex, and judging by the size of the apartment, it wasn't cheap.

The carpet was thick and white, as were the walls, furniture, and fireplace. She must not have any children, he thought. White wouldn't have been the best color choice for little ones.

He walked through the apartment, careful not to touch anything. The kitchen was immaculate like the living room, as well as her bedroom, with the exception of the bright splashes of color, contradictory to the space that'd welcomed him. Pictures lined her dresser, proving she had many friends and hopefully family.

The bed was made with an expensive comforter and lined with several plush pillows. Nothing looked out of the ordinary. The investigator padded along the carpet, noticing a second full bath and spare room.

Expecting another organized room, he was shocked to find it in total disarray. It appeared to be ransacked until he took a closer look. Two computers were lined against the wall, side by side. Bookcases lined the other three walls, each so full that additional books were stacked on the floor at least twenty deep.

The trashcan was overflowing with wadded up balls of paper, and the floor was strewn with newspaper copies of the local serial killer's rampage. He stared blankly at the articles until hearing a voice behind him.

"She's a newspaper reporter for *The Seattle Times*," Pablo Valdez, the building manager, said. "Kind of a workaholic.

Never saw her except when she left for her office. Friendly young woman though. Always spoke to everyone."

Valdez handed the trooper a piece of paper with her emergency phone numbers on it. "Has four siblings and both parents are still alive. They live right outside of town."

The officer nodded his thanks, handing the key back. He studied the information; grateful he didn't have to engage in further conversation.

Back at the precinct, a social worker began making phone calls. It was not yet known if the victim would survive, which alleviated any time for personal visits. Reaching the mother first, she broke the news, ending with the name of the hospital caring for her daughter.

It was the panic and grief-stricken voice she'd heard many times, and it caused her muscles to grow stiff. Sitting up straight, she tried to clear her mind.

There were many other calls to make.

Chapter 6

Erin lay deep in a coma, unaware of the life-threatening injuries her body sustained. Her mother and three of her siblings sat in the cold, faux leather chairs in the waiting area, hoping to get word from the doctor soon. Her father paced the floor with a cigarette hanging limply from his mouth.

The *No Smoking* sign posted prominently on the wall was large and red, but he wasn't even aware of it. No one would stop him. They couldn't possibly at a time like this.

The doctors worked slowly and meticulously to stop the internal bleeding and repair her crushed facial bones. It had initially appeared unlikely they could save her, but luck had been on their side as they wheeled her into the recovery room. The only thing left would be to hold their breath and wait.

An attractive, middle-aged doctor faced the growing crowd with a stern face. She'd learned years ago to detach herself as much as possible from her patients. However, this was going to prove to be a difficult case with a daughter of her own about the same age as the victim.

"Hello," she said, reaching out her hand to the first person she encountered. "I'm Dr. Hazlett. I've been in surgery with Erin." She measured the weak and hopeful looks wishing she had better news to share with them.

Erin sustained numerous injuries from her attack. The most serious being internal bleeding. We've removed her spleen and gall bladder and stopped the bleeding, however, that may only last temporarily. She had several fractures to the skull resulting in an epidural hematoma."

Dr. Hazlett paused for a moment to let the information sink in, measuring the looks of confusion on their faces. It was times like these when she struggled between being clinical and using layman's terms. It was often easier to revert to doctor mode than to relate with emotions. She shifted her weight from one foot to the other before deciding to pull up a chair and sit among them.

"Erin is in a deep coma and not responding to pain. However, during the surgery, we were able to reduce the pressure on her brain by draining the blood and fluid caused by the skull fractures. She was treated as promptly as possible after arriving, and we expect minimal brain injury. Erin's condition will be monitored closely. Should there be any change, we'll react immediately."

Before the family could ask the inevitable question, Dr. Hazlett answered them. "It's touch and go at this point. The next twenty-four hours will be crucial. Erin will be in intensive care under constant watch. I don't want to give you false hope," she said, then stood and turned to walk away. There was nothing more the doctor could share with them. The answers to any further questions would be hypothetical.

The Detectives seemed to swarm the family, an inappropriate time, but it couldn't be helped. Unfortunately, they got the usual answers in an attack such as this. Erin didn't have any enemies, only good friends. She had a good education and a steady job. Her family had money, and she lived in a safe and guarded apartment complex. If they were aware of anyone capable of hurting her, they'd refused to admit it. Both detectives spoke briefly to the doctor before leaving the hospital.

Chapter 7

Detective Jose Ramirez got up from his dented and rusty desk, grabbing his stained overcoat from the coat rack. His job had become his life, and he didn't have much to go home to except a ridiculously small apartment that resembled nothing more than an unkempt bachelor's pad.

The freezing rain fell on him like needles as he ran to the parking deck. In ten minutes, Jose was at his apartment with his key already in the lock. Flipping on the dim overhead light, he tossed his coat on the nearest piece of furniture. It would wait there for him until the following morning. He dropped his mail on the kitchen table and it landed quietly onto the growing mound already resting there.

He grunted as he opened the refrigerator and only saw two light beers, a bottle of ketchup, and a bruised apple. Grabbing a beer and tossing the top into the trash can, he ambled into the living room, pushing newspapers to the side, clearing a spot to sit on the sofa. Kicking his shoes off and consciously ignoring the holes in his socks, he glanced up at the bulletin board hanging on the wall. It contained gruesome color photos of the serial killer's five murders. The detective looked into the faces of each woman. The pictures had a way of luring him into their web.

Jose had beaten himself up trying to find a link between the girls but had yet to do so. They were random choices, one predictable characteristic of a serial killer. None of them had been street people, which was odd. The victims had all been young and belonged to families, had jobs or were students, and would be missed. That was a risk for the killer, but it was likely something he enjoyed. Jose had initially thought he was someone the victims might've known, but none of them knew each other or even had the same friends or hangouts.

Sighing heavily, he turned from the pictures. Pulling the recycling bin over to the couch, he stacked the papers neatly without investing much time, then tossed them inside. Jose forced a smile when he could see the color of the couch.

Grabbing the last beer from the fridge, he went back into the living room and settled down with the remote. It was eleven o'clock, time for the late-night news. His favorite anchor, a young woman with long black hair and haunting eyes, flashed her pearly white smile, welcoming him to the local channel.

"Tonight's top story is the attack on crime journalist Erin Sommers from *The Seattle Times*. Sommers, twenty-six, was assaulted and left with life-threatening injuries on Interstate 82 late Sunday night when she'd apparently pulled her car over during the heavy rain. As of yet, her attacker has not been found, and few leads have been forwarded to the police. The latest report has her listed in critical condition at an undisclosed hospital. Doctors are refusing comment at this time."

Jose Ramirez's face dropped, along with his stomach. "What the…? I can't believe this!" he said to himself.

Grabbing his coat, he jogged to his car, furious he had been left out of the loop. Ramirez smirked at the anchor's comment that Erin had been taken to an *undisclosed* hospital. It wasn't as if the town had many options. With severe injuries such as hers, Harborview's Trauma Center was the only place to send her.

Jose had mentored Erin since she'd joined the staff at *The Seattle Times*. Her interest in solving mysteries was one she hadn't been able to dismiss. Erin had contacted the detective division when she first took the job at the newspaper. Her call had been directed to him and he'd found her to be a valuable ally in many of the department's investigations. Jose was always impressed by her determination.

He couldn't believe that no one had called him about her attack. His first thought went to the serial killer. He and Erin had been working on the case since it'd become apparent that the department was dealing with more than an isolated murder.

Jose hoped Erin hadn't been one of his victims. The thought of her suffering at the hands of the man they'd been studying was more than he could stomach.

The rain remained persistent as he pulled the big undercover Caprice into the parking deck. Jose often wondered how the department still considered those big monstrosities inconspicuous vehicles.

The lighting was bright in the garage as Ramirez pulled into the nearest space. It was well after visiting hours, so it made sense that the parking deck was virtually empty. Jose grabbed his badge from the seat, intending to use it as his admission ticket. It'd worked wonderfully so far.

The hospital was eerily quiet as he waited for the automated door to slide open. The pit of his stomach knotted up as it always did when he entered a medical facility. The smell of disinfectant mixed with urine always made him nauseous. Pulling his badge from his back pocket, he flipped the leather binder open, flashing it to the woman at the information desk.

"Good evening," he said, in a professional tone. "I'm Detective Jose Ramirez, here to see Erin Sommers."

"Detective," the older woman said in a firm and condescending tone. "Don't you think it's a little late to be visiting?"

He sat dumbfounded for a moment then answered in an equally condescending voice. "It may appear that way, Ma'am, but we have a crime to investigate, and time is of the essence. We have to move as quickly as possible."

Jose was proud of himself for not allowing her to intimidate him. Her judgmental facial expressions didn't change, but her irritation bled through as she pounded out the information on the computer that he was searching for. She made him wait longer than necessary before telling him that Erin was in the intensive care unit on the third floor.

Jose grudgingly thanked her and made his way to the elevator. The doors opened right away, and he stepped inside, pushing the button for the third floor. Ramirez was afraid of what he'd find, but at least he knew she was still alive. That was a comfort. He buzzed the nurses' station from outside the double metal doors of the ICU and waited impatiently for a response. A male nurse stepped through and met him outside.

"How can I help you?" he asked impatiently.

"I'm here to see Erin Sommers. I'm Detective Jose Ramirez."

"Mr. Ramirez," he said, in the same tone the woman at the desk had used. "Are you aware we have visiting hours, especially in the Intensive Care Unit?"

"Yes, I'm painfully aware of that. However, it's imperative we get any information we can to pursue her attacker. The quicker we pick up on any leads, the better chance we have of taking the perpetrator into custody."

"I understand, Detective, but are you aware of the fact Ms. Sommers is in a deep coma?"

"I was hoping she'd come out of that."

"No such luck. But, assuming she does, she'll most likely have little, if *any*, recollection of the event."

"I'd still like to see her. Maybe her injuries will give me some insight into the assault she sustained," Jose said, struggling not to sound desperate.

"I'm sure your department has taken photographs," the nurse said bluntly.

"Yes, they're extremely thorough. However, pictures aren't quite the same as viewing the victim personally."

"*Viewing?* I would hardly think that's the *appropriate* word. She's neither in the morgue nor in a mortuary," the nurse sneered. Silence reigned until the nurse finally conceded. It was obvious he was dealing with a persistent man and he had more important things to do than argue with a stubborn, unreasonable detective. What could a few minutes with a comatose patient hurt?

"Five minutes, and that means exactly what I said. Five minutes, no more."

"Thank you for your time. I will be out in five." Jose held his breath as he entered the unit. *Damn, it gave him the creeps.*

The nurse pointed in the direction of Erin's room, telling him to take the fifth door on his right. Jose made his way past the nurses' station and entered the dimly lit room. The dismal, repetitive sound of a respirator, breathing in and out for her, was almost too much for him. Then, Jose saw her. Erin lay there like a bloated and bruised corpse.

Her face was swollen more than he'd seen in all of his years of police work. Deep purple bruises covered most of her battered body. Jose slowly drew closer, holding his breath. He reached out to touch her hand, but couldn't bring himself to do it. It reminded him of surgical gloves that nurses blew up into a balloon to ease frightened children. He was angry with himself for being so repulsed by his friend. Jose leaned over and whispered to her.

"I'll get this animal. If it's the last thing I do, I'll get him."

Erin didn't respond or give him any reassurance she'd heard him. Jose watched her eyes as they moved back and forth beneath her lids. He heard his own voice saying a prayer for her.

Detective Jose Ramirez got on the elevator aware of the perspiration beading on his forehead and upper lip. It was his usual reaction to a hospital. He was grateful for the rain now. It was cool on his face and the back of his neck. He took his time getting to the car, oblivious to the fact he was getting drenched.

Chapter 8

Jose was seated in his Captain's office, expecting to have his ass chewed for his persistence at the hospital the night before. He'd been out of line, and he knew it. Fortunately for him, the Captain hadn't found out about it.

"What's your theory on the latest double homicide?" the Captain asked.

"Perfect match for our serial killer, no doubt about it. He's getting bolder."

"How do you figure?" Captain Graham asked.

"He killed two this time. One of them could've screamed loud enough to alert a neighbor, especially in an apartment. He left them to suffer, again taking a risk someone could've found them in enough time to get a description from them."

"Maybe it's a copycat."

"Not a chance. He's killing them the same way, and a lot of this information hasn't been leaked to the press," Jose countered.

"Do you think he's in the medical field? He hasn't left a witness alive yet, and they only have one stab wound. That's taking a big chance they might live," the Captain continued questioning.

"I've thought about that, but it doesn't take a rocket scientist to figure out hitting a vital organ will eventually cause death, especially if it's not treated. I've got to tell you, he's a bold son-of-a-bitch," the detective answered.

"Yeah, heartless as hell too. I reviewed the photos of the scene. Gruesome sight. Made me sick. I couldn't help thinking of Alyssa. She's going to college next year, you know. Seems like yesterday we brought her home from the hospital. It's a scary world out there, but young people refuse to believe it," Captain Graham sighed.

"That's how we all were at that age. Maybe this will keep them on their toes," Jose added. "Our killer has to be right under our nose. These girls, well young women, are all in proximity to one another, which means he has to have an anchor of some kind nearby. Maybe it's his residence, a relative's or friend's residence, or even a place of employment or education."

"Frightening, but true. Did you hear about your protégé? They found her beaten damn near to death the other night."

"I heard," Jose answered, stepping lightly out onto the ice, feeling out the Captain to see if he knew anything about his visit to the hospital the night before.

"Do you think it's our man?" Graham asked.

"I considered that, but she sustained a beating, not a stabbing. He left her for dead, but there was always the potential she could've survived even a serious beating. I don't think it was our man."

"Have you pondered the thought it could've been a warning for her to quit nosing around the investigation?"

"I hadn't thought about that," Jose answered, his stomach churning. "That makes sense, but on the other hand, who knew about her investigation? The newspaper didn't even know."

"Maybe you're right," Graham said.

"Besides, he would have to know she was coming down that stretch of highway and take the chance she'd pull over.

There's too many *ifs*. It just doesn't sit well with me. I feel responsible for letting her get involved in this, she's just a kid," Jose said.

"Erin's young, but I'd hardly say a *kid*, Ramirez. She's out of college and has a good job. We were already with the department at that age."

"Maybe you're right. I just hate to see females put their lives at risk."

"I'm with you, but this day and time, we'd be considered male chauvinists and taken up on charges of harassment. But screw that. I'm too old to change my ways. Keep an eye on your girl. I'm concerned about her."

"Do you think we should put an officer at her door?" Jose asked.

"I'll check with the brass, but I doubt they'll authorize the funds. They'd have a fit if they knew you had involved her in the investigation. Our asses would be over the fire, and it wouldn't be a pretty sight."

"Well, do me a favor and check, I'd sleep easier," Jose persisted.

"Okay, Ramirez, now get the hell out of my office! You aren't the only child I have to lead around by the nose. Get to work!"

Jose snickered under his breath as he shut the Captain's door behind him. Graham always ended every meeting the same way. Ramirez sat down at his desk just as the phone rang. It was Dr. Malone from the Medical Examiner's office.

"Yeah, Ramirez," he started, irritating Jose from the start. "I thought you might like to take a look at these bodies."

Ken Malone smiled on the other end of the phone. He'd intentionally called Ramirez because he liked to watch him sweat when he came by the morgue. Malone enjoyed any chance he could get to make the detectives squirm. *They were so damned arrogant, thinking they knew his job.*

"Uh, yeah," Jose stalled. "I guess I need to do that. How about an hour? Would that work?"

"Sure. Just don't make it any later." Malone hung up the phone, ending the conversation.

That always infuriated Jose. "Asshole," he cringed.

The morgue had the same smell as the hospital, so the detective took one last, heavy breath before stepping inside. Several lab techs were sitting at the front desk eating a sandwich, motioning for him to go on back. *Jeez, how in the hell do these people eat for Christ's sake?* Ramirez thought, sighing heavily.

Malone was in the autopsy room in between two metal gurneys. He had on a stained lab coat and a hair net. "Come on in," he said, without looking up.

Ramirez swallowed hard as he looked at the two naked bodies, their abdomens gaping open.

"Put one foot in front of the other and get your ass over here."

Ramirez didn't give him the pleasure of acknowledging his remark but made his way over to the cold metal slabs, tying on an apron, and sliding protective goggles over his eyes and face as he went.

"One gash to the liver on both victims. Painful death. May not have died if it hadn't been such an oversized blade." Malone handed over the plastic bag that held the knives.

"My God," Ramirez mumbled. "He wasn't taking any chances, was he?"

"That would be my bet. The internal bleeding was unbelievable."

"Did you get anything from under the fingernails? Skin fragments maybe?"

"Nope, not a thing. I don't know how he restrains them so quickly. He must just startle the hell out of them. This one," Malone said, pointing to Ashley Gregory, "had a broken collarbone, almost splintered actually. It looks like she was hit with something, possibly a door. That'd make the most sense."

"Her name is Ashley," Ramirez said coldly. "She isn't *this one*."

"Name 'em if you want to, but it's not my style. If I looked at them like that, I'd be crazy. I'd make my wife and kids crazy too. Listen, you've got to quit taking these cases personally, or you're gonna have a breakdown. Maybe you're in the wrong business. There are a lot of social work positions open out there, ya know?"

"Screw you, Malone," Jose answered, furious with himself for allowing the ME the pleasure of pissing him off.

"That should do it. If you don't have any questions, then don't let the door hit you in the ass," Malone said smugly.

"Call me if you find anything else," Jose answered placidly.

"Ramirez, you should know by now I do it right the first time."

"Yeah," Jose grunted.

The door slammed behind him as Malone smiled.

Chapter 9

Dr. Ken Malone slapped the weighed and dissected organs back into the gaping body cavities and sewed them up with the careless precision of a butcher. If the bleeding-heart detective had been there, he would've demanded a better job.

"Stupid, naïve son-of-a-bitch," Ken Malone snickered.

He finished just in time for the mortuary van to pick up both girls. It was the most affluent funeral home in the city, but Malone had expected nothing less. The employees transferred the girls into their own body bags, after wrapping them tightly in bright, white linens.

"Another case finished at last," he said to the old, wrinkled fellow who was rolling the women out.

"Know what you mean. I'm sure there are a lot more of 'em to take their place."

"You got it. My job is never done. At least that counts as job security. Can't beat that," Malone said.

"Yep, people are always gonna die, that pretty much keeps me in business too," the old man responded seriously.

Malone laughed. *Keep him in business? Ha! He was nothing more than a van driver. Who did he think he was fooling?* Malone sneered as he wheeled a train wreck victim into the autopsy room. "What the hell were you thinking, you careless idiot?" he asked the mangled body as if it would speak back.

Ramirez phoned the hospital as soon as he got back to the office. Erin wasn't out of the coma, not that he'd expected anything different. He thought about asking to speak to someone from her family on the waiting room phone, but decided against it. Jose wasn't sure if she'd told them about her crime pursuits, and he didn't want to be blamed for her attack. His own conscience was already heavy enough, and he didn't need anyone adding to it.

Pulling all five social security numbers up onto the computer, Jose hoped he'd find any criminal activity on the girls. He hadn't found one the other three times he'd looked, but he tried once more anyway. The results were the same. The detective had hoped he might hit the jackpot and find they'd been involved with the police at least once. Of course, that'd mean it would implicate an officer, but if the evidence led him to another uniform, then so be it. Ramirez was desperate for anything.

Jose called the Captain and told him he'd be out for most of the afternoon. Grabbing his umbrella, he drove to Ashley and Jennifer's apartment. The yellow crime scene tape still stretched across their door, a dim reminder of what had happened there. With the key the manager had given him, he unlocked the door, stepping under the tape. It was still as they'd left it on the night of the murders, and a familiar shiver went down his spine. Jose walked over to the ceramic lamp on the end table and switched it on. He was still amazed at the amount of blood that had saturated the sofa. *Jeez, how could they have had any blood left?* He let his eyes roam over the apartment, turning his gaze from the brutal scene.

The apartment was typical of two, young college roommates, a coffee and kitchen table covered in schoolbooks and scattered papers. A pair of reading glasses sat unfolded on top of an open book. The refrigerator held a plastic container of cut up fruit, four cartons of yogurt, and a two-liter diet soda.

There were pizza-stained paper plates in the trash while the sink was empty of any dirty dishes.

Jose passed the sofa again, walking down the hall to the bedrooms. The bathroom was the first door he reached, so he flipped on the light and peered in. The counter was covered with cosmetics, a blow dryer, and a curling iron. The shower had the latest body gels and expensive shampoos, something even struggling young women splurged on.

The bedrooms were average, boasting a few pictures of drunken sorority girls snuggled up with good-looking frat boys. Their bedspreads looked worn, suggesting they were from their younger years. Dirty clothes were thrown on the floor while clean ones lay spread across the bed appearing to be laid out as a choice of dress for the weekend. Beyond that, he found nothing out of the ordinary. It was another dead-end. Jose hadn't been sure what he was looking for, but he hadn't found it.

"I thought I'd find you here."

Jose jumped, turning to find the Captain standing in the hallway. "My God, you scared the shit out of me!"

Captain Graham ignored the comment and cut straight to the chase. "Found another one. Same MO, I need you at the scene."

"Jesus, why can't I find him?" Ramirez seethed.

"Hey, it's one of those things. We can only work with what we've got. You're a damn good detective, but you won't stay one for long if you beat yourself up over it."

"I'll follow you over, where is it?"

"Five blocks away at another apartment complex. Young Caucasian girl. Her roommate found her this morning when she came home from an all-nighter with her boyfriend. The ambulance crew is sedating her. She's in shock. We haven't been able to get jack shit out of her," Captain Graham answered.

"Can't say I blame her. A slaughtered roommate is probably the last thing she expected to come home to."

Jose slipped his fingers into his front pocket, retrieving his keys. He shook them indicating he was ready to go. It took them less than two minutes to get to the scene. Blue lights were flashing, making it look like a cheap fly-by-night carnival had come to town. It was overkill, and always infuriated Ramirez. The unnecessary show of uniformed cops hovering over a bloody corpse sickened him.

"I think you can get these men out of here," Ramirez said bluntly to the lieutenant. "It doesn't look like we have a problem with crowd control."

The Lieutenant looked at him with resentment as he turned to call off his troops. Ramirez shooed some of them out of the apartment. "Damn, they know better than to contaminate a crime scene!" he shouted to no one in particular.

The apartment was similar to the one he'd just left…two college kids living away from the supervision of home. The girl had apparently been surprised at the door like the others. She lay right inside on the outdated shag carpet, a butcher knife in her abdomen.

Jose scanned the room to avoid looking too long at the body. There wasn't a need to gawk at her as he'd seen the haunting sight for the sixth time now. The Captain stood beside him, shaking his head from side to side.

"You know Cap, I've been thinking. What if this is a good-looking college kid? There has to be a reason these girls would open their doors to begin with. They have to know what's going on with the murders. The media is certainly putting the word out. It only makes sense they'd trust a handsome guy about their age. I can't imagine them opening it to someone who looks suspicious, even to an older man."

"You've got a point there, especially with the University and the Junior College so close in proximity. Girls are always a sucker for a good-looking face. That's how I got Irene." Jose looked at him with a dry, judgmental expression.

"Just trying to lighten up the mood. Damn, Ramirez, can't you take a joke?"

"Not these days I can't."

Jose passed Malone as he walked out of the apartment and to his car, but didn't feel the need to speak to him. He could feel the quickened footsteps of the Captain hurrying to catch up to him.

"Gone so soon?"

"Yeah, I'll read the report of the first officers on the scene. I'm going to *think*. I'm going to think about who this evil creature is."

"How about a drink? I could use one of O'Hara's T-bones and loaded potatoes. Their draft beer ain't too bad either."

"How's their scotch?" Ramirez asked without even a glance in the Captain's direction.

"Couldn't tell you, I'm strictly a beer man myself, but I've never had anything there that's disappointed me."

"You talked me into it. I'll meet you there in a few. I'm going back to the precinct for one of my folders."

"Don't be too long. I hate to drink alone."

"Yeah, I bet," Ramirez laughed, as he got behind the steering wheel, slamming his door loudly, and shutting off the world.

It was a few minutes before five p.m. The office was mostly cleared of the day shift detective staff. Jose was one of a few who continually burned the midnight oil. He often wondered how any of their cases could get solved between the hours of nine to five. Fumbling through the drawers of his disorganized desk, he pulled out a thick folder that held brief synopses of the victims.

He'd take it to the restaurant and go over it with his Captain, that's if he'd allow it during dinner. Jose had to admit to himself he was getting anal. Actually, borderline morbid.

O'Hara's was already filling up with its usual happy hour crowd. Detective Ramirez squeezed through the crowded doorway spotting Captain Graham. He was flagging him down with one hand, the other holding a chilled mug, the froth running down the sides.

"I know I don't see a folder tucked under your arm. You can't possibly think I'm going to look at autopsy photos while I'm eating. That might even ruin my zest for beer. Damn, Ramirez, this is supposed to take your mind off of it for a while."

"There aren't any autopsy pictures," Jose said defensively. "I just thought…"

"That's the point, Detective. Don't think."

Jose motioned for the nearest waitress and ordered a Dewar's and water. "What are we eating? I'm not that hungry, but I have a feeling you won't let me out of it."

"I took the liberty of ordering, my treat. I have to do that sometimes to keep morale up. Anyway, we're having two king-sized T-bones, loaded baked potatoes, and a salad. Ranch dressing. You can change that if you want to."

"No, that's fine."

"In fact, it should be rounding the bin any time now."

He was right. The salad was slid in front of him almost as soon as the Captain finished his sentence. It was full of everything Jose liked: olives, cherry tomatoes, onions, cucumbers, bacon bits, and an excessive slap of dressing. Sprinkling salt and pepper, he dug in. Although he didn't feel hungry, it was a damn good salad. Maybe he did need to eat more regularly.

It was after eight when they left the restaurant. Jose could feel the light-headedness that accompanied too much to drink. He'd let Cap talk him into one, or two, too many. At least it had taken his mind off of the latest murder. Four other detectives had come in and joined them. It was something Jose rarely took part in. He was too absorbed in his job and craved the quietness of home. But, he'd enjoyed tonight and decided he should do it more often.

The others in the department never knew how to take him. The detective was self-absorbed and quiet, but they respected his dedication. They shared an envy of him that Jose never noticed, just like he never noticed the women who gazed at him everywhere he went. He was a damn good-looking man, even the men recognized that in him.

Ramirez was six-two and 220 lbs. He had a small thirty-four-inch waist, which led to broad shoulders and well-defined, muscular arms. His thick, dark hair was always cut short and neat, and his dark eyes were large and curious, just like a child's. Women, almost everywhere he went, pursued him, but he stayed clear of a social life. His parents had been dead for years now, and twice, women who didn't want to live the life of a cop's wife had broken his heart. It was easier to stay alone.

Jose had become so immersed in his work he rarely even noticed the emotion of loneliness. It was far better that way, he'd convinced himself.

Chapter 10

Captain Graham was sitting behind his desk with the phone hanging limply from his ear. His face was beet red as it often was when the top brass was demanding the impossible. He motioned with his thick middle finger for Ramirez to sit down.

"Yeah. We're working on it," Graham muttered sarcastically.

A long pause followed before the Captain rebutted.

"He's a damn kid for crying out loud. What the hell are you people thinking? Besides his lack of investigative experience, it could be dangerous. I don't want the responsibility, plain and simple."

The Cap's face flushed a darker crimson.

"Send him down," Graham conceded.

"Do you want the latest shit from upstairs?" he seethed, turning to face Ramirez.

"I think I see what's coming."

"You got it, Buddy. You're getting a partner. Seems he has connections upstairs and after six months of writing parking tickets, he's joining our clan. One of those college boys that doesn't know a damn thing about detective work. The higher powers seem to think an expensive education can take the place of common sense and gut instincts."

Jose slammed his fist on the desk and stood up, pacing the floor of the small, overcrowded office. It was out of character for him, and for a moment it left his superior speechless.

"Hey, Ramirez, it can't be that bad. Just give him some grunt work and keep him out of the field. We've dealt with this bureaucratic bullshit before."

"Yeah, but not on a fucking serial killer case! They can't possibly be serious. I do much better on my own. You know that. Give him to somebody else. I'm not the only one on this case."

"Yeah, but you're the best and everyone knows it. If they want him to get some good, productive experience, then you're the one."

Ramirez started to continue his angry tantrum when he heard a light tapping at the door. He turned to see a young kid as green as the proverbial *grass on the other side.* The Captain motioned impatiently for him to come in.

"Hi there, Captain Graham," he said in a weak, uncertain voice.

"Yeah. Sit down. We've got work to do. I have to tell you, Officer?"

"Chatham, Officer Daniel Chatham."

"Chatham, we aren't too thrilled about having a rookie, an inexperienced rookie at that, on a serial killer case."

Daniel opened his mouth to say something, but instead shifted his gaze down toward the floor.

Ramirez almost felt sorry for him, then thought about his babysitting duties, and it immediately left his mind.

"What's your experience with murder cases?" Captain Graham demanded.

"None in the field, Sir," he answered, making a failed attempt to look the Captain in the eye. "I do have a master's degree in Criminal Investigations."

"You're about to find that don't mean shit here in the *real* world. Ramirez, get this kid out of here. I'll see you both first thing in the morning."

Ramirez opened the door as the scrawny rookie walked out into the hallway.

"Let's go. We're headed to visit Erin Sommers at the hospital."

"Listen, Detective Ramirez, I don't mean to be a problem. I just want to practice what my education has taught me. I'll stay back and observe. I'm sure I can learn a lot from you, that's all I want."

"Yeah, just stay back."

The hospital was crowded, which didn't thrill Jose. He noticed the kid looked as uneasy as he felt.

"Look, Chatham, I don't feel too comfortable in these places either. They give me the damn heebie geebies."

"You just don't know what you might see next."

"Yeah. Unpredictable. But it's nothing like a murder scene. You're going to see some horrible things that'll never leave your memory. I hope you can handle it."

He looked pale but nodded his head in agreement. "That's part of it. I knew it before I got into this."

"Good, because I'm not going to have time to coddle you."

They got off the elevator on the third floor and walked back to the double doors. A young, attractive nurse answered the bell this time. She was much more accommodating than the male he'd dealt with several nights before.

She let them in without hesitation, and Ramirez led the kid back to her room. Erin was still in a coma, but the swelling and bruising appeared much better. She was beginning to look like herself again. Chatham stood at a distance, uncertain of what to do with himself.

"This is Erin Sommers, the journalist from *The Seattle Times*. She was attacked almost two weeks ago."

"I heard about it," Chatham murmured.

"She's a friend of mine and a damn good investigator."

"Did she work for the department?"

"No, Erin just had a strong interest in solving murders. Actually, its kind of hush, hush. It was sort of a mutual agreement. She got to work on crimes, and I got the benefit of her mind."

"I see. Do you think this assault had anything to do with the serial killer?" Chatham asked.

"Well, college boy, what's your take on it?"

"It has to make you think twice. Her attack was different, and although she could've died from her injuries, there was the possibility she could survive, thus implicating her attacker."

"Not bad, not bad at all. Anything else?" Ramirez asked.

"I read the report. She wasn't found far from the road, making it fairly easy to locate her. He could've buried her in the woods. But if he was afraid of being seen, then he could've just driven her in his own car, or even hers, to a more secluded spot," Chatham said.

"Right again," Ramirez answered, waiting for the kid to continue.

"Maybe this was just a warning. She may have gotten too close."

"Even I didn't think of that, kid. Maybe you'll be worth something after all. Let's go visit her apartment. Erin keeps all of her notes there. If she were onto something real, she would've shared it with me. We'll take a look anyway."

The apartment was the same as it'd always been when Jose visited. It was neat and clean, but the air-conditioning was now turned off, making it hot and sticky. Jose walked straight to her office without hesitation. Accustomed to its usual mess, he found something he wasn't expecting. He put his hand on the doorframe as he looked around the room."What's going on here?" Ramirez demanded of no one in particular.

"Looks fine to me." For a moment Chatham thought the veteran detective was going to hit him. Daniel stepped back two full steps before looking up at Jose again.

"It sure as hell isn't okay. This room is always a mess, and I mean a *disaster*. It was like a tornado blew through it. Now it looks like a cleaning service has spent two days in here!"

Jose took his hand off the door, slapping it down to his side. His burgundy Bostonians took one step into the room when Officer Chatham stopped him with a forceful tug on his shoulder.

"Man, maybe we shouldn't go in there. It could have some clues, you know, be a crime scene or something. You said she did her research in here. It could be possible our

killer came and stole the information," Daniel Chatham
stammered as his face flushed.

Ramirez studied his colleague, knowing he was right,
but hating like hell to admit it. It was obvious the attack on
Erin had taken its toll on him, and he wasn't dealing with it
objectively. Maybe he needed a vacation.

"You know what," he said, looking at Chatham with an
exhausted set of eyes, "maybe we should just call it a day.
It's your first one in homicide. You probably need to get a
good night's rest. Tomorrow might turn into an all-nighter.
You can't ever predict this job."

Chatham wanted to argue with him and to suggest
calling in the crime scene unit, but thought better of it.
He'd been pushy enough for one day.

Chapter 11

By Saturday, the weather had cleared up, giving way to bright sunny skies and warmer weather. It was peculiar to feel the change in temperature, especially in the middle of March.

Jose stepped into his apartment with his morning newspaper, bagel, and black coffee. He walked five blocks every morning to the *Mom and Pop* grocery store down the street. It'd been the only one in the area when he'd first moved here, and it was hard to transfer his loyalty to a chain store. Besides, they were like family.

The Gellars had owned the business for three generations now. Their son Zac had started delivering Jose's groceries when he was just eight, now he was twenty-two. Jose had not only become fond of him, but proud as well. Zac still worked for his parents, had recently married, and was expecting a child of his own.

Jose continued to tease him about his red hair that never seemed to lie down on his head, and his red freckles that stood out like fluorescent lights on his cheeks. Even at twenty-two, he still looked so much like the little kid who'd first delivered his groceries.

Zac's wife Angela had been in the store that morning, and she looked as if she were going to pop. Zac had insisted Jose touch her stomach and wait for the baby to kick, but the little one just hadn't cooperated. Angela looked embarrassed, but mostly proud and anxious. For a few moments, Jose had been terribly envious.

Back at the apartment, the phone rang. Jose debated answering it. He knew who it was going to be, and also knew he couldn't get out of the departmental family picnic.

Shit, why do I have to go to these things? It's not like I've got a family, and I don't feel like oohing and aahing about everyone else's. The ringing remained persistent until he grabbed the receiver and barked a hello.

"Damn, Ramirez," Captain Graham said. "You answer the phone like that every time we have a picnic."

"Then catch a clue, Cap. I hate these functions."

"You sound like a whiny brat who doesn't want to go to Sunday school. Get over it."

"You know, I think we have this same conversation every year. Why do you have to call and make me dread it even earlier than I need to?" Jose snapped.

"Somebody has to make sure you don't skip town for the day. See you at the park at 2:00. Don't forget to bring some sodas."

"Yeah, I've had that reminder on my fridge for weeks," Ramirez answered sarcastically as he slammed down the phone. Graham snickered on the other end.

Jose turned the television on and watched the local news as he ate his bagel and drank the strong black coffee. There wasn't any news on Erin or their serial killer. Just as well, no news was good news. He caught up on the results of his latest missed ball games, and the five-day weather forecast.

"Damn, another thunderstorm headed our way," he grumbled. He wasn't fond of the rain for two reasons. It kept him away from his jogs in the park, and it seemed to be the kind of weather that brought out their serial killer. That was one of the first things he and Erin had narrowed down. They hadn't, however, figured out exactly why he only struck when it rained. Maybe it camouflaged him to some extent.

His mind went back to the evening before, to Erin, and to her apartment.

Who would've cleaned her office? No one was allowed in there but him, and her housekeeper was well aware of it. Maybe her family thought they were helping out. Still, something didn't sit right with him. He felt a rumbling of uneasiness settling in his stomach. As his mind pondered the possibilities, he was startled by a knock on his door. Glancing down at his watch, he grumbled a few choice words before getting up to answer it. "Yeah, who is it?"

"It's me, Officer Daniel Chatham, Sir."

"Shit," Jose muttered as he opened the door. "What are you doing out on a Saturday morning? I thought young people liked to sleep late."

"Yes, Sir, I'm sure many do. It just isn't my style."

"I see," Jose answered, giving in to the fact he was going to have to ask his partner inside. "Come on in."

Chatham walked in and stood there awkwardly.

"Have a seat. I'm sorry I don't have any coffee. I buy mine down the street every morning. I might have a soda I think."

"Oh, I'm okay. I've been thinking. You know, kind of brainstorming."

Ramirez threw the morning's newspaper on the coffee table and sat down on the couch, motioning for Chatham to take a seat in the recliner.

"Shoot…"

"Maybe Ms. Sommers did have something to share with you, only she didn't get a chance. Let's say someone else knew what she was onto and they got a hold of her before she could consult you about it."

"That's a possibility, but Erin's a smart girl. She wouldn't have taken any chances with her life. I just can't imagine her doing that."

"What exactly have you two gotten so far?" Chatham asked.

Jose laid his head back on the sofa shutting his eyes. "Let's see. Not a whole hell of a lot. We have about as much as the media does right now." He sat upright on the couch and interlocked his fingers. "He isn't matching the profile of a serial killer except in a few instances. He's only killing white women, meaning he's most likely white himself. They're all about the same age, college girls. I think he's some good-looking kid like Ted Bundy."

"That was my guess, too. Young women can be naïve, but they're also aware of the dangers out there. They don't typically open doors to people they don't know."

Jose looked up at the young kid's face. Daniel Chatham was a handsome boy, just so damned young. His blond hair was full, his face was scrubbed clean, making him always look fresh and alert. His big blue eyes would definitely make him a hit with the women. They were so innocent looking, not piercing and suspicious like this job would soon make them.

He was so eager to learn, that for a moment Jose pitied him and decided to start cutting him a break. Chatham was a smart guy. Ramirez had to give him that. As much as he hated to admit it, there was a possibility he could help.

"Did the girls know each other?" Chatham asked, looking hopeful for the first time.

"No, I haven't found any links at all. But there's the possibility they shared a mutual acquaintance. Maybe they frequented the same bar, or restaurant, who knows? Why don't you look into the local college hangouts? You're young, why don't you visit some of them?" Jose suggested.

"That's a thought. Did you talk to Erin's family to see if they had her office cleaned?"

"No, not yet. I thought I'd visit her later today. There's bound to be some family there."

Chatham stood, his lanky body slowly reaching its full six-foot height.

"Hey, Chatham, have you even started shaving yet?" Jose laughed.

"Screw you, Man."

Chapter 12

Ramirez pulled the paper grocery sacks out of the passenger side of his car and grudgingly made his way toward the crowd in the park. He felt a twinge of guilt for not wanting to be there as he looked on at the youngsters throwing their Frisbees and flying their cheap, paper kites.

This was about the only time of year he half-heartedly wished for a family of his own. Captain Graham was under one of the large tents donning his chef's hat, and waving a spatula around as he told some outlandish story. This was truly his day. He looked forward to it every year and remained on the planning committee to see to it the tradition was never lost. Jose plopped the sacks on the drink table and pulled a beer from a galvanized tub.

He was surprised to find it was a fairly expensive import. Good thing they hadn't assigned beer to him, it would've been Busch. He noticed Chatham standing alone, looking more than a little uncomfortable, so he meandered over. Besides, he really didn't have anyone else to talk to.

"I see you got bullied into this crap, too," Jose said.

"Yeah," he laughed. "I couldn't exactly turn down the invite being the new guy."

"Well, they don't ever let you turn it down, actually. In fact, the less you want to come, the more they hound the hell out you." They both laughed and their moods began to lighten.

"Hey, can I get you a beer?" Jose asked. "You look like you don't know what to do with your hands."

"Yeah, sounds good." Daniel Chatham was still in an uncomfortable stance when Jose returned. He slugged two long swigs before he started to sip on it.

Captain Graham had shed his apron and was making his way over to his team.

"Oh shit," Ramirez said under his breath. "He's going to make us mingle."

He was right. Graham scolded them both, leading them into the growing and jovial crowd. Jose knew almost everyone and tried to appear attentive as they introduced their families, just as they did every year. He smiled to himself as he watched the rough, calloused men he worked with dote on their wives and children. He spotted the Captain's wife and started over to speak to her. Graham was instantly at his side. Chatham hung back a few paces but followed them just the same.

"Good afternoon, Mrs. Graham," Jose said, smiling and reaching out with his right hand.

"Irene, please," she said, bypassing his extended hand, and hugging him lightly.

She was an attractive and dainty woman, which never ceased to amaze Ramirez. His Captain wasn't a handsome man and certainly didn't appear to have much in common with his wife. *Opposites attract, I guess,* he thought.

"You've met our daughter, Alyssa," Mrs. Graham said, pulling the young girl's elbow as she guided her over into their conversation.

"Yes, I have. It's nice to see you again." Luckily, she'd taken after her mother. She, too, was petite and pretty. She wore a white sundress with matching sandals and her hair was pulled back in a ponytail with a bright ribbon. Alyssa had always stared at Jose like a young girl with a big crush, making him uncomfortable.

"It's good to see you again, Mr. Ramirez," she said with a shy smile. Jose didn't offer his first name, instead nodded slightly at her.

"I hear you are starting college next year," he said.

"Yes, Sir," she responded. "I'm going to Tuft's University."

"Wow. Impressive," Chatham piped up. "You must be a good student."

Alyssa blushed. "I've tried."

"Heading to the East Coast," Ramirez smiled. "Brave girl." She obviously didn't like the reference girl.

"Yes, it's too far away," Irene sighed. "Now both of our children will be on the other side of the world."

"Oh, Mom, it's only across the US."

"It might as well be on the other side of the world."

Captain Graham rolled his eyes behind his wife. "Okay, Honey," he said. "Let's not get the empty-nest- syndrome yet."

"How is your son?" Jose asked, reaching into the depths of his memory to grasp his name.

"Chad is fine. He graduates next year from U.N.C. at Chapel Hill. Yeah, all that money and he wants to teach school. Can you believe that shit?" Captain Graham said in disgust. He'd always made it clear he wasn't impressed with any of his son's choices.

Jose looked around at the crowd, then back at Alyssa. "That's an unusual necklace," he said, as he looked at the gold amulet dangling from a short chain.

"It brings good luck and comes from an old Indian proverb. It was a gift from my mom."

"Nice. Well, take care."

Irene hugged him again before turning to speak to several of the other women.

"Still can't figure out how you got her," Jose kidded the Captain.

"Sheer luck of the draw. When are you going to venture out and find a wife?"

"You sound like one of my elderly aunts. When it's meant to be, it's meant to be."

"Well, if you're waiting on one to show up at your door, it's not gonna happen."

"You never know, Cap, you never know."

Jose was relieved when he finally pulled away from the crowd. The two hours had seemed like an eternity. He smiled, thinking it'd be another full year before he had to do it again. Jose was letting the air-conditioning cool off when he spotted Chatham walking to his car. The kid stretched before he got into a sporty, silver Corvette with a black convertible top. Jose shook his head. *Yep, he thinks everything is picture perfect. It won't take him long to realize it isn't.*

Chapter 13

Erin's physical appearance had gotten back to normal. She now appeared to be in a deep sleep, unaware of her broken body. Her family was starting to show the exhaustion that inevitably came along with waiting helplessly in a hospital.

Jose slid two boxes of glazed doughnuts across one of the tables where they were spending their vigil. He tactfully showed his badge and stated the snacks were from the police department.

"We're big fans of her column and share your concerns." He didn't wait for a reply, just nodded, as they did to him with their red-rimmed eyes and slumped, exhausted bodies.

Jose walked down the hall, rang the ICU button, and waited impatiently for a response. Unfortunately for him, it was the male nurse from the night of his first visit. *Shit, it had to be him, didn't it?*

The nurse looked at Jose with a sour, disdainful look, but motioned for him to come in. He didn't need to see the badge, or ask if he was family, he remembered the son-of-a-bitch. Jose made his way to Erin's room and sat by her side.

He would've brought flowers if they'd been allowed in the unit, but he'd been told they weren't. She wouldn't have been able to enjoy them, but they would've brought him some peace of mind. Jose rubbed his fingers across Erin's tiny, smooth ones, and closed his eyes in a silent prayer. The doctor came in and cleared her throat.

"Hello there," she said quietly. "Are you family?"

"No, Ma'am, I'm not. I'm Detective Jose Ramirez, I'm also a friend."

"I see," she answered, offering nothing more.

"Could I ask how she's doing? Is there a possibility of her getting better?"

Dr. Hazlett paused for a moment, and Jose could see the wheels turning in her mind. "I really shouldn't be discussing her medical status with you, as it's not relevant to her assault at this time." She looked at him and detected a concern that went further than police work.

"Oh, what the hell. The good news is she's made it through the first crucial hours and days. That's not to say she's out of the woods."

Jose nodded, instinctively removing his hand from Erin's, and placing it in his lap.

The doctor continued, "Her brain waves are normal, which is obviously another good sign. With the blows she sustained, it's nothing short of a miracle. The internal bleeding has been stopped, and the swelling in her brain has ceased."

"So, the coma, when…?"

"In all my years of medicine, I've never been able to predict that. As far as modern medicine has come, it's perhaps one of the most unpredictable situations I encounter. I don't want to give you too much or too little hope. They can last for days, weeks, months, and even years. Unfortunately, it can also last until death."

Jose felt his nose, throat, and eyes burning. He swallowed hard. "I guess I should go and let you do your thing, Doctor."

"We're doing all we can," Dr. Hazlett assured him.

"I'm sure you are. Thank you."

Jose walked to the elevator, deliberately diverting his eyes from Erin's family. Using the back of his hand, he wiped the lone tear that escaped his right eye. He was almost to the door when he realized he hadn't found out more about Erin's clean office. He cleared his throat in hopes of keeping the knot from rising any further. Jose stepped into a nearby restroom, turning the water on in the sink, letting it run for a few seconds before cupping both of his hands, and splashing his face with the cool liquid. It brought instant relief but was gone almost as soon as it had come. He stared into the mirror, and it told him, with brutal honesty, how worn out he really was. He pulled two paper towels from the metal dispenser and held them on his face with his eyes closed.

There were four people in the waiting area that had been filled with Erin's family. Jose walked over, standing straight, and trying to appear professional. He remembered meeting her parents, and introduced himself again, as he reached out his hand. As her father motioned for him to sit down across from them, he could feel the damn knot rising again.

"I'm sorry to bother you at such a difficult time," Jose started.

"Why haven't you found this coward, son-of-a-bitch, huh?" her father demanded, his voice rising louder with every word.

His wife reached over for his hand, but he jerked it away. "No, I won't sit here and wait for some lazy-ass cop to find her attacker."

Jose was taken aback, but he'd been in this situation many times since joining the homicide division. It was a usual response to tragedy, especially when the family was rendered helpless.

"Detective…" Erin's mother said softly.

"It's okay, Ma'am," Jose smiled tenderly. "I can't say I understand what either you or your husband are going through, but I'd like nothing more than to find out who did this to Erin."

"Don't talk about her as if you know her," her father said indignantly. "She's much more than just a bruised victim in ICU. She is…"

"She's a beautiful, young woman, filled with talent and promise," Jose interrupted kindly. "She's small in stature, but big when it comes to heart and courage. She's my friend, Mr. Sommers. I respect her very much."

Mr. Sommers looked ashamed for a moment, then his attitude twisted to skepticism.

"You're a little old to be seeing my daughter, aren't you? She never spoke of you."

"We aren't romantically involved, Mr. Sommers. Her work at *The Seattle Times* often sent her to the department for a few more details to add to a story. She usually contacted me."

His head hung forward as Jose saw a few large tears splatter on the polished floor.

"I'm sorry, Son," he said, his head still bent over. "I just want to help her. You understand that, don't you?"

"Yes, Sir, I do. And believe me, I'll do everything I can to bring this monster in."

"Thank you," Mr. Sommers said, glancing up this time to meet Jose's stare.

"No need to thank me, Sir. It's my job, and unfortunately, it's also my friend in there. I hate to ask you questions at this time, but it's imperative. Did any of your family clean Erin's home office, or maybe hire someone to do it?"

"Why heaven's no," Mrs. Sommers quickly answered. "We were told it could be a crime scene and the last thing we want to do is to hinder any possibility of the police finding evidence. If Erin had needed any personal items here at the hospital, we would've simply gone out and bought them. In fact, I haven't any desire to see the place. My duty is here with my daughter."

"Thank you for your time," Jose said, as he rose to his feet. Pulling a business card from his coat pocket, he handed it to Mr. Sommers. "Should you have any questions or concerns, please feel free to contact me. My number at the precinct and my cell number are both on there."

The three nodded to one another, then Jose found himself back at the elevator. The doors opened and closed with a jolt.

He spotted Chatham sitting in one of the plush chairs in the lobby. "Damn it. Not now!"

Chatham stood up quickly, as if he were about to be chased with a belt by a parent. "Detective Ramirez," he began. "I thought you'd be here. Can we talk?"

"Yeah, meet me at the precinct."

"I thought maybe over lunch. I'm…I'm still struggling with the sneers from the other detectives."

"You'll have to get used to that. This job requires a thick skin." Jose knew he was being a hard-ass and for some strange reason, he instantly regretted it. "All right, I'll meet you around the corner at Joe's. If you get there before I do, sit in the back."

Chatham didn't answer, but hurried out of the hospital, his posture stiff and upright.

Jose held back a laugh. Oh, to be young and ambitious again…

Chapter 14

As Jose had expected, the kid had beat him there and was sitting in a booth in the back. He had a black leather portfolio lying on the far side of the table, next to the wall.

"Not the greatest place, but get used to it," Jose said, as he slid onto the greasy, plastic seat. "It's cheap and the food's not half bad."

Two menus sat unfolded on the table as Chatham reached for his leather-bound notebook. Unable to meet Jose's eyes with his own, Chatham began.

"I've made a few notes and thought I'd share them with you."

"Listen, Kid, you have a good head on your shoulders, but you've got to grow up. Get some damn confidence, it's not the first day of preschool."

His face turned a bright shade of red, but he continued without acknowledging the remark. "The knives, can we trace them? How's he hiding such big-ass knives from his victims?"

Jose smiled at Chatham's first use of profanity, a necessity in police work. Crude, but for some reason, it just went with the job. Before he could answer, a waitress, with dyed hair and a beehive hairdo, walked over to their table.

"What'll it be?"

"The usual, Rosie. Make it a diet coke today."

"Why bother with that?" she asked with a loud cackle. "A Rueben with a diet coke. What sense does that make?"

"Hey, the last time I checked, this was a restaurant. That means I can order whatever the hell I want."

She laughed again, shook her head, and turned to Chatham. "What do you want, Kid?"

The blood returned to his face, but he managed a faint smile. "I think I'll have the same, but a real coke, please."

"Smart one, you are." She was gone as quickly as she'd come.

"As I was asking…" Chatham continued.

"I've checked on the knives," Ramirez interrupted. "Henckels is one of the most popular brands in the US. The first J.A. Henckels office opened in Berlin in the early

1800s. They're massed produced and don't have any lot numbers or other markings that can tie them to one shipment destination. Hell, you can purchase one anywhere from Amazon to Target. They're damn good knives, but they aren't cheap."

"They may be widely produced, but wouldn't it be odd if somebody were to purchase an excessive amount of them?" Chatham asked.

"Hell, he wouldn't be stupid enough to buy them at the same place."

"Maybe we could look at videotapes from local stores."

"Do you seriously have *that* much time on your hands?" Jose asked impatiently.

"Maybe they could go through the receipts, giving us a time frame of purchases," Chatham suggested, undeterred by his new partner's frustration.

"Yeah, right. Not without a warrant. They have better things to do. Besides, there's no way of telling how broad of a range he travels to get them. Then there's the chance they were purchased at thrift stores or yard sales. Just a hell of a lot of possibilities."

Chatham's shoulders went up in a heavy sigh as he looked down at the table.

"Hey, pick your head up, Kid. It was a good idea. It just didn't work out for us."

The Ruebens arrived, and the two men ate in silence. Chatham ate with the vigor of a college football player and ordered an apple pie a la mode for dessert.

"Where do you put all of that?" Ramirez asked.

"Just an inherited metabolism, I guess."

They finished their meal as Jose motioned for Rosie to refill their sodas. "What else do you have in that binder? I have a feeling that wasn't the only thing that's been on your mind?"

"We can't find a link to friends or hangouts, but what about dentists, doctors, hair stylists? Maybe they all have certain types of designer dresses or shoes? It's worth a shot."

"I must be getting old," Jose laughed. "And on top of that, I've had too little contact with the female gender. I'll talk to Erin's family. It might be better for you to talk to the surviving roommate. She may be more apt to talk to a young, strapping lad such as yourself."

"I'll get on it, Sir. I'll see you later this afternoon back at the precinct."

Ramirez looked over at the Chatham and for the first time realized how mature he actually was. He wasn't as useless as Jose had anticipated, and was far from a slacker. Ramirez was ashamed he hadn't been the mentor the department had wanted.

"Sir?"

"Yeah?"

"You were kind of spacing out there for a minute."

"Too much in this little brain, I guess," Jose laughed. "Hey, Kid," he began before corrected himself. "I mean, Chatham.

I say we give it our all today then take a little break. The weather's supposed to be clear for a few days, hopefully holding our killer at bay. I have a little, allow me to stress *little*, cabin about an hour and a half out of town, right in the belly of the most beautiful mountains you've ever seen.

It's nothing fancy, two bedrooms, a bath, a kitchen, if you can call it that, a den, and a big front porch. What do you say we grab a few beers and head up there for a couple of days? We can relax, and if the desire hits us, brainstorm about all of this shit."

Chatham looked embarrassed and shocked, but mostly flattered. "That sounds good."

"Did I tell you about the big stream in front that's filled with the biggest trout you've ever seen?"

"No, Sir, but I bet we'll be frying some up."

"You got it."

Chapter 15

Jose went back to the hospital for the second time that day. Erin's parents, who'd long been showing symptoms of sheer exhaustion, were not very happy to see him. Their memories were blank, at the moment, and they weren't willing to strain to remember. Her mother started crying and her father refused to talk anymore.

"Maybe later," he said. "Leave us be for now. It's simply too much to tax our minds when our daughter's lying in a coma. Surely, you can understand."

His tone had changed from earlier in the day, and Jose knew not to pressure them any further. It was probably best for both parties. He, too, was burned out and needed a break. He'd follow up after his weekend in the woods.

Jose got into the police cruiser and headed to his apartment, but not before stopping at the liquor store. He bought a case of Heineken, a splurge for him, a canister of mixed nuts, and two bags of chips. He was going to call it a day.

Chatham went directly to the survivor's apartment and was shocked to find it empty. Literally, *empty*. No furniture, nothing. A maintenance man was taking his time painting the walls, and he could hear the whirring noises of another worker cleaning the carpet in the back of the apartment.

"Shit, shit."

The maintenance man turned around and looked at him, but never said a word.

"I'm Detective Chatham. Where did the latest tenant go?"

Setting his brush down, the maintenance man appeared pleased at the distraction, and walked the few feet over to Chatham.

"Can't say as I know. The Super might know, but it ain't none of my business. I'll tell you though, it's spooky as hell in here. Ain't ever painted an apartment where there's been a murder. Had to use three coats of primer just to cover the blood."

Chatham cringed and turned away. This guy obviously didn't have any information. He walked out without so much as a good-bye.

The Superintendent wasn't happy for the interruption. He let Chatham in after seeing the badge, then returned to his ragged recliner. A forty-ounce can of malt liquor was on the end table beside him, and the television was on some seedy talk show.

"What do you want?" he asked gruffly.

"I'm looking for Chrissy Ozette, the latest occupant of 206."

"I know who you're talking about. Hard to forget a killin', Detective. I ain't that insensitive."

"I apologize," Chatham forced himself to say. "I didn't mean to imply that."

"What do you want with her? It's pretty obvious she ain't here no more."

"Actually, I need to speak with her. Is it possible you may have any numbers for her?"

He grunted, took a swig of his beer, and struggled to lift his overweight body from the chair.

"Got a number for her folks from her lease. You might find her there."

"Thanks. I appreciate it," Chatham said politely, his patience thinning.

"Yeah, just remember it when I get my next speeding ticket," the Super responded rudely.

"I'll remember," Chatham assured him.

It took him over thirty minutes to find the information. Papers were crammed into a makeshift file cabinet that held three times more than its capacity. The Super shoved it at Chatham and sat back down. "That's it. Close the door when you leave."

Back at the precinct, Chatham made the phone call. Her mother answered the phone on the fourth ring.

"Hello?"

"Yes, is this Mrs. Ozette?"

"Yeah," she answered, offering nothing else.

"I'm Detective Chatham. I was wondering if I could speak to your daughter, Chrissy. I wanted to ask her a few questions."

"She ain't here," she answered flatly. "We haven't spoken in years. The little bitch left home at fifteen, and we haven't seen her but twice since. Ungrateful brat."

Chatham was speechless for a moment, and then, surprisingly, was able to regroup. "I see," he said. "Is there a chance you might know where she is now?"

"Chrissy whacked out after that murder thing. She wanted to come back home, but her father wouldn't allow it. She admitted herself into some asylum."

Chatham hated the outdated word. *Asylum sounded so cruel.* "Would you possibly know the name of it?"

"Lobale, or something like that."

It immediately rang a bell for Chatham. It was one of the few hospitals that still took in those without insurance. He refused to refer to them as indigent. Some just weren't fortunate enough to have jobs that were concerned enough to take care of their employees. "Thank you for your time, Mrs. Ozette."

She hung up the phone leaving him dangling the receiver from his ear. Chatham shook his head as he wondered what kind of home life the young woman must have endured.

He placed his next call to Lobale, telling the receptionist who he was, and requesting a visit. He could hear her chewing gum, cracking it actually, and it made him cringe. He recalled how his mother had always complained about how unprofessional it was to chew gum in the workplace.

"Hold, please. I'll transfer you to her unit nurse."

Again, he stated his business and waited for a reply that didn't come right away.

"I'll have to talk to her doctor. She's not doing well, and he has her heavily sedated. Now might not be a good time."

"Could you please call me back? It's imperative I get some information from her."

"What's your number?"

Daniel gave her the precinct's number and assured her he'd wait there for her call.

"It may be awhile, Detective. I have several patients to attend to and so does the doctor."

"Yes, I understand. There isn't a rush."

She appreciated his patience and respectful tone. "I'll get back with you."

It was thirty minutes later when his phone rang, and Chatham picked it up right away. It was one of the few calls he'd received at his desk.

"Detective Chatham?"

"Yes." He recognized the nurse's voice.

"The doctor said he's still in the early stages of Ms. Ozette's treatment. He's willing to meet with you next Wednesday at 2:00. Is that possible for you?"

"I'll make it work. I look forward to meeting you."

"You too," she answered kindly.

Chapter 16

Before going home, Chatham decided to stop by Ramirez's apartment. He knew he was wearing out his welcome but wanted to share what little information he'd gathered. Hopefully, his partner had fared better.

The knock at the door didn't surprise Jose this time. He knew it was Chatham. "It's open," he yelled from his recliner.

The young detective entered with a little more confidence.

"Grab a beer out of the fridge. There's a bottle opener on the counter."

"This isn't your usual beer. What's up?" Chatham asked, holding the beer up and wearing a look of feigned confusion.

"Just getting ready for my vacation."

"This opener is kind of rusty, don't you think?"

"Just use the damn thing. I haven't died from it yet, and I've been using it for years," Jose answered sarcastically.

"So I see."

"Listen, smart-ass, what did you come over here for, to insult my home?"

"Actually, I wanted to share what I've gotten. It seems Chrissy is not on the best terms with her family and that's putting it mildly. At any rate, her apartment is empty, and the painting crew is already preparing it for the next tenant.

Time is money, I guess. Anyway, to make a long story short, the young lady has checked herself into Lobale Mental Hospital and is basically catatonic at this point. The doctor is willing to meet with me next Wednesday."

"You did much better than I did. Erin's parents are walking zombies. They can't remember anything and aren't willing to try. I didn't push it."

"That's probably best."

Jose threw an unopened bag of chips over to Chatham and got them another beer.

"I'm not quite ready for another one yet."

"Listen, if you're going to run with the big boys…"

Chatham finished off his first beer and stifled back a burp.

"Let's discuss our trip. I have some old friends that own a supply shop a few miles from the cabin, so we can stop there. Not a big variety, but we're not going gourmet."

"Anything special I need to bring?" Chatham asked.

"Just bring the beer, and if you have a deck of cards, bring those too. I'm sure mine are around here under the mounds of clutter, but I'm not willing to invest the time to look for them."

Chapter 17

Captain Graham was more than a little perturbed at the unexpected vacation of his two lead investigators. "Could you boys have picked a worse time to pull a stunt like this?" he demanded.

"Look, Cap, its just a little break to clear our minds. We'll work on the case while we're there," Ramirez assured him.

"Like hell you will. I know how you are when you go to that cabin, it takes you away."

"Yeah, it does. I come back with a clear, relaxed mind, ready to get back to business."

"Just get the hell out of town. You're going anyhow. I'm not in the mood for a migraine."

Jose smiled as he heard the phone slam. He knew the Captain felt it was best, and if he'd thought of it himself, he would've recommended it.

At seven the next morning, Chatham showed up, cooler in hand.

"Prompt, aren't you?" Jose teased.

"It comes from home training."

"You haven't talked much about your home life."

"Not much to tell. My father raised me, and did pretty well, if I must say so myself." Chatham didn't offer any more than that, so Jose didn't press.

They didn't talk much on the way to the cabin. It was a scenic route, and both of them needed the respite.

"See that shack right ahead, the one leaning to one side?"

"Yeah, don't tell me someone lives there."

"Of course not. It's the supply store," Jose answered.

"Oh, Jesus, did you ever reel me in," Daniel sighed skeptically.

"'O ye, of little faith. Come on in. You'll love the Everetts."

"Is it safe?" Chatham asked.

"Get out of the car!" Jose demanded.

As it was every time they saw Jose, the couple rushed to greet him, and Mrs. Everett met him with a kiss.

"My, my," she smiled, as she held his hands tight. "If you don't just get better looking as the years pass."

"Oh, you say that to *all* your customers," Jose laughed. "This is my new partner, Daniel Chatham. We just call him Chatham."

"It's very nice to meet you, Daniel," Mrs. Everett said kindly.

Chatham felt awkward hearing Ramirez use his first name. "It's nice to meet you too, Ma'am. Ramirez, I mean Jose, has said wonderful things about the two of you."

"Don't believe it," Mr. Everett said. "Don't believe anything you hear, and only half of what you see."

"He's been telling me that for years," Jose laughed.

"Have you been up to your place yet?" Mr. Everett asked.

"Not yet. I can't wait to see it."

"Well, let's get you on your way. What can I get you?"

"How about some lighter fluid and charcoal, a couple of those thick rib eyes, a bag of potatoes, a dozen eggs, bacon, and a case of Busch beer. I don't know what kind the kid brought, but I'm sure it's out of my league."

"That wouldn't take much," Mr. Everett laughed heartily. "I'm throwing in your usual bait. The trout are biting like you've never seen. Your oil and flour can't be good. Throw some of that in too, darlin'."

"I already thought of it," Mrs. Everett answered.

It only took one trip to load the groceries into Jose's jeep. The Everetts waved until he was out of sight.

"Nice people," Chatham said.

"Yep. Those are the kind of people you meet out here. Just good folks."

The ruts in the road got rougher, and the jeep tilted back and forth like a small boat on a rough sea.

"Damn, don't flip this thing. Didn't they tell you when you bought it that it could turn over?"

Jose gave him a scouring look as he pointed up a small hill. "There she sits, like an old friend."

It was definitely antiquated, but Chatham liked it right away. It had character, and the surroundings were beautiful. The sound of the river rushing by was one he'd only heard on television. His vacations were always to much more exotic places. He liked it though, so far anyway.

Jose got out of the vehicle, stretched his arms upward, and arched his back. "Back to nature. It doesn't get any better than this, Chatham. Take the groceries in. I'll go around back and turn on the water and electricity."

The inside was comfortable, yet small, as Jose had promised. The walls were covered in cedar boards, and the kitchen was ample. There was a rock fireplace and a worn sofa.

"So, what do you think?" Ramirez asked.

"Not bad."

"Have you ever slept on a feather bed?"

"No, can't say that I have."

"Well get ready for the best night's sleep you've ever had."

They walked the twenty yards or so down to the small, winding river. It was fairly shallow, making it possible to see the rocks worn smooth from years of rushing water.

"Do you smell that, Chatham?"

"What's that?"

"It's the smell of fresh, clean, unpolluted air. The smell of mountain laurel and honeysuckle. Let's grab our poles.

We only bought dinner for one night. We better catch something for tonight."

Chatham squealed like a girl when he caught his first fish. He pulled it to the shore, admiring it with a big grin. Jose smiled to himself. He was glad he'd brought the kid and glad he'd taken a chance on him.

"My first," Chatham laughed. "Damn, it's a big one."

"I certainly hope it isn't the only first in your life," Jose teased. "That's not a scrawny fellow, throw him over there into the bucket. He'll fry up just right."

Dinner was better than either of them had expected. Fried fish, French fried potatoes, along with the pint of coleslaw Mrs. Everett had slipped into one of their bags.

"I couldn't eat another bite."

"I've seen you eat, Chatham. You have a hollow leg. Let's build a fire and grab a beer," Jose said.

"Sounds good to me. I have a few ideas about the case." Jose feigned a sigh but was more than willing to talk about it.

Chapter 18

It wasn't long before Jose had the fire going strong. It was apparent Chatham wouldn't have been able to start one if his life had depended on it. Jose motioned toward a few large logs, and the men rolled two of them over, sat them upright, and used them as stools. He pulled a Busch from the cooler while Chatham chose a dark, lager ale.

"What drives one to drink that shit? Is it peer pressure? Is it the need to feel better than those of us that drink domestic beer?" Jose questioned.

"That brings me to a question. Why would someone be so obsessed with what others choose to eat or drink? Do you feel intimidated by my finer tastes?"

Jose laughed as he reached over to slap Chatham on the back. "Guess you got me. Anyway, what's your latest take on our killer?"

"I've always had a certain interest in killers, more specifically, serial killers. I almost went on to medical school to become a psychiatrist, you know, attempt to find out what makes them tick."

"What the hell would you do with that information? Sell it to the FBI, or better yet, the textbook writers? Even though it's undeniable many of them share some of the same traits, they each have their own histories."

"That's always interested me. You know, how it starts to rear its head in childhood. The bedwetting, the cruelty to animals, etc." Chatham continued.

"That's been proven beyond the shadow of a doubt as well. Maybe it's an imbalance in the brain chemistry, who knows? In either case, they're animals who desperately need to be taken off of the streets," Ramirez added.

"No doubt. The scariest part, to me, is how they appear so normal. Did you know most of them have above average intelligence?"

"Chatham, I know you have a master's degree, but all of this is common knowledge, especially to anyone who picks up a paper or listens to the news."

Chatham looked frustrated but continued. "We're dealing with a *spree* killer, not a *serial* killer."

"That's a matter of semantics."

"Whatever. He doesn't require the cooling off period of a serial killer. He doesn't have to wait for the urge to kill to come around again. It makes sense in our cases because he doesn't feel the need for sexual gratification. He fits the profile perfectly. Just someone who suddenly snaps. Did you know Bundy's alter ego didn't appear until his college days?"

"Nope. Didn't know that." Jose answered.

"Did you know that Charles Manson's mother once tried to sell him for a pitcher of beer?"

"Am I supposed to break into tears now?"

"Damn it. I'm just trying to sort things out," Chatham said, sounding frustrated.

"I know, and you're doing a fine job. All of those statistics are important, but I'm not the type of guy who really gives a shit why people do what they do. I just want the bottom line. *Who the hell is doing it?*"

The two sat in silence as they pulled another beer from the nearby cooler.

"He's got to know there isn't a man in the house," Jose said. "He wouldn't be able to overpower both a man and a woman without someone screaming for help."

"O.J. did it," Chatham countered.

"He got lucky. Element of surprise. Anyway, the fact that he hits apartments says something. I'm not quite sure what though."

"One theory could be he knows the girls are young, and the odds are they have female roommates. Married couples are more likely to purchase homes. Besides, the neighbors are constantly changing in an apartment complex, unlike a neighborhood," Chatham offered.

"Good answer. I think we have established a few things so far. He's a young, white male… statistics… he's good-looking, at least enough so to get them to open the door. He attacks in torrential rainstorms, most likely to hide his appearance from any outside witnesses. If he should be seen running from the scene, it wouldn't appear strange. There are a few holes. He doesn't take them anywhere to dump them, either because he doesn't want to get caught, *or* because he doesn't have anywhere to take them. Maybe he's married, you know, the guy next door with the good job and two and a half kids," Jose said.

"Maybe so. But we can't disparage the notion he wants them to be found. He could be angry, along with the need to feel dominant."

Jose laughed as he stoked the fire with a long, skinny stick. "We could ponder it forever, but I can't help pointing my finger at all of the assholes I know."

"You don't know *that* many people," Chatham laughed. "Who's at the top of your list?"

"Ken Malone."

"The medical examiner?"

"Yep. He's a heartless son-of-a-bitch. It's as though he enjoys seeing the guts and gore. Young, slaughtered victims don't seem to affect him any more than older people dying natural deaths. It doesn't sit right with me. There are so many things that rub me wrong about that guy."

"I've heard he's a bear to work with, but let's face it, that's a macabre career. You have to be detached from all you see and deal with."

"I've given that a great deal of thought too, but look at all we have to see. A homicide is never a pleasant thing.

Maybe I'm in the wrong field, but I don't ever want to get to the point that they become objects to me. I just have to wonder what his life is like outside of the job. How would he react to the death of someone in his family?" Jose asked.

"We'll probably never find out, but let's see if he would have motive and opportunity," Chatham said.

"He can come and go as he pleases. He could tell his family he has to go to the morgue, he could tell the morgue he has to go home. As long as the autopsies are performed, who would give a damn?" Jose said.

"Okay then, motive?"

"Maybe he just enjoys the gruesome shit. He also gets thrown into the limelight every time there's a homicide. Malone's on the scene when the media arrives with their cameras and hot reporters. Some people get off on that type of attention," Jose continued.

"Makes sense. It could be his wife looks like a sea hag and holds out on him. Have you ever seen her?" Chatham asked.

"No, but I intend to when I get back."

"That's taking things a little far, don't you think?" Chatham asked.

"Can we take things too far?" Jose demanded.

"I hate to say it, Ramirez, but I'm starting to think Erin's attack didn't have anything to do with our killer."

"That's been foremost on my mind, but it's difficult for me to deal with. I'll think about it later. Right now, I just want her to get better."

As the fire turned to embers, the two men retired to the cabin. It was late, and the beer, along with their full bellies, had made them excellent candidates for a good night's sleep. Jose had enjoyed the conversation. It hadn't made things clearer, but it helped to work his mind.

The feather bed was all Chatham had been promised, and he was asleep as soon as he felt it mold around his thin, taut body.

Chapter 19

Both men bolted upright in bed as they heard the shattered glass from the kitchen window.

"What the…?" Jose asked, as quietly as he could. "Chatham, are you okay in there?"

"Yeah, man. What the hell's going on?"

They were both on their knees as they met each other in the small hallway.

"Where's your gun?" Jose asked in a harsh, steady whisper.

"I didn't bring it. You said this was the most peaceful place on earth."

"You fucking rookie," Jose hissed. "Mine is in the jeep. I'll have to slide outside and try to get it before the gunman gets closer. Lay low."

"Maybe it's just a hunter," Chatham said, his voice quivering like a child's.

"Hell no, it's not a hunter. They don't hunt near cabins, and they don't hunt in the middle of the night."

"What then?"

Jose didn't answer. Crawling along the floor, he reached up quietly, turning the old crystal doorknob. He could see his breath expelling in the cold, night air, and feel his heart as it pounded out of his chest. His ribs were starting to ache as the adrenaline flowed so fast he almost lost his bearings.

With one last gulp of air, Ramirez reached for the handle on the jeep, aware the overhead light would illuminate him as soon as he did so.

What's going on? Chatham thought. Please God, let this be a dream.

Jose reached into the jeep, grabbing his nine-millimeter from under the seat, just as a bullet took out the front tire beside him. Even though he expected it, it startled him just the same, sending him backward onto the wet ground.

"Shit, he isn't playing!" Jose screamed toward the cabin. "Stay down, Chatham!" He fired three rounds in the direction of the assailant, knowing he was merely pissing his ammo away. But he needed to bide a few more seconds to get another clip and his small backup weapon.

Jose felt the smooth metal of the extra clip just as a bullet seared through his right thigh. "Fuck!" Dragging himself into the cabin, he sat on the floor with his back pressed firmly against the door. His breathing was irregular as he struggled to calm himself.

"Is that you, Ramirez?"

"Hell no, it's the boogeyman."

He could hear Chatham's sigh of relief, along with the fear consuming his body.

"I found a flashlight. Do you want me to turn it on?" Chatham whispered.

"Yeah. Head over toward me."

He did as Jose had told him, then yelped like a puppy that had its tail stepped on. "Jesus, you're hit, man. You're hit. Damn, that's a lot of blood. I'm not a medic! What am I going to do?" Chatham asked, his voice now a high-pitched whisper.

"It's not *your* fucking leg. You aren't going to do anything. It's not that bad, blood can be deceiving. Go into the kitchen and get a dishrag or towel, the bigger the better.

It needs to fit around my thigh to put some pressure on the wound. Chatham?" Jose asked quickly.

"Yeah?"

"We're gonna be all right, okay? Breathe slow and easy. You're a cop, you'll be fine. Now shut that damn flashlight off until we absolutely need it."

Two more gunshots hit the cabin, penetrating the wooden siding, but not entering the interior. Jose listened as intently as he could for anyone drawing closer. It was difficult this time of year. The thick, damp pine needles were covering the ground, making it next to impossible to hear someone until they were right up on them.

"He's getting closer if he nailed you," Chatham said.

"Either he's a bad shot, or he meant to hit me in the leg. In that case, he doesn't intend to kill us. Take this," Jose said, pushing the weapon toward him.

Chatham looked at the gun. "What the hell is this supposed to be?"

"It's a .38 asshole. I know it's not that accurate from a distance, but it makes a hell of a backup. Besides, it beats the hell out of what you brought."

Chatham didn't respond. His panicked breathing was so loud it was beginning to sound like a snore. The gunshots were becoming louder, indicating they were getting closer.

"Whoever it is, they're making their way to the cabin. We can't take our chances staying here. We'll have to split up. He's coming south, down the mountainside. I'll go left, taking me further into the woods, and I'll go as far as I can. Then I'll lay low, be quiet, and hope that morning comes quickly. You run parallel to the road and try to get into town," Jose said calmly.

"You'll never make it with that leg," Chatham retorted.

Jose pulled the rag a little tighter, cringing with pain. "I'll *have* to make it."

Chapter 20

Apparently, it was closer to morning than the men had anticipated. The panic that seemed to have lasted only a few seconds was far longer. As the sun hit the horizon, Jose felt safer as he headed back to the cabin. The gunfire had long since ceased.

He assessed the damage to the Jeep's tire and would've kicked it if he weren't in so much pain. His leg was bleeding through the towel, so he took off his T-shirt and wrapped it tightly around the already bloody rag. Tears of pain ran down his already sweating face, making it difficult to distinguish between the two.

Jose unlatched the spare from the back of the jeep, rolling it to the front. It took what seemed like hours to jack it up and replace the new one. Several times, he struggled with unconsciousness. Turning the wrench with all the strength he could muster, Jose decided it'd simply have to suffice.

Luckily, it cranked immediately, meaning the tire was the only thing that'd been hit. Using his left leg and a long stick, he was able to both shift gears and push the accelerator. Waves of nausea were sweeping over him, forcing him stop several times to heave out the window. Each time it became more difficult to operate the vehicle. Another mile up the road, he saw Chatham running, waving his arms, and screaming for him.

"Stop! Stop, right now!" Chatham screamed.

Jose pulled up beside him, struggling to stop the vehicle. "Of course I'm going to stop, you idiot. Do you think I'd ride past your ass?"

Blood dripped from Chatham's face, saturating his shirt.

"Are you okay?" Jose asked.

"Yeah, flesh wound. But that's not the bad part. It's the Everetts."

Jose felt his stomach drop. He was too afraid to ask any questions. "Get in and drive. Make it quick."

It was still too early for the small town, if one could call it that, to awaken. Jose spat on his dirty watch, rubbing it against his shirt. "Seven thirty a.m."

Less than two minutes later, they were at the store. Chatham ran around, helping Jose out of the jeep, supporting him by wrapping Jose's arm around his neck.

"I don't know if you should go in, man," Chatham warned.

"Pull me in there if you have to. Now!"

The front door had been kicked in, and it hung onto the frame by one rusty hinge. Jose struggled to keep his breathing under control, but he was hyperventilating. He couldn't imagine losing the Everetts. They were the only semblance of a family he had left. Chatham insisted on helping Jose to the nearest stool. Bags of chips, crackers, and bruised tomatoes littered the floor.

"If they've been hurt, I need to find them. They'll need help," Daniel insisted. "You'll be unconscious yourself soon from blood loss. Sit down and let me look around."

Jose knew he was right. He was of little help, and soon wouldn't be of any at all. The possibility of anything happening to the Everetts had erased any thoughts of his own pain, so he held up his hands in surrender. "Just find them, hurry!"

Chatham raised the backup weapon that Ramirez had given him earlier and quickly began scanning the small supply shop. Although his breathing had quickened, he was surprised at how calm he remained. Deep in his gut, he knew if they'd been attacked, he wouldn't be able to help them. Aside from the place being ransacked, thankfully there weren't any bodies in sight. For that, he heaved a big sigh of relief. "Looks like we're in luck, Ramirez. No sign of blood, or the Everetts."

"Are you sure, partner?" Jose asked, sounding much weaker.

"Yeah, everything appears clear," Chatham answered, then looked up and spotted the large knife stuck deep into the counter, adjacent to the cash register. "They may not have been attacked, but this was clearly a warning they may not be safe for long."

Chapter 21

Jose's body finally gave in to the loss of blood, and he lost consciousness. The state police arrived, along with a medical chopper, to airlift him out. Chatham rode with them in the jump seat. With his head bent over, braced in his cupped hands, he prayed silently. Maybe he *was* in over his head. Jose had been right. There wasn't anything in any of his textbooks that could've prepared him for this.

The red medical target came into focus as the blades started to slow. Chatham could see a band of nurses and doctors waiting below with a gurney.

It all happened in such a whirlwind. Jose was removed from the chopper, quickly rushed to the waiting gurney and raced inside. The rotors slowed to a light hum, then went silent, a silence that was deafening. The pilot stepped calmly out of the helicopter and stretched his arms and legs. Chatham waited for his own legs to move forward.

His mind was telling them to go, but they stayed planted, heavy as cement.

"You all right, man?" the pilot asked.

"Uh, yeah. I'm going in," Chatham answered. He carried his weighted legs through the emergency doorway but was immediately shooed away by the staff. He could see them hovered over his partner, each yelling directives to the other. A shiver went up his spine that shook his entire body.

"Tell me what's going on," he said to one of the nurses as she pushed him forcibly out of the trauma area.

"We don't know anything yet. It's very critical. You've got to get out of here."

Her final push led him through a set of metal doors and into an empty, polished hallway. Chatham didn't know where it'd lead, but there was nothing to do but follow it. He took it to the end and turned right, his only choice. He could see the swarm of blue uniforms, their heads bowed, peering into their lukewarm cups of coffee. They looked up at him with a combination of hopeful and skeptical glances. It was one of those, *you want to know, but you don't* situations.

They stared at him, waiting for him to make the first move. Finally, the Captain stepped from the back of the group.

"What's going on?" he asked, not giving Chatham a chance to answer before he went on to his next question. "I don't believe this shit. We haven't heard anything other than we have an officer clinging to life in there. What the hell's going on?"

"He was shot in the thigh," Chatham said, watching as all of the officers leaned forward to hear his response. "He's lost a great deal of blood. I don't know Cap, I just don't know," he said, choking up and weaving his way to the nearest chair.

"Give him some room!" Captain Graham barked. "Somebody get him some water and a cold rag. We can't have him going into shock. That's all we need."

A nurse followed behind the officer carrying a cup of water. She scurried over to check Chatham's blood pressure.

"Pretty high," she said. "I want a doctor to check him and clean that wound on his face. I'll get him placed into a room, but he'll need rest. That means no visitors, no questions, nothing."

"We can respect that," Graham said. "Look, Kid, you did a hell of a job out there. Let that nurse get you a room."

Chatham nodded, ran his fingers through his matted hair, and followed behind her. The nurse turned into the first empty room they came to and closed the horizontal blinds. She started an IV, gave him a sedative, and cleaned his facial wound. He never said a word but thanked her softly with a nod as she left.

"Try to get some sleep now," she said kindly.

Chatham knew he wouldn't sleep, even though it'd be hours before Ramirez was out of surgery. Although it'd only been a couple of weeks, he already felt the unspoken loyalty of one partner to the other.

There was a double tap on the door before it opened just enough for Captain Graham to squeeze through. "The guys and I figured you could use a real meal." He pulled the dinner tray up to Chatham and opened two takeout boxes. He also pulled a Styrofoam cup out of a leaking bag containing a watered-down soda.

"Thanks, Cap."

"Look, I know you may not feel like eating, but you need your strength. Ramirez will be counting on you when he comes out of this. Sorry, but I've got to get out of here. That nurse of yours should've been a prison warden."

Chatham laughed, picking up the burger as Graham slid through the skinny opening he'd made for himself. He turned on his television set, flipping from channel to channel, as the anchors interrupted the regularly scheduled shows with the breaking news. They all had the same bits of information, and reiterated them over and over again. Finally, Chatham turned it to ESPN, but found himself drifting off into a restless sleep, only to be awakened by his nurse.

"I hated to wake you, Mr. Chatham," she said.

"What? Is it something about Ramirez?"

"Yes, it is. You can't excite yourself like this."

"Tell me, dammit. Oops, I'm sorry."

She appeared unfazed by the profanity. "Detective Ramirez is out of surgery. He required a great deal of blood. In fact, the doctors were amazed he made it here alive. He's listed in critical but stable condition. He's still under sedation, but you can see him in a couple of hours."

"Oh, thank God," Chatham said as he leaned back on his pillow and wept.

Chapter 22

For the first time in almost three weeks, Erin Sommers' eyelids flickered. She strained her eyes to bring them into focus, rotating her head from side to side in an attempt to determine where she was. Nothing looked familiar. She tried to sit up but failed miserably.

The shift nurse came in to check her vital signs and was so surprised to find Erin awake, she had to do a double take. "Well, good afternoon, dear," she said, gently rubbing Erin's arm.

The confusion in Erin's eyes asked the nurse all the questions she would've expected.

"Erin, you're in Memorial Hospital. You were injured in an accident. Do you recall that incident?"

She shook her head no, attempted to speak, but her mouth and throat were so parched, she almost gagged.

Panic set in. Pointing to her mouth, she tried to speak again, but her tongue stuck to the roof of her mouth.

"Would you like some water?" the nurse asked.

Erin shook her head affirmatively, indicating how desperately she wanted some.

The nurse returned within seconds with a small paper cup. She raised the bed, gently placing the straw in Erin's mouth. It took a great deal of effort, but slowly Erin was able to get some fluid through the straw. It didn't satiate her thirst as she'd expected. Her mouth was still left with the rough, dry feel of her bloated tongue. When the nurse took the empty cup from her mouth, Erin motioned for more.

"Let's give it just a few minutes to see how your body handles it. It may make you nauseous." Erin's eyes pleaded with her. Holding her hand, the nurse began to ask her questions. "If you understand what I'm saying, squeeze my hand, okay?" A faint squeeze followed. "Do you understand that you're in the hospital?" Another squeeze. "Do you work at the hospital?" Nothing. "Do you work for the Newspaper?" Another squeeze. "Very good, dear."

Erin's eyes closed as she drifted back into a deep sleep. Her few moments of consciousness had exhausted her.

Chapter 23

Jose opened his eyes to the wrinkled forehead, and worried face, of Daniel Chatham. In fact, his face was so close to his that Jose drew in a startled breath.

"Oh, thank God, man. You almost didn't make it. You scared me to death."

Ramirez couldn't help himself as he smiled. *Damn, he's a good kid.*

"Tell me everything," Jose said, struggling to speak.

"It was terrible. Do you remember anything?"

Jose nodded, as a sharp pain seared through his body.

"First, let me get the nurse. They'll need to know you're awake," Chatham said.

"No, tell me first."

It was too late, Chatham was skirting out of the room.

A pleasantly plump, middle-aged nurse entered the room with a broad smile. Jose didn't want to smile, and he didn't want to see anyone else smile, either.

"I see you're awake, Mr. Ramirez. Do you have any pain?"

"Yeah," he whispered.

"We'll get some more pain medicine in your IV. Do you want some water?"

"Um hmm."

She poured some from a nearby pitcher and held the straw up to his mouth. He sipped slowly, savoring each small splash as it wet his mouth, then his throat.

"Anything else?"

Jose held his hand up, indicating he didn't need anymore. She reached for the blood pressure cuff and took his vitals. "Not bad. The doctor will be in soon. Let me take a quick look at that leg." She slowly folded the sheet down, touching the bandage lightly. "Looks pretty good, too. I'll change it later today."

Jose closed his eyes in frustration. He wasn't looking forward to that. His thigh ached with a pain he hadn't known before. He lifted his arm slightly, pointing his right index finger toward his leg.

"You took a pretty bad hit. Luckily it didn't splinter the bone," Chatham said. "You won't have those tight thighs you once had, but hey, you're alive. The surgeon said a little more to the left, and you wouldn't be here. It's amazing how you made it through those woods."

Jose wanted to ask about the Everetts, but he was too weak. His eyelids struggled to stay open, but he could no longer control the strong urge for sleep. Chatham awkwardly patted his forearm as he sank back down in the chair by the bedside.

Captain Graham opened the door and motioned for the young detective to come outside. Once in the hallway, they could talk without Ramirez overhearing them.

"The evidence is coming in," Graham said quietly. "I don't know, Chatham. This is the first time the killer used a weapon other than a knife. It's confusing *and* alarming. Appears our perp used an AR-15 like the sniper used in D.C. The good news is the .223 caliber rounds he used tapered into small projectiles, most likely saving Ramirez's leg."

"What do you think it means?" Chatham asked.

"I don't know. It'd only be hypothetical at this point anyway. How do you think he found you guys, and why would he follow you?"

"I guess he followed us. Why? I don't know. Maybe it's getting personal with Ramirez."

"Looks that way. I heard he woke up for a few minutes," Captain Graham said.

"Yeah. He was weak and in a great deal of pain, but he was coherent. He wanted to know all about that night, but he fell asleep before I could tell him."

"That was probably for the best."

"You're right," Chatham agreed.

"Listen, you need to go home. You look like hell, and you don't smell so good, either. I'll stay with him. Get some sleep, and a good meal, and come back tomorrow morning," Graham insisted.

It was obvious Daniel didn't feel right about leaving, but Captain Graham shoved him toward the stairway. "Get out of here, Kid, or I'll call security." With that, Captain Graham walked into Jose's room, shutting the door behind him.

Chatham knew he was right. He needed a good night's sleep in a bed, instead of a poor excuse for a recliner, and as he thought about it, he was hungry too. The only things he managed to grab over the past few days were from the vending machines.

Daniel went through the drive-through at McDonald's on his way home. Pulling his car into the parking garage of his building, he was relieved to be home, to be away from the hospital, and the thoughts of a killer that none of them could catch.

He ate, showered, and climbed into bed. He slept for twelve hours and woke up feeling like a new man. Daniel got some orange juice out of the fridge and sat down to the latest edition of the newspaper, which boasted that Erin Sommers was out of her coma and doing well. Ramirez would be thrilled to hear the good news. There was little about the killer, only a small blurb indicating he was still at large. The department had done a good job in keeping it as much under wraps as they could. Opening the windows, he sat back to enjoy the cold air coming in. His mind went back to that night, and he rolled it around in his head. *Maybe it was possible that Malone was their killer. He'd take it* personally with Ramirez. He hated cops, and most of all, he hated Ramirez. It made sense, but then again, why would he do it? Questions, questions. Would there ever be anything else?

Chapter 24

Erin looked much better than the last time Chatham had seen her. Her hair had been washed and combed, and she was sitting up in bed eating from a hospital tray.

"The food isn't their greatest quality here at Harborview, is it?" Chatham asked, startling her.

"No, it isn't," she smiled.

"I'm Detective Chatham, Jose Ramirez's new partner."

"I know he's thrilled about that," she laughed. "He doesn't like to share his time with many people. But I'm sure you've gathered that by now."

"You've got that right," Chatham agreed. "But things are going okay. Do you feel like talking, or would a later time be better?"

"Now is as good as any, I suppose. I don't have much to offer you."

"Anything is better than nothing. Tell me everything you remember about that night. No detail is too small."

Erin started with her weekend at the lodge, ending with the hand wrapping around her mouth until she lost consciousness.

"That's it. That's all I remember. The next thing I knew, I was here in the hospital," Erin said.

"Did you hear a voice, see any clothing, anything?" Chatham pressed.

"Nothing. It was raining cats and dogs. I just remember seeing a form. I can't tell you how tall it was, or even if it was emaciated or obese."

"Do you think it had anything to do with the serial killer?"

Erin took a bite of red Jell-O then pushed her tray out of reach. "From my injuries, I'd say no. Besides, it'd be a remarkable coincidence. How would the killer know I'd be traveling that highway, or better yet, stop?"

"We've already thought about that. Did you recently discover anything new about the killer? Anything you hadn't had an opportunity to share with Ramirez?"

"No, not really. We stayed in close contact. Always."

"I don't want to worry you, but…"

"Look, nothing could worry me any more than this already has."

"Are you aware someone cleaned your office? Ramirez was extremely concerned about it, saying you always kept things in your own organized clutter."

Erin sat silent for a moment, appearing deep in thought. "No, I wasn't aware of that. The security, as I'm sure you know, is fairly tight at the complex. It's unsettlingly that anyone could get through the gates, much less enter my apartment." She wrinkled her face. "But a cop could've easily gotten in there."

"You might just be as good as Ramirez said you are," Chatham said.

She smiled, then her expression turned quickly to concern. "Why are you here without him? He hasn't visited yet."

Chatham sat silent.

"Tell me," she said.

"He was shot…"

She gasped as her hands flew up to her face.

"It's not as bad as it sounds. He was hit in the thigh. He's downstairs in a room, irritating the hell out of the nurses to get up here. They aren't very fond of him here in ICU."

Another laugh. "I'm moving into a room this afternoon, thank God. I want to see him desperately."

"He shares the sentiment."

"What happened? I want to hear about everything."

It took over an hour for Chatham to tell her about the events at Whispering Hollow. Erin stopped him several times to question him further about specific details.

"Why would anyone follow you two up there? It doesn't make any sense. Up until now, it's only been young women. Actually two things don't make sense. First, why you and Ramirez? You were both left with life-threatening injuries, but you weren't killed. And, why the Everetts? I've heard Jose speak of them. It had to be a vindictive act. Nothing else would make sense. The killer used the same MO, making it deliberate so we'd know it was the same person. The knife was left there as a warning."

"Ramirez isn't ruling out Ken Malone."

"Who in the hell would open a door to that creep?" Erin asked sarcastically.

Chatham snickered. "You've got a point there. I'm going to let you rest now. I've overstayed my welcome. You're going to need your strength when they move you into your room. I'll share our conversation with Ramirez."

"Thanks. Tell him I expect a speedy recovery. We've got work to do."

Chatham entered Jose's room feeling better than he had since the weekend in the mountains. Ramirez was alert now, and irritable, almost to the point of running Chatham out of the room.

"I just saw Erin."

"How was she?" Jose asked eagerly.

"Good. Just as anxious to see you as you are to see her. She didn't give me anything to go on. Apparently, it was raining too hard for her to make out her assailant. But, after the attack on you, I'm convinced it's our killer. Nothing else makes sense."

Jose shook his head in disgust. "You know, Chatham, we must be closer than we think."

"I hope so. At any rate, I've got to make a showing at the precinct. They're about to take me off the payroll."

"Look, man," Jose started. "I appreciate all you did. I won't forget it."

"It was nothing. I'm sure you would've done the same. Besides, all I did was run like hell."

Ramirez released a good, hearty laugh that seemed to come from his gut. Chatham could still hear chuckling as he shut the door behind him.

Daniel stepped out of the hospital and felt the coolness of the light breeze. He looked up at the sky and swore out loud. "Son-of-a-bitch, it's about to rain."

Detective Chatham found the precinct empty, realizing he'd arrived too late to make an appearance. Furious he hadn't noticed before parking and getting out into the rain, he trotted the hundred yards back to his car. Grabbing a sweatshirt from the passenger seat, he wiped his dripping hair and face. The rest of him would have to wait until he got home.

Daniel decided on a hot shower and a delivered pizza. The weather had been too miserable to stop at the grocery store, and he hadn't felt like cooking since he'd been partnered with Ramirez. Within the hour, he'd finished off a vegetarian pizza and a two-liter of soda.

Chapter 25

Elle Jenkins had been on the police force for three years. Lucky for her, she'd been able to get on as soon as she'd turned twenty-one. It was a fringe benefit of having a city councilman as a father, and she didn't mind taking advantage of it. Besides, she'd become one of the best beat cops in the city. She was pretty, kind, and the people on her beat trusted her. It was a perfect fit. Unfortunately, she was stuck with Tuesdays and Wednesdays off. But, Elle was still low on the totem pole, so it was to be expected. She didn't mind today; the rain was back.

Elle knew she'd lain in bed too long, but she enjoyed the comfort of the warm bed, mixed with the sound of rain. Dragging herself from underneath the down comforter, she showered, dressed, and made her way to the kitchen. She was having company for dinner. A mutual friend had introduced them, and they'd hit it off from the beginning. Elle was sure it was getting serious.

* * * *

Not being much of a cook, she prepared spaghetti sauce out of a bottle, hoping it'd make up for the lack of a decent home cooked meal by putting extra effort into the salad. The clock gave her just enough time to put on some makeup and pick up the scattered newspapers and dirty clothes. The doorbell interrupted her before she was able to begin. Scott was early, which wasn't his style. He didn't want to appear too desperate. Two hard knocks followed the buzz of the doorbell.

"Okay, okay, I'm coming." She looked out the small, smudged peephole before swinging the door open. "This is a huge surprise," she said, hugging him hard. "How great to see you."

"Same here. How's the world treating you?"

"Not too bad, you know, the life of a cop."

"All too well."

"Take off that big rain poncho and come sit down. I'm expecting company, but we have a few minutes. What brings you to this section of town?"

"I was just riding by and thought I'd stop by to see the new place."

"It's not exactly new anymore, you know."

"Since I haven't been over this way, I still consider it new. I didn't know if you'd still be here or not."

"Like I could afford anything else on my salary."

He carefully lifted his poncho, but instead of removing it, he hastily reached inside the hidden pocket for the concealed butcher knife. Plunging it into her midsection, Elle only had time to let out a small gasp.

"You," she whispered, as blood drained out in spurts. "I can't believe it."

Grinning a sick, frightening smile, he turned to make his exit. Darting past Elle's boyfriend, the plummeting rain prevented Scott from even noticing him.

When he knocked and didn't receive a response, Scott turned the doorknob, peeking in. "Elle, it's me. I don't want to startle you." Again, he didn't get a response, so he walked, in assuming she must be in the shower. It wasn't like her to leave the door unlocked. As a cop, she knew better.

He took a few steps before seeing her there, covered in blood, lying on her left side.

"Oh, my God!" Scott screamed, running over to grab her. Checking her pulse, he detected a faint one, but she was unresponsive.

He reached 911, only after dialing four other numbers. It was strange how the most well known number could leave one's mind in such a situation.

"Help!" he screamed into the phone. "It's my girlfriend. She's been stabbed. She's barely alive."

"Hold on, sir, while I ask you a few questions. I need you to stay on the line."

"Fuck that, you idiot. Get an ambulance here!" With that, Scott slammed down the phone and ran to Elle's side. Her pulse was getting fainter by the second as he pleaded with her to come to. "I love you, Baby. I know I took too long to say it, but I'm saying it now. Please, hang in there."

Two minutes before the ambulance arrived, Elle Jenkins drew her final breath.

Chapter 26

Ramirez was finally able to wheel himself into Erin's room, but it was a bittersweet reunion. He was able to visit his friend and see her alive, but he'd also come to bring the latest news.

"You're looking good, Kid," he spurted out, for a brief moment forgetting the horrible news he had to share.

"You couldn't possibly know what you've put me through."

"Sorry about that, but you didn't cut me any slack either. How's that leg?"

"It's nothing. Not anything a cold beer and a couple of days of R&R can't handle," Jose said.

"Right. Sounds like you came close to death's door too, you know."

"We both cheated death. That's all that matters."

"What's with the look?" Erin asked.

145

"What look?" Jose asked innocently.

"That one you get in your eyes when something bad has happened," Erin continued.

"You're good Erin, you're good. I hate to share this with you, but it'll hit the paper and the news stations soon. There's been another murder. Elle Jenkins, the young beat cop."

"Oh, no! I don't think I've met her. Same guy?"

"Yep. We've got work to do," Jose said.

"You know what that means, don't you?" Erin asked, suspicion in her voice.

"Yes, I do. It's a cop."

"I knew it, Jose. I knew it from the beginning."

"Me too. I just refused to admit it. But, I still have my suspicions about Malone. Sick bastard. I'm going to set up surveillance on him when they let me out of here," Jose said indignantly.

"I'm going with you. I figure I can get about a month's sick leave from *The Seattle Times* if I play my cards right."

Jose laughed. "You're a trooper, but you need recovery time."

"And what about you?" she asked, pointing at his injured leg.

"We need to get on this. I'm getting out today, no matter what the doctor's say. I can recoup better at the apartment."

"I'm not even responding to that. You're too hardheaded to waste my time."

Jose called Chatham, demanding he pick him up. Against his better judgment, Daniel drove to the hospital.

Ramirez's attitude had left much to be desired, and Chatham cursed himself under his breath for being so gullible. "Why did I pick you up?"

"Because I told you to. We have a lot of work to do. Do you think I have time to be tended to by that nurse, or should I say prison warden? Stop by a gas station and pick up some beer, maybe a sandwich or something," Ramirez demanded.

"Don't tell me you're hungry enough for a gas station sandwich. We'll stop at a drive-through."

Chatham was able to make the two stops without pushing Ramirez out of the car and running over him, but it'd been difficult. Navigating the stairs in the apartment had been a challenge, to say the least.

"Would you just quit bitching. I didn't *have* to pick you up at the hospital."

"Listen, Chatham, I hurt like hell, and just need to solve this case."

Daniel tried desperately to resist the guilt trip Jose was putting on him, but failed miserably. Ramirez was soaked with sweat when they reached the apartment, so Chatham helped him take his shirt off, replacing it with a clean undershirt. He also handed him a cool, wet washcloth to put on his face.

"Should I turn this fan on?" Chatham asked.

"Might not be a bad idea."

Chatham opened two beers and grabbed two plates from the cabinet. He filled both of them with fried chicken, coleslaw, baked beans, macaroni and cheese, and a biscuit. He passed the plate and beer to his partner along with a couple of napkins. "Maybe this will help your mood. You're acting like a teenage girl with PMS."

"Screw you," Ramirez said.

"Yeah, whatever."

"Listen, we need the files and pictures from Elle's murder. Can you get them from the precinct?"

"I'll try, but they're still working on it, Ramirez, it just happened last night. Malone probably hasn't even started the autopsy."

"Just get what you can. Everyone will be gone in thirty minutes. Let's eat, and I'll ride with you and wait in the car."

"You need to take a pain pill now then. You screamed like a baby the whole way home from the hospital."

"I don't think I'd say *screamed like a baby*. In case you haven't noticed, I've got a serious injury."

"Yeah, one that should be treated in the hospital. Captain Graham's going to chew your ass when he hears you left without discharge papers."

"He'll get over it. While we're out, let's put some surveillance on Malone. I've got a gut feeling," Ramircz said.

"Shit."

Chapter 27

Ramirez was drenched with sweat again by the time they made it to the car. It took well over five minutes to get into the Corvette.

"Why would *anybody* buy a piece of shit like this? Why didn't you get a real car?" Ramirez said sarcastically.

"Why does *anybody* buy cheap beer?" Chatham countered.

Jose mumbled a few choice words before he sank into the seat in exhausted silence. He waited impatiently as Chatham went into the precinct.

"What were you doing in there, socializing?" Jose grumbled.

Chatham refused to put any energy into arguing with him. "I had to practically steal the damn thing. Lucky for us, we work with men who lack ambition. They were filing out for the day."

"Hand it over," Ramirez demanded.

Chatham sighed sarcastically, thrusting the folder over to him. Jose read, looked at the pictures, and then shook his head in disgust as he always did at homicide victims.

"Tell me, damn it. I went in to get it, why should I have to wait to look at it myself?"

"Her boyfriend found the door unlocked to her apartment, which is crazy for a police officer. I find it hard to believe she'd do that. Apparently, the boyfriend found it strange too. He entered the apartment to find her barely alive on the floor, incoherent, of course, until she died. The killer couldn't have been far behind, but the boyfriend didn't notice anything unusual. The fucking rain, it's the devil, I swear."

"You know what this means, Ramirez. Elle knew her assailant. She had to know all the details of our killer, and wouldn't open the door, even to a good-looking guy in distress."

"You got it, which leads us to either a cop or Malone."

"I hate to agree with you, but I'm left without a choice. Where do we go from here?"

"The medical examiner's office. Malone won't know your car, park across the street, and we'll tail him."

"I don't feel good about this," Chatham said hesitantly.

"I hate to pull rank on you, but sometimes it has to be done. Hurry up, he should be getting off soon," Ramirez said, as he reached down to rub his injured leg.

The two only had a fifteen-minute wait before Malone sauntered out of the building toward his car. It was a new Lexus four-door.

"I didn't know they paid public servants so well," Ramirez said, in between sudden bouts of pain.

"Maybe the wife has a good job," Chatham suggested.

"Don't be an optimist, Chatham. I hate that shit."

They followed at a safe distance as the Lexus made its way into a seedy part of town.

"What's he doing?" Ramirez asked, craning his neck to see what would happen next.

"Let's wait and see," Chatham answered impatiently.

They continued two more blocks as Malone pulled up beside a shady character, thrusting his rolled-up cash out of the window. The man looked around, took the money, and handed him a clear baggie of what appeared to be crack cocaine.

"Son-of-a-bitch," Ramirez said. "He's buying drugs. I told you something wasn't right with him."

"Look," Chatham said. "He's pulling up next to a hooker. I can't believe it. She's getting in the car."

Both men sat in silence, watching from a distance. Chatham had turned his headlights off, feeling uneasy in the crime-riddled neighborhood. Malone sat in the car a few minutes before driving off with the young prostitute in his vehicle. The silver Corvette pulled out and tailed him at a safe distance.

"He's going to notice us soon, Ramirez."

"Keep going."

Riding for over five miles, Jose was beginning to get a little uneasy himself. They pulled into an old, vacated, concrete factory, and again Chatham switched off the headlights.

"Get out and see what's going on," Ramirez instructed.

"What are you thinking? Are you crazy? I can't do that," Chatham said defiantly.

"You've got two legs, don't you?"

Chatham shook his head then got out of the car. He felt like a sick stalker, but he made his way toward the Lexus. Just as suspected, Malone was utilizing the services he'd undoubtedly paid for.

Quietly opening his car door, Chatham slid back behind the steering wheel. "He's enjoying himself. I could've lived my whole life without seeing that. Now, I'm going to get a mental picture of it every time I see him."

Ramirez attempted a laugh but found it difficult.

"Holy…" Chatham said frantically. "Your leg's bleeding like crazy. We're going to the hospital."

"Not before we find out if Malone returns this girl safely," Ramirez persisted.

"What have I done so bad in my life that they stuck me with you?" Chatham asked.

"You're just a lucky man."

Five minutes later, the Lexus pulled out of the factory.

"So much for romance," Chatham commented.

"That's not what you get a whore for," Ramirez said.

"Please spare me the *whore* word. It's so degrading."

"My God. Don't tell me you're one of *those*."

The Lexus dropped the girl off at the same spot, and she got out blowing a kiss at Malone.

"I'm gonna puke," Ramirez said. "Sick bastard."

"Look at my floorboard, Ramirez. I'm going straight to the hospital, you're bleeding!"

"Not until we follow Malone home."

"No, we aren't! I'm taking your ass to the ER. I can get a nurse out there before you can get out of this vehicle," Chatham said.

Jose was too weak to argue. Maybe it was a good idea. "Let me take the folder. I'll look at it and share it with Erin."

Chatham knew he should get it back to the precinct, but reluctantly agreed. It was a compromise to get Ramirez to the hospital.

Chapter 28

The following morning Chatham showed up bright and early at the precinct for the first time in two weeks. Captain Graham stood in the doorway of his office and motioned for him to head his way. Chatham's heart beat a little faster as he felt his face grow red. *Damn it*, he thought. *I knew this was going to happen.*

The Captain waited until Chatham sat down before he slammed the door, ensuring it was loud enough for the whole floor to hear. It was a scare tactic, and it'd worked.

"Are you a fucking doctor, Detective? Is that what you think we pay you for? Our unit has had a meeting every day since the incident at Whispering Hollow. Do you not feel obligated to join us?"

Chatham opened his mouth, but the Captain wouldn't give him clearance to speak. "You were brought in here as a political appointee to put your education to work. You weren't sent to be a nursemaid for a grown-ass man!"

He slammed his balled fist on the desk, making Chatham lean back in his seat.

"Do you want a job, Detective, because if you do, you've got a shit load to catch up on."

"Yes, Sir, I do. I apologize for getting sidetracked."

"We don't get sidetracked in homicide, Detective."

"Yes, Sir. It won't happen again," Chatham said, regret resonating in his voice.

"You better not be blowing smoke up my ass. I only give one warning around here. We don't need any dead weight," Captain Graham threatened.

"I understand, Sir."

"And do you, Detective, have any idea where Officer Elle Jenkin's file might be?"

"Um, well…"

"Listen, Son, you're on thin ice."

"Actually, I dropped it off with Ramirez. He wanted to take a look at it, Sir." Chatham held his breath. He knew what was coming.

"That arrogant son-of-a-bitch! I suggest you take your ass over there and get it. Now!"

"I'm on it, Sir. I'll be right back."

"We're meeting in an hour. Oh yeah, a nurse called for you from Lobale Mental Institute."

Oh shit, Chatham thought. How could I have forgotten?

Ramirez had his leg propped up on the recliner in Erin Sommers' room, his mind deep in thought. Erin had the crime scene photos spread across her legs on the bed.

"Look you two, I've got to have that folder. The Captain is *raving*, and I'm in deep shit."

"Sorry about that, partner. I should've known. Listen, they're officially releasing us as of tomorrow. I've talked Erin into leaving the physical comforts of her apartment and staying at my place. It'll be much safer."

"That should be quite a change of venue," Chatham laughed. "Have you washed any sheets in the last two years?"

"Yes, as a matter-of-fact, I have. Besides, I have clean ones for the guest room. Do you think you could get my police cruiser and drop us off?"

"Yeah. I'll be here in the morning. Gotta run," Chatham said as he straightened the photos and returned them to the folder. "We're having a meeting in an hour, oops, a half hour now."

The meeting was exactly the joke Chatham had anticipated. They all knew there wasn't anything to go on and weren't willing to go the extra mile to identify any potential leads.

What a waste of taxpayer dollars, Chatham thought. Where did they find these bozos, and how can they criticize Ramirez and me?

The detective finally had an opportunity to share both his experience in the mountains and what few leads he was investigating. He knew the Captain was impressed, but he'd never admit it.

"Let's hit it, Ladies and Gentlemen," Graham said, tossing his pen onto the mounds of paperwork. "Do what you can. Chatham, you and Ramirez are the only ones assigned specifically to this case, or cases rather. These other guys have other cases besides this one."

"Yeah," several sneered, walking out of the conference room.

Chapter 29

"Lobale Mental Institute, how may I direct your call?"

"Yes, this is Detective Chatham. Could I speak to Chrissy Ozette's unit nurse, please?"

"One moment," the woman replied.

It was less than five minutes before the nurse picked up the receiver.

"Hello, Detective," the nurse said, sounding a little frustrated.

Chatham recognized her voice as being the one that'd assisted him earlier.

"Hi there. I was calling about Ms. Ozette."

"Her doctor was not very pleased when you missed your appointment. He has very little spare time."

"I understand that... Nurse?"

"Nurse Sally Spriggs."

"I hope I can offer a decent excuse for my absence, Ms. Spriggs. My partner and I went camping the weekend before, and he was shot. A life-threatening injury, actually."

"Oh, how horrible," she said, sounding much younger than she had before. Her voice had broken away from the professionalism that had initially greeted him. "My apologies for being so nasty to you."

"Nurse Spriggs, I'd hardly call that nasty. I'm a police officer. No one is ever happy to talk to me."

With that, she laughed. "Please, call me Sally."

"Thank you, Sally. Do you think you might have enough pull to get me back in to see the doctor?"

"Yes, Detective, I think I can do that. If you'll give me your number one more time, I'll get back with you."

Chatham opened a can of soda that he'd let get too warm for his taste, but he needed the caffeine anyway. Nurse Spriggs had given him forty-five minutes to get to the institute. He took three aspirin and a swig of soda, its temperature and carbonation almost making him choke. He now had Ramirez's cruiser, and compared to his Corvette, felt as though he were navigating a large ship.

He pulled up to the facility within thirty minutes. It was as lifeless and generic as a penitentiary. Chatham had studied the history of this type of facility enough to know that the patients were treated much the same as the inhabitants of a prison. Some were better than others, but he wasn't getting a good feeling about this one. The interior gave him the same sick feeling hospitals did, and he found himself wishing Ramirez were there to lean on.

Sally Spriggs came out to the information booth to greet him. She was probably twenty-four or five and quite attractive. That was the last thing Chatham had even considered. He hadn't dated in several months and now found himself wondering why. Her blonde hair was shoulder length, and as full and smooth as the shampoo models on television. Expecting blue eyes, he was surprised to see dark, with a slight hint of hazel.

"Detective Chatham?" she asked in a friendly voice.

"Yes. Actually, it's Daniel," he answered, feeling awkward at the sound of his own first name.

"Well, Daniel, it's nice to meet you," she countered. "You can come with me. No one is allowed back in the patients' living areas, but as you know, you're an exception.

162

I'm sure you get to see behind the scenes of many interesting places," she added with a smile.

"Oh yes, and many you wouldn't believe if I told you." Chatham shared a laugh with her, helping to put him at ease. He followed her through thick metal doors in a maze that left him feeling as though the place really was a prison. It was an extremely sterile environment, and he took in small, shallow breaths so as not to breathe in the fumes of ammonia and various other disinfectants. The maze abruptly ended at a nurses' station, very similar to the one in the hospital's intensive care unit.

"The doctor will be out shortly," she said, motioning to a few chairs for him to choose from.

Chatham walked over, picked the middle seat, and then wiped his forehead to dry the sweat forming there. Glancing down at his watch, he wondered what Ramirez was doing.

"Detective Chatham, I'm Dr. Ronald Easton," a middle-aged man said, extending his hand. He was much like Chatham had suspected, a short, rounded man with a shiny baldhead.

"Thank you for seeing me, Doctor. I know how valuable your time is. I hope Nurse Spriggs explained the unfortunate circumstances that kept me from my last visit."

"Yes, she did. My sympathies to both you and your partner," Dr. Easton said.

"Thank you, Sir. It appears to be tied to the serial killer who murdered Ms. Ozette's roommate, which leads me to why I'm here."

"I understand you're here to question her in reference to that murder."

Chatham nodded his head in agreement. "Will that be possible?"

"I must tell you, I don't know what she's blocked out and what she hasn't. Ms. Ozette is in a severe depressive state at this time. In fact, so much so that she's only started verbalizing her needs in the last couple of days."

"I understand. We see that a great deal in survivors and witnesses," Chatham said, trying to sound seasoned, and hoping it worked.

"I'll take you back to her. She's expecting you. Although she's still heavily sedated, Chrissy is aware of what's going on."

"Thank you, Doctor."

Chatham felt a deep hollowness in the pit of his stomach, the uneasiness that comes from the unknown. He followed the doctor down the hallway to a door that had a small windowed opening covered with heavy, wired mesh. The walls were a light attempt at army green and the door, institutional beige. Dr. Easton tugged at a roll of keys attached to his belt until finding the correct one. Taking his time, he detached the key ring and twisted a key into the door. It was driving Chatham crazy, and he had to force himself not to shuffle his weight from one foot to the other. The lock clicked as the doctor motioned for him to enter.

"I'll be back in about fifteen minutes. Should there be a problem, there's a button on the wall for you to push, kind of a nurses' button, if you will."

Chatham looked back at him and continued staring at the door long after he'd heard it lock. He was frozen by the fear of what he'd see when he turned around, but slowly Daniel twisted his body to confront Chrissy. It wasn't as he'd expected. For some reason, his mind had led him to believe she was going to be a monster, not just a young woman who'd been through a tragic event. She was sitting upright on her bed, her legs drawn up to her chest, her thin arms wrapped around them. Her hair was past her shoulders, but unkempt, like someone who'd spent the past few days in bed with the flu. Her eyes were bloodshot and swollen, and small blotches of pink hives were running up her neck. Chrissy didn't look at him. Her eyes were transfixed on the woolen blanket that covered her small, twin bed. She reminded him of a frightened child, and Daniel was ashamed of himself for fearing her.

"Good afternoon, Ms. Ozette," he said softly, as he made his way over to the chair by her bedside.

She didn't move her head, but her eyes shifted to his chest. When Chatham sat in the chair, Chrissy was looking him in the eye.

"My name's Daniel," he said, hoping the use of his first name wouldn't be as intimidating. "I'm with the police department. I'm very sorry about your friend."

She didn't respond, but pools of tears began forming in her eyes.

"I'm here to see if you remember anything that might help us to find who did this to her."

Daniel paused for a moment as he watched the tears overflow from the rims of her eyes. She looked so vulnerable, fragile. He cursed himself for not carrying a handkerchief. She instinctively used the sleeve of her hospital gown to wipe the tears, then her nose.

"I know this is hard for you," Chatham began again. "I'm sorry I have to ask you these questions, but it's very important."

She wiped the thin, cotton sleeve across her eyes again, then nodded in response.

"Can you tell me what happened that night? It might be easier to start from the beginning," Daniel said, his voice quiet and soothing.

Chrissy cleared her throat, and Chatham watched, as her chin quivered. Her voice was much softer than he'd expected. "I… I was out with my boyfriend. We went to a party and drank too much. I spent the night in his dorm room."

The tears were flowing one by one down her cheeks, but she continued to speak. "I felt guilty that morning because I was supposed to pick up something for Bridgette to eat and bring it back to her. I forgot."

"Is that your roommate?" he asked, making sure her recollection was clear.

"Yes."

Chatham gave her a minute to get herself together before asking if she could go on.

"We stopped by the party and started drinking beer. They had four kegs, and everyone kept pushing the beer on us. They didn't want it to go bad."

With that, she broke into sobs, her shoulders heaving up and down, in sequence with her breaths.

"Do you want me to leave, Chrissy?" he asked, reaching for her shoulder, then deciding it'd be inappropriate to touch her.

"No, I need to tell you everything," she answered. "We drank too much, and I forgot about Bridgette. She didn't come with us because she wasn't feeling well. She had a bad headache. I was going to pick up some Tylenol and a hamburger for her. Instead, I got drunk, and screwed my boyfriend."

She spoke with such anger that Chatham reached out and patted her shoulder anyway. "It wasn't your fault, Chrissy. Even if you'd brought her dinner, it wouldn't have changed anything. Besides, it may have happened before you got back with the food. The important thing is for you to be strong."

"It was raining, really bad, even the next morning when I got home. My boyfriend dropped me off, but he didn't walk me to the door. I found her by myself. It was, oh God…" Her voice broke into uncontrollable sobs.

"It's okay, Chrissy. I saw the pictures. Don't think about that moment when you found her. Was there anything out of the ordinary in your apartment?"

"No. I didn't really look around, but nothing stands out in my mind. I was so upset about Bridgette, that…"

"I know. I mean, I can't imagine. You're a very strong young lady. Did Bridgette have a boyfriend?"

"No. She dated her schoolbooks. It used to piss me off, but then I realized she made the perfect roommate. She was different from me, she had money and a family, and I, well, I was damn lucky to get into college, and that was on financial aid. I liked her though."

"Did she have many friends?"

"Yeah, she didn't party like I did, but she had her own friends. Kind of the nerdy crowd, I guess. She stayed home mostly. Sometimes I could talk her into going out with Trey and me."

"Trey is your boyfriend?"

"Yes. Trey Young. He goes to the University with me."

"I see. Did you and Bridgette go anywhere together, like a certain place to eat, or shop?"

"Sometimes. We had classes that ended at the same time on Thursdays. We'd meet at a sub shop across from the campus at Elm and 10th."

"Did she know people there? Maybe some of the employees?"

"Nothing stands out. It was just a place where all the students went."

"What about shopping?"

"We didn't share the same taste. She did her own grocery shopping, and I did mine. We didn't wear the same clothes, either. Oh yeah, we did shop at the mall at Bare Necessities. We usually went once a month and spent about an hour in there, smelling all the latest scents. You know, bath gels, body lotion, all of that stuff."

"They seem to be big sellers right now."

"Yeah, everyone goes there. They have the best prices and the best selection."

Chrissy suddenly realized she was talking about bath gels and not about the death of her friend. "God," she said, the tears forming again. "I can't believe I'm talking about freaking shower gel right now."

"It's important for me to hear everything. Are you feeling better?"

"I'm doing better than I was. It totally freaked me out and I couldn't even talk about it. I checked myself in here because I really..." The tears tumbled forward and she didn't attempt to wipe them away this time.

"It's okay," Daniel said, patting her lightly on her shoulder. "You're doing great."

"I didn't have anywhere else to go," she blurted. "I didn't have anywhere else to go." Chrissy Ozette sobbed until Chatham thought she was going to vomit. He heard the key sliding into the lock, then looked up to see Dr. Easton.

"The point of you being here, Detective, was not to upset my patient!"

"Yes, Sir. I'm very sorry. It won't happen again."

"You're damn right it won't. Now get out. There will be no more visits!"

Chatham didn't have the nerve to look back at Chrissy. His heart ached for her. Where in the hell was her boyfriend? He was there to get her drunk and into the sack.

Sally Spriggs met him at the nurses' station. "I heard you weren't exactly a big hit with Dr. Easton."

"That's putting it mildly. He wouldn't win a personality contest, would he?"

She laughed, covering her mouth with her hand. Chatham noticed she didn't have on a wedding band. That was a relief.

"I'm on my way down to the cafeteria for lunch. Would you like to join me?"

"I, uh, well…" Chatham desperately wanted to spend more time with her, but eating at this place wasn't what he had in mind.

"I'm sorry, Detective. I know you're a busy man. I'll show you the way out."

"No, it's not that," he answered. "I just have this kind of fear of hospitals. I'm not sure I could eat. Suppose I take you to lunch somewhere nearby?"

Sally laughed, tucking her arm into his. "I'm not allowed to leave the premises during working hours. But, I think you might be surprised at our cafeteria. I promise, you won't even know you're in a place like this."

"A man's first mistake, trusting a woman!" Chatham said good-naturedly.

Chapter 30

Detective Chatham pulled the cruiser up to Ramirez's apartment and got out. It'd been a long, exhausting day, but it'd also had its high points. He'd obtained information from Chrissy and enjoyed lunch with a pretty nurse named Sally Spriggs.

Erin answered the door, greeting Chatham with a hug. He was glad to see her. "So, what have you two bums been doing today? Recuperating?"

"Yep," Ramirez said.

"Let me hear the latest news," Chatham said.

"I was telling Erin about Malone," Ramirez started.

"That man is sick," Erin interrupted. "I'm dying to see his wife."

"Will you two give it a break? Damn, if I didn't know better, I'd think you were both obsessed with him. What's the deal with his wife? I don't think she can help the fact her husband's a creep."

"I just want to know what the deal is with him," Erin responded defensively. "What drives him to be such an asshole? Why would he cheat on his wife with a prostitute?"

"Have you two ever thought he may be an asshole because he was born an asshole, or he may cheat on his wife because she's dog-ass ugly and won't put out?"

"Damn, Chatham, are you screwing him?"

"Fuck you, Ramirez," Chatham answered, then had to laugh. "I'm getting a round of drinks. I can see we're going to need them. What's for dinner?"

"Pizza. The number's on the side of the fridge. Will you give them a call while you're up? Order whatever you want. He that orders, payeths."

"Why am I not surprised?" Chatham sighed. He took off his shoes and settled into the recliner, knowing it'd be his bed for the night. He was drinking too much to drive. He shared his experience with Chrissy Ozette, her boyfriend, the sub shop, and the store at the mall.

"I'm not so sure the mall could lead us anywhere," Erin said. "Unfortunately, every college student, high school student, and young professional like me, shops there. It's kind of like saying all the girls eat at McDonald's once a week."

"So, you've been there?" Chatham asked.

"Every week."

"There have been expensive gels and lotions at every crime scene," Chatham responded.

"Every crime scene has been at a young woman's apartment," Erin countered.

"Were any young men working at the store?" Chatham asked.

"No, I think I would've remembered that," Erin said.

"Do young men ever shop there?"

"Young men shop wherever they can find an easy gift that's sure to satisfy their girlfriend. It's a dead-end," Erin said defiantly.

"Okay, enough with bickering over the small stuff," Ramirez said. "There's one common denominator we all share. We think it's a cop."

Erin and Chatham nodded in agreement.

"Well, the only way to research that is to get into all of the personnel files," Jose said.

"And how are we going to do that, Ramirez? We aren't internal affairs."

"You're right, but we have something stronger than IA."

"Dare I ask?" Chatham asked, skepticism clear in his voice.

"We met with the Mayor today. Actually, he came here. Erin had an inside number, you know, the unrelenting media."

"Go ahead, Jose," she said. "You can both thank me later."

"Well, as I was saying, he came here, imagine that." Ramirez laughed.

"Okay, damn, the Mayor came here. Do you want me to put a sign out front? Tell me about the meeting," Chatham demanded.

"Getting a little arrogant isn't he, Erin?" Ramirez retorted.

"Jose, please!"

"Okay, okay. The Mayor also felt there was reason to believe it could be a cop. He also agreed that even Internal Affairs didn't need to know about the investigation. So if IA can't find out, then that means absolutely nobody can find out."

"I know that, Ramirez. So how do we get the files?" Chatham asked.

"The Mayor confirmed he calls for them randomly every year or so to appear to be in the loop. Reelection is coming up, so they'll just think he's trying to get a jump on revamping the department. They'll be so scared that they'll have them over to him in the morning. One of his assistants will drop them off."

"Hot damn! You sneaky son-of-a-bitch!" Chatham said, clapping his hands together.

"I'll take payoffs later. We won't sleep for another week," Ramirez said sarcastically.

"Erin, how are you feeling?"

"Pretty good, Chatham, thanks."

"Are you comfortable here?"

"And why wouldn't she be?" Jose asked.

"It's just hard for a woman to leave her own place."

"We're safe as little mice. The only thing I have to worry about is Mr. Sommers beating the door down and killing me. He thinks Erin needs to be with her parents."

Chapter 31

Chatham awoke early the next morning to the smell of bacon and eggs cooking on the stove. Erin was up and dressed, her hair pulled into a short ponytail, and a spatula poised above the morning's breakfast.

"Do I smell coffee?" he asked.

"Shhh, Jose is still asleep. Let's let him sleep as long as he can. As soon as we get those files, you know he won't sleep until he's reviewed them all himself."

Chatham folded the throw blanket Erin had put over him the night before and laid it across the back of the recliner. He walked over to the tiny kitchen and took a cup of steaming coffee out of her hand.

"Thanks. Why aren't you asleep?"

"I'm used to running on little or no sleep. Believe it or not, journalism is very much like police work. We're both following the next case."

180

"Ramirez and I respect what you do. It's a difficult job."

"You wouldn't blow smoke up my ass, would you?" Erin laughed.

"I'm too hung over to do that." He sat down at the kitchen table as she handed him a large plate of fried eggs, bacon, and buttered toast.

"So, this is why men marry?"

"Eat, Chatham," Erin demanded.

Daniel did just that, then as he rinsed his plate in the sink, he turned to Erin. "I need to go home, shower, and pick up some clothes. Hopefully, I won't need them, but if we're keeping a constant vigil over those files, I'd better be prepared. I'll grab today's paper too."

"Sounds good. Give me a call from your apartment. Jose may need you to pick some things up."

"Will do."

Chatham cranked the obese car, heaving a sigh of relief at the thought of trading it out for his sports car. He rode across town to a more expensive area and pulled into his garage. He parked, foregoing the elevator, and jogged up the three flights of stairs to his apartment. Throwing the keys in the basket by the door, he went straight into his bedroom and hit the shower. It felt good. Even in college, he'd never gotten accustomed to being out all night without bathing. He showered until the water started to run cold, then grabbed a towel and stepped out. It was apparent he also needed a good shave. Daniel dressed in jeans, a polo shirt, and dock shoes, and packed two outfits for Ramirez's. He took one last glance around the apartment.

Everything seemed to be in place, but he noticed the red light flashing on his answering machine. It'd been Sally thanking him for lunch and leaving her number. He wrote it down on the back of a piece of scrap paper before tucking it into his pocket and picking up the phone to call Erin.

"Hello?" Jose answered.

"This is Chatham. I'm on my way back to your place. Do you need me to pick up anything?"

"Erin phoned in an order at Gellars Grocery Store. It's right down from the apartment. It should be ready when you get there."

"No problem. Listen, how am I going to get away with working at your place? The Captain's already crawling all over me about not being at the precinct."

"I took care of it this morning. I told him I've got you doing some cold call interviews with neighbors, etc. He bought it. The Cap is catching so much shit about this case that he knows not to piss me off."

"Good. I'll be there in a few. Have the files arrived?"

"They're en route."

Chatham stood awestruck as Zac Gellars loaded sack after endless sack of groceries into the car. He was glad he'd decided to bring Jose's cruiser back instead of his car. He'd thought the three of them might need to take a field trip. Zac closed the heavy door with a thud and turned to Chatham.

"That should be it, Detective."

"I hope so," Chatham answered. "Is he expecting an army I'm not aware of?"

"I'm not sure. I think it may be his friend's idea to cook at the house."

"Here, man," Chatham said, holding out a five-dollar bill. "I appreciate it."

"Thanks, and Jose asked me to tell you to pick up beer and wine. I'm sorry, but we don't carry it here. My parents say they've survived business this far without selling it, and they won't give in to it now."

"Wise decision. That always brings a different type of clientele."

"Yeah, we don't need that. Tell Jose that Angela's scheduled to have the baby tomorrow. I'll call him later."

"Will do."

It was afternoon when Chatham arrived, arms full of grocery bags, at Ramirez's door. He was only able to see through a small crack between bags.

"Yo, who is it?" Ramirez blurted.

"Who do you think is bringing this shitload of groceries to your house?"

Jose opened the door, and walked back to the couch, without offering to help.

"Thanks, Chatham," Erin said, looking a little tired. "Can I help you?"

"No, thanks. You need to rest. I'll have everything up here in a few hours. Are we expecting the Mayor's office to eat with us?"

"No, we aren't silly, I just like to cook. Besides, I thought two bachelors would appreciate it."

"Oh, we do, *don't* we Chatham?" Ramirez yelled from his seat.

"Yes, we do."

Chatham was on his final load when he spotted a dark, Lincoln Town Car pulling up to the curb. He carried the bags on up, then hurried back down to meet the vehicle. Two men got out of the car in shiny, double-breasted suits.

"Excuse me, are you two with the Mayor's Office?"

"Who's asking?" one of the men in the outdated suit asked.

Chatham wanted to slug them both but refrained. "My apologies. I'm Detective Daniel Chatham, and we're waiting for someone from your office."

Neither of them responded but motioned for a moving van to pull up alongside them. "These men should have what you want," the driver said, then literally turned on his heels, and was gone. It was so comical that Chatham struggled to contain himself.

The passenger got out of the van, opened the side door, and pulled out a hand truck. "I see you've met the brains behind the operation," he said mockingly. "Just be glad you won't have to see them again."

It didn't seem like many boxes, but as they started to stack them in the apartment, it became overwhelming. Neither Erin, Jose, nor Chatham said a word until the men had gone.

"What're we going to do, Jose?" Erin asked. "The killer will hit a hundred more times before we can go through all these boxes!"

"We'll just have to be logical while we go through them. I thought Chatham could take the files from the cops with the most seniority. He may find something that we can't. When you know somebody so long, you tend to become biased. Erin, you take the younger cops. You might see something that triggers a red flag for you. I'll take the rest, the ten to fifteen-year cops, and the detective divisions. Is everyone in agreement?" Ramirez asked.

"Sounds sensible to me," Erin answered.

"Me too," Chatham agreed.

It took them most of the day to merely separate them into categories, but hopefully things would begin to go quickly from there.

"What exactly are we looking for, Jose?" Erin asked.

"That's the sixty-thousand-dollar question. Maybe they'll be *too* normal, or maybe their record will stand out somehow, either positive or negative. We're fairly safe in breaking it down into two areas. White and male. Other than that, it'll just have to be instinct."

They read for the next six hours, placing hot pink post-it notes on folders suggesting doubt. Finally, Jose stood up, stretching his body. "We've got to take a break. After a while, Joe Blow and John Doe will start looking too much alike."

"I agree," Erin said. "Besides, I'm starving. What about you guys?"

"Do me a favor and don't ask Chatham that. This grocery bill is going to kill me."

Erin prepared sandwiches, and they all sat at the kitchen table. She opened the curtains; the sun was out and the bright light flooded in. "See, there's a whole world out there."

"Yeah," Jose answered. "And thank God it isn't raining."

"I'm going to make a quick call," Chatham said, pulling out the worn piece of paper from his pocket.

"Who is it, Daniel?" Erin teased.

"Oh, it's nothing," Chatham's answered evasively.

"Come on, Chatham. We're a team around here," Ramirez laughed.

"It's nothing. Damn. Isn't there enough in those boxes over there to occupy your minds?"

"Oh, this must be good," Jose said to Erin. "He's getting a little too defensive for me."

"It's the nurse, okay? The nurse from Lobale Institute. I had lunch with her when I visited Chrissy Ozette."

"Hmm," Jose said as he rubbed his chin with his index finger. "What does she look like?"

"That's it. I'll call her from home."

"No, Daniel," Erin intervened. "Jose, we've taken it a little too far. Is she a nice girl?"

"From what little I know of her, she seems to be. I wouldn't know much about anybody since they put my ass with Ramirez. They're either dead, or I don't have enough free time to get past their first name."

Jose shrugged his shoulders in an attempt to look innocent. Daniel rolled his eyes in response.

"I've got a great idea," Erin said. "Why don't you ask her to dinner?"

"We don't have time for that shit!"

"Jose, please. I'm starting to agree with Daniel about your attitude. We're going to be stuck here for days together. We need to take breaks. Besides, a new face now and then would help. I'm cooking Lasagna if she'd like to join us. Say eight o'clock?"

"That's very nice of you Erin, but, maybe some other time." Daniel walked into Jose's room and got Sally on the first ring. She sounded genuinely happy to hear from him. It was her day off and she wanted to know if he'd like to get together.

"It sounds great, but I'm stuck here at my partner's place reviewing a case. Maybe soon."

Before she could respond, he felt the receiver floating out of his hand.

"Hello, Sally. This is Erin Sommers. I'm here with Daniel, and we'd love to have you for dinner. Daniel was embarrassed to ask because he thought you wouldn't know how to say no."

Chatham wanted to die, better yet, he wanted to wrap the phone cord around Erin's neck and strangle her. He could hear Ramirez chuckling in the other room.

"What is this shit?" Chatham seethed at Jose. "This is low, even for you. I can't believe it. Come on, man, I thought you were better than this."

"I'm sorry," Ramirez said. "Really, I am. It was all Erin's fault. I swear I had nothing to do with it. She didn't mean any harm. It's a girl thing."

"Screw that. Give me a box of files. I'm out of here. I don't need this shit. It's one thing to be embarrassed, but it's a whole different ballgame when you're humiliated!"

Erin came bouncing out of the bedroom, oblivious to the damage she'd caused. Chatham was putting on his coat and stuffing files into a box.

"What's going on?" she asked.

"What's going on? Do you honestly have to ask? I'm not in fucking junior high, Erin. Jesus, I do have my pride."

"Are you upset at me?" she asked, clearly surprised by his behavior.

"She's kidding right, Ramirez?"

Jose was trying to stay out of it but couldn't any longer. "Chatham's right Erin," he answered. "You went too far. He just met this girl."

"She loved the idea," Erin said, looking hurt and dejected. "I gave her the directions, and she'll be here at eight o'clock." She turned on her heels and returned to the kitchen.

"Ah, shit," Ramirez said. "We don't have time for this petty crap. Take care of it, Chatham."

"Why me?" Chatham demanded.

"*Now*, Chatham!"

Over the next thirty minutes, they mended hurt feelings and were back to work. It'd been touch and go for a while, but Daniel realized Erin was only trying to help.

"Look, Ramirez," Chatham said, holding up a file. "This guy was terminated from the department."

"We have a lot of those. Just make an extra stack. We'll review them together."

The stacks were simply shifting from one area to another.

"Are we really making progress?" Erin asked.

"Let's hope so," Jose answered.

"Well good, because it's 6:30. I'll start dinner while you boys freshen up."

"It's already 6:30?" Jose asked. "You're going to have to walk the nurse to the car fairly early tonight. We've got a lot of work ahead of us."

"You're right," Chatham answered.

Chapter 32

Daniel had changed shirts, wet his fingers, ran them through his hair, and brushed his teeth. When he came out of the bedroom, he could already smell the Italian spices simmering into the lasagna's sauce.

"It smells great, Erin."

"Thanks, Chatham. You look nice."

"What's the latest?" he asked.

"Nothing. The media is tired of reporting on something they can't further substantiate. I just don't want this city to start believing they can let their hair down again, know what I mean?"

"Yep. But I bet it takes a lot of heat off the department," Chatham commented.

"Yeah. You're right. That's the bottom line, unfortunately. What did you find in today's files?" Jose asked.

"Not much, except for a few discrepancies."

"Hey, there will be none of that," Erin yelled from the kitchen. "We'll share and share alike. No fair not including me."

Jose opened his mouth to respond, but the doorbell rang. Chatham stood quickly but didn't move any further.

"What are you waiting on, man?"

Chatham didn't answer, but instead made his way toward the door. Looking through the peephole, he could see her blonde hair.

"Hello there," he said, as he opened the door.

Sally was more beautiful than he'd remembered. She looked different in something other than her uniform. She had on a tan, linen outfit that matched the hazel swirl in her eyes. She seemed taller, but looking down, he noticed it was due to the latest style of wedge sandals. Her makeup made her look like a cover girl commercial. Her lips were pouty, and full, and traced with a pink lipstick.

"Hi," she answered. "Thanks for inviting me over. Something smells great."

"Come on in. I'll introduce you to everyone." He held his breath, wondering how Ramirez was going to handle himself.

"This is Jose Ramirez, my partner."

Jose stood up, walking the few steps over to her. "Sally," he said, extending his hand, "it's very nice to meet you. I'm sure my partner would've much preferred to have taken you to a restaurant with better ambiance, but unfortunately for the two of you, this is what you're stuck with."

Sally offered a warm smile. "I much prefer this type of environment. I'm a homebody."

"Come in and have a seat. Chatham tells me you're a nurse."

"Yes, I am. My work more or less consumes my time, so I enjoy my down time."

"A nurse, huh?" Erin's voice came from the kitchen before she appeared in the den. "Hello, Sally, I'm Erin Sommers. We talked on the phone. So nice to meet you."

"You too. Can I help with anything?"

"I'm just waiting for the bread to finish, then we'll be ready to eat. So, tell me," Erin questioned, "what led you to nursing?"

Sally laughed. "I can't say I was *led* actually. It was one of those things that happen when you bomb at everything else. I wish I could make it sound noble and tell you I've wanted to be a nurse since I was a child."

"Yeah," Ramirez said. "I think if a little kid dreamed of growing up to be a homicide detective, then he might end up at the Lobale Institute."

"Well, I always did," Chatham interrupted abruptly.

"That explains a lot," Jose laughed.

****

"This was a great meal, Erin," Jose said sincerely. "Why did we always order takeout when we stayed up to work on cases?"

"I offered to fix a meal or two, but you refused to let me stop and take the time to prepare one," Erin answered.

"Oh yeah, I remember now."

"What are all of these boxes?" Sally asked, waving her hand in the direction of their organized mess.

"We're investigating the serial killings," Jose answered. "Obviously, we aren't making much progress."

"Oh, my goodness. I guess you guys will be busy for some time," Sally said.

"Unfortunately, you're right."

"Do you have any leads?" she asked, showing her apparent interest.

"Let's not call them leads, as of yet. They're more *gut feelings*," Ramirez answered.

"It's such a shame. Those poor girls. I just have to wonder why in the world they'd open the door to a stranger." Sally commented.

"That's what we're trying to figure out," Chatham answered. "At least you know not to open the door to anyone."

Sally looked down at the floor, remaining silent for a few moments. "I had a friend in college who was raped in her dorm room. She refused to report it to the police and eventually had a nervous breakdown. I think that's one of the main reasons I chose to work at Lobale. Many people don't realize your mind can become as sick as your body. It's terribly sad."

"So, what do you think about Chrissy Ozette?" Chatham asked. "Will she will be able to overcome this?"

"With time, and by that I mean she'll be able to come to terms with it. But, she'll carry that burden with her for the rest of her life."

"What a tragedy," Erin intervened. "Do tell me, what happened to your friend?"

"She committed suicide," Sally answered quietly.

Chapter 33

"Thank you so much for dinner," Sally said, hugging Erin and Jose. "It's been so long since I've enjoyed myself like this."

"We're glad you came," Ramirez answered.

Chatham had enjoyed the evening. He handed Sally her jacket and walked her to the car. She was all he'd hoped for, intelligent, fun, and beautiful.

Erin stood at the window looking down on the street below.

"What are you doing?" Jose asked.

"I'm just watching. They're so cute together, don't you think?"

"We aren't their parents for God's sake. Sit down before they see you."

Erin skipped over to the couch, plopping down beside Jose in a burst of giggles.

"How old did you say you were?" Jose laughed.

"Old enough," she said, as she leaned over and kissed him lightly on the mouth.

"Erin…"

"Shhhh," she said, placing her index finger across her lips, "don't say anything."

"It's just that…" Ramirez said, his voice trailing off.

"It's just what? Do you not find me attractive?"

"Erin, please. I think you're beautiful, but I'm forty years old. You're young and vibrant, and I'm a burned-out, old cop."

"Stop it. You wouldn't be so wrapped up in this case if you were burned out. You're a loving and caring man, and I've been in love with you from the moment I met you."

"Erin," Jose gasped.

"I'm sorry, but I had to say it. When we both had our brushes with death, I decided I'd let you know how I feel. I realize you think of me as a kid sister, but I had to tell you anyway. I love you, Jose Ramirez."

He pulled her close, their noses almost touching. "And I love you too, Erin Sommers." He held her, kissing her soft mouth. It'd been such a long time coming. Jose brushed her dark hair away from her face, then sat back to look at her.

"I didn't ever think this would happen. I'm a cop, Erin, and that's not an easy life for anyone."

"You're right, Jose, and I'm a journalist. Tell me the difference."

"You've got me there," he answered, hugging her to him. She smelled so sweet and clean, and she was so tiny, so damned tiny he was afraid she might break in his arms.

"Wait," Jose said, pushing Erin away as he moved forward on the couch. "Look at the forecast."

"Oh no," Erin groaned, looking over at the television. "Not again."

"Can you see Chatham from the window?"

"Yeah, he's still down there," Erin answered.

"I'll try his cell phone."

Chatham grudgingly answered the phone on the fifth ring. "Yeah?"

"It's Ramirez. Does Sally live in an apartment?"

"Hell, I don't know. Why?"

"Just ask her. Now!" Jose could hear him bashfully asking her.

"Yes, she does."

"Bring her back upstairs for the night. It's about to storm."

Sally looked confused and worried. "What's going on?" she asked as she walked back into the apartment.

"It's supposed to rain all night," Erin answered. "That's when our killer attacks, and it's always single young women that live in an apartment. Jose didn't want you to take the chance. You're welcome to stay here for the night."

"I couldn't possibly impose, you already have a crowd."

Chatham wore a look of concern. "Sally, they're right. It's not a good idea for you to be alone. If you could stay tonight, I could take you home tomorrow. We just can't take any chances."

"This is really serious, isn't it?"

"Yes, it is," Chatham answered, "and we're starting to think it's getting personal with Jose and me. The killer doesn't want to get caught."

"So, tell me," she asked, "what's in all of these boxes exactly?"

Jose answered first. "The three of us are the only ones who know. We have reason to believe the killer could be one of us. A cop, I mean. These are personnel files."

"Oh goodness. Could I be of any help? Maybe I could review their psychological exams or something. I'm certain your department does a psychological inquiry on every applicant."

Jose smiled. "As a matter-of-fact, they do, Sally. Sounds like we could use the help."

It was after four a.m. when Jose finally demanded they call it quits for the night.

"Let's get a few hours of shut-eye before reviewing the folders we've red flagged. Erin, you can take my bed and Sally you can have the guest room. Chatham and I will enjoy the comfort of my den."

There weren't any arguments as they dispersed and fell right to sleep. Erin was the first to awaken. She pulled her pillow close to her face breathing in Jose's scent. She turned to face a rustling sound in the doorway.

"Good morning," Jose smiled. "I have to know. Are you sorry about last night? The kiss, I mean?"

"Not for one second. Are you?"

He walked over and sat on the edge of the bed. "You're so beautiful, Erin," Jose smiled. "How could I ever regret loving you?"

Erin sat up in bed, meeting his lips with her own. His broad shoulders enveloped her instantly, and they kissed until he felt his way under the covers.

"Make love to me, Jose," she whispered into his ear.

"Not now," he whispered back. "I want it to be special. We have an apartment full of people and a murder case to solve." He slowly slipped out of the bed, grabbed a clean pair of boxers and jeans, before making his way into the bathroom for a shower. "I love you," he mouthed.

Chapter 34

"Yeah," Jose said, as he grabbed for the telephone, the wet towel still hanging around his waist.

"What the hell is going on, Ramirez?" Captain Graham growled.

"Hey there, Cap. Good to hear your voice."

"Don't give me that bullshit. Where's your partner? He's AWOL."

"I told you where he'd be. I have him in the field asking questions about the investigation."

"The little prick seems to think he's better than the rest of us. He hasn't shown up for any of our meetings. Damn college boy. I think it's time to go up top and get him out of here."

"Easy, Captain," Jose interrupted, surprised at the anger in his superior's voice. "He's not a bad cop. I hate to eat crow, but he's become quite an asset to this investigation."

"Quite an asset, huh? Well, what has he solved for us so far?" Captain Graham demanded.

"Come on now, that's below the belt. None of us have come up with anything solid." Ramirez said.

"I'm giving him two more days in the field and then his ass had better start reporting to me. Don't let the fact he babysat you in the hospital lead you astray. If Chatham really cared, he would've been out there catching the son-of-a-bitch who shot you. As far as I'm concerned, he fits what we're looking for."

"Hey now, that's enough. You know that's a crock of shit, Captain, and I won't even listen to it," Jose said, agitation growing in his voice.

"Look, Ramirez, I'm sorry if I offended you, but this investigation has gone on far too long. The killer has to be looking us dead in the face."

If you only knew, he thought.

"We're all tired, Cap," Jose said, cringing as he heard the phone slam.

"What's going on?" Erin asked.

"We've got two days to find the killer. Graham's fired up and wants Chatham back at the station."

"I guess that means we need to get busy." Erin rolled over and sat on the edge of the bed. Her hair was ruffled, and her eyes were glazed over from lack of sleep. Jose threw on his jeans, blowing her a kiss as he went out into the den.

"Get up, Chatham," he grunted. "Cap's pissed off. He's given me two days before you have to report to the station. I hope the sleep you got last night is enough to tide you over for the next forty-eight hours."

Chatham grabbed his extra set of jeans and headed to the shower. He knew it'd undoubtedly be his last for a while. He paused long enough to linger in the doorway of Jose's guestroom to smile at Sally. She was propped up on her elbows with a look of exhaustion on her face.

"What's going on?" she asked.

"Just another day in the life of a cop," he answered. "It's 6:00 a.m. What time do you have to be at work?" Chatham asked.

"I can call in if I need to. I think you guys could use an extra set of hands," Sally said.

"I wouldn't ask you to do that. I'd love for you to be here, but…"

"Then say no more," she interjected with a smile. "A shower and a cup of coffee, and I'll be like new."

"You're a woman after my own heart. Just don't tell Dr. Easton I had anything to do with this," Chatham said sarcastically.

With that, Sally shooed him away as she started to get out of bed.

The personnel files were placed in three official stacks. Those with excessive disciplinary actions, those who'd been terminated, and those that had proven themselves to go above the call of duty numerous times. The system seemed to make the most sense to the four of them. Unfortunately, the stacks were so large it virtually defeated the purpose of the investigation. It'd take weeks to look into every one of the files.

"All four of us have gotten this far in our careers on our gut instincts," Jose said. "We're just going to have to do that again now. Let's each take turns reading through these folders out loud and see if anything stands out. It's worth a shot."

"Maybe you're right, partner," Chatham answered. "We're not getting anywhere otherwise. I'll start."

Four hours later, they'd narrowed a list of sixty, down to eight.

"If we keep this up we just might get somewhere," Erin answered. "Time to eat."

"My God, for somebody so small, you sure do eat a lot."

Chapter 35

Night fell like a black curtain as the group contemplated the evening's events.

"Erin, you need some rest, and Sally, we appreciate all you've done, but I'm sure you need to get home and rest up for work tomorrow," Jose said. "We've already asked too much of you."

"Where is this headed, Jose?" Erin asked suspiciously. "You're going somewhere, aren't you?"

Ramirez looked over at his partner. "I think we should go over to Malone's office. I haven't found anything in those files that makes me feel any different about him."

"I know you don't expect us to break into the man's office. That's not what you're implying, is it?" Daniel asked incredulously.

"No, Chatham. I just thought we'd ask him to stay late for coffee and a doughnut! Of course I mean break into the damn office. How else are we going to find what we're looking for?" Ramirez asked sarcastically.

"And what are we *looking* for exactly?" Chatham questioned.

"Are you with me or not? Last I heard you didn't have any better ideas."

"Are you suggesting we leave Erin here alone? It's dark for Christ's sake, Ramirez. I don't mind looking for the killer, but let's not put all our eggs in one basket. I have at least three other potential leads I feel strongly about," Chatham said.

"Grab the files. We'll check them out, too. Erin will be safe here. The weather's clear, she has a gun, and we have cell phones."

"I'll be happy to stay with her," Sally said. "I don't have to be at work until ten in the morning. I wouldn't feel right about leaving her."

"Are you sure?" Chatham asked.

"Really, it's fine. In fact, I'd enjoy it. We can rent a movie and share some popcorn. You know, have a girl's night out, or *in* rather. I think Erin needs to take her mind off of murder for a while."

"You know, Ms. Spriggs, nothing could be closer to the truth. You have yourself a real winner there, Chatham. I appreciate it." With that, Jose turned to his partner. "Now, let's talk strategy."

"No, let's pick up a movie for these women. What'll it be, ladies?"

"Oh, surprise us," Erin answered.

****

They pulled back up to the apartment with three of the latest chick-flicks and microwave popcorn. With those delivered, they headed to the morgue. Luckily, it was dark, except for several security lights keeping vigil over the building. Malone's Lexus was gone, and the only cars in the lot belonged to night security. With the budget in such a bind, everyone else was on call. Bodies were logged in through security, and held until the morning, unless the situation required other measures.

Ramirez clenched a pain pill between his back molars, then swallowed. He should've taken it much earlier, but it was too late now. He rubbed his thigh, as if to offer it some encouragement, before easing out of the car. "Let's go, partner. No time like the present."

"How're we going to get past security?" Chatham asked, his voice full of skepticism.

"Just follow me. I was doing this before you were a twinkle in your daddy's eye."

Chatham followed Ramirez around the back of the building to the drop-off bay.

"Oh, this is lovely. Could you have picked a more illuminated area?"

"We're going through the side door over there," Ramirez said, pointing his index finger in the direction of the entrance. "I'm going to slide my county ID across the pad and hope for the best. Let's just pray it doesn't beep when we enter."

"What? You don't know if it makes a noise? You don't *remember*? Oh, hell's bells, Ramirez."

"If it does, we'll just walk away. If someone comes, I'll say we were coming to see Malone, and he's not here. Damn, we haven't even done anything yet. This isn't the Federal Reserve. We *are* cops, you know," Ramirez scoffed.

"Yeah, cops about to go into someone's office without permission," Chatham rebutted.

"Shit, go back to the car, I can't handle this. I feel like I'm about to be reprimanded by a nun schoolteacher wielding a large ruler."

"Okay, okay. Let's go," Chatham conceded.

The illumination of the loading dock soon faded, giving way to long, dim hallways. Jose cringed as he struggled to maintain a slow, steady gait. They could hear the nightly cleaning crew buffing the floors off in the distance as Jose motioned for Chatham to veer to the left. They both felt more comfortable where the lighting wasn't as bright.

"Let's see," Jose hesitated, "I think it's down here on the right. Yep. There it is." He fumbled with a plastic credit card, then a thin, metal tool, until he freed the locked door. He opened it wide enough for them to enter then pulled it shut as soon as they entered. They stood in total darkness.

"What the hell...?" Chatham whispered.

"Give me a minute," Jose whispered as he fumbled in his jacket pocket, retrieving a small flashlight about the size of a pencil.

"You'd think the top dog would have a window office," Chatham complained, as he felt his way around to the back of the desk.

"Maybe the top dog didn't *want* a window. Maybe the top dog wanted some *privacy*," Ramirez stated coldly.

"Yeah, well, what exactly are we looking for? I'm not particularly fond of playing the *Hardy Boys*."

"I don't expect to find anything, really," Jose answered, his voice weary from exhaustion. "He's too smart to hide anything here. I'm just hoping he had a moment of weakness and left something that could be considered evidence."

The file cabinets were locked, which wasn't a surprise, but with a little work, they too were pried open as quickly as the door. His records were neat and well kept, obviously by an administrative assistant and not himself.

The autopsies of the murder victims weren't found in the metal filing cabinets, so both men went to work on his personal desk drawers. As soon as they were opened, it became painfully obvious the assistant hadn't been in charge of them. There were dirty tissues, Hall's cough drops, half-eaten bags of M&M's, and loose change. As they dug deeper into the larger drawers, they found the files of the murder victims. There wasn't anything unusual about any of the files.

Dr. Ken Malone had made the same type of entries into their records as he had done in the various other murder cases throughout the city. One thing about Malone that Jose hated to admit was he was thorough and competent.

"So, Malone has the files somewhere separate," Chatham started. "That doesn't mean anything."

"Maybe you're right, but what do you make of this?" Jose asked. He handed a stack of *instamatic* photos to Chatham and stood up to shine the small light on them.

"Oh, my God. What the hell?" Chatham gasped.

"I told you the son-of-a-bitch was sick, didn't I?" Ramirez sneered.

Chatham flipped through the photos of the naked bodies, posed in various positions, on the autopsy table. Some were in vulgar, enticing poses while others looked as though they were waiting for their husbands to lay down beside them. It was repulsive, and Chatham felt the sudden urge to vomit.

"What're we going to do, Ramirez? We can't take these with us, and we can't even tell the Captain about this. He'd kill us. This would blow the whole investigation out of the water. We better get the hell out of here before we get caught!" Chatham exclaimed.

"I won't argue with that," Ramirez answered, fumbling to get everything back in its proper place.

There wasn't any way to lock the drawers back, so they wiped off as many fingerprints as they could. Malone would, no doubt, call the precinct about the break-in. He'd hide the pictures, and any evidence in the future, wouldn't be found in this office. Ramirez had made a rookie mistake, all because of a personal vendetta. He wanted to kick himself in the ass. Chatham wanted to be second in line. They made it out of the building with little problem, and slid into the car, with their adrenaline flowing.

"Well, now we know. He's the one, Ramirez, but we'll never have any evidence to prove it. He'll have everything burned and buried by the time we get a search warrant," Chatham barked.

Ramirez sat silent. He deserved anything Chatham threw at him. If another girl died, the blood would surely be on his hands. He sat slumped in the seat with his head hanging forward. "Let's just get back to the girls."

Daniel slid the key into the ignition with a snort of disdain. He'd known better than to come tonight and he should've put his foot down. Ramirez was not in his normal frame of mind. He was tinkering on the edge. Chatham should've been the bigger man. He slowly pulled the car forward and out of the parking space along the street. The morgue was not in a good area, and several of the streetlights needed to be repaired, but he could still make out the looming shadow, of a large vehicle, pulling out behind their cruiser. It was several lengths behind them, but he'd learned to tune in his senses in the past few weeks, and something just didn't feel right. He debated whether or not to share it with Jose, then realized he'd be crazy not to. Ramirez was far too intuitive not to figure it out soon anyway.

"We've got a tail about fifty yards back. They pulled out when we did," Chatham stated.

"Lovely. Could this night get any better? How many are in there?"

"Can't tell. The damn streetlights are out, and their headlights are off. Call the girls. They need somebody with them, this feels like a diversion." Chatham said.

Ramirez grabbed his cell phone and dialed two numbers before they felt the strong hit from behind. It threw them both forward as Chatham struggled to maintain control of the car.

"Speed up!" Jose screamed. "Hit the freeway."

"They know that's what I'm trying to do. They're not going to let me," Chatham screamed back as he held tight to the steering wheel.

Ramirez pulled the gun from his ankle holster and rolled down the window with firm, confident hands. He'd had enough. He fired twice before he even looked back. They waited for the sound of return fire, but never heard any. Jose leaned out the window, firing two more rounds, this time hitting the windshield, and the front headlight. The car swerved, taking a sharp turn onto the next small street.

"Shit, turn around, Chatham," Ramirez screamed. "He's getting away."

"You're damn right he is. We're checking on the girls. Call them now!"

"He's not armed. He would've fired back. He just wanted to scare us. Go back, now!"

"Give me the fucking phone, Ramirez," Chatham screamed, adding to the chaos that was taking place in the vehicle.

Jose drew back his right fist and was barely able to stop himself before it struck Chatham in the face. The car screeched to a halt.

"Hit me, you crazy son-of-a-bitch! Hit me! That'll solve this whole damn thing, won't it? It'll solve everything. Then we can go home and get a good night's rest."

"Okay! Okay! I'm losing it, but you don't have to treat me like I need to be in a fucking mental institution. I just want to catch this asshole. It's making me crazy," Ramirez said.

"Pull yourself together because I can't handle the investigation, the Captain, someone trying to kill me, and your crazy ass too. You're going to have to deal with your own issues and get your shit together. Understand?" Chatham fired back.

"Yeah, I understand."

"Now, I know in an ideal world, we would've gone back and gotten that brazen piece of shit, but this isn't an ideal world. You're not in the best of health, we just broke into the medical examiner's office, and two women we care about may be in a great deal of danger. Now, find the cell, get them on the phone, then call the department and have a unit get to them before we can," Chatham demanded.

"Done," Ramirez said.

"Thank you."

"Now let's get our stories straight, in case the Captain hears about this, and wants to know what the hell we were doing in this area," Ramirez said, his voice quivering from the pain pulsating in his injured thigh.

Three hours later, after the patrol units had left, the foursome sat around the kitchen table, trying to figure out what was going on. They hadn't seen anyone follow them when they'd left, and they hadn't noticed anyone pick them up along the way.

"It's weird," Chatham said. "Almost like Whispering Hollow. Who knows our schedule?"

"Nobody could have," Jose said, rubbing his forehead.

Sally was resigned to the fact she'd be was spending one more night. She couldn't deny she'd been frightened with all that'd transpired. Chatham liked her, but couldn't see how a relationship could form under these circumstances.

"I don't know when I'll be able to see you," he said as she walked into the guest room to get ready for bed. "This case is going to keep me so busy."

"I know," she said gently, reaching over to touch his cheek. "You're such a great guy, Daniel."

"Is that a nice way of saying it was fun while it lasted?" he asked.

"Oh, my goodness, no way. I hope this is only the beginning. I haven't met anybody like you in so long. I hope you'll call me."

"Of course I'll call you," he said, obviously pleased with what he'd heard. "Just promise me you'll be careful. You really shouldn't stay in your apartment alone."

"I've been thinking about that. My sister just had a baby. Maybe I'll stay with her for a few days. I'm sure she could use the help."

"Now that's an idea. It's too dangerous to stay by yourself right now, especially with your shift work," Daniel continued.

"I know." She leaned up, kissing him tenderly on the lips. He closed his eyes as he breathed in the sweet scent of lavender.

Chapter 36

Jose started off the next morning with four aspirin and a Mountain Dew.

"Breakfast of champions," he grunted as Chatham walked into the kitchen.

"So, I see. I say we go talk to the Captain today. If we don't, I'm going to be fired, and none of this work would've been worth it. We need to tell him about last night. He knows the kind of crazy shit you do, so one more thing isn't going to send him into a rage. We also need to share those eight files with him. Not the actual files themselves, but our concern about the officers. Let's just tell him we have our sources, and something doesn't feel right about those particular cops. That'd open the door up for me to start investigating those guys without getting fired."

"Yeah, you're right. It's time to move forward with this investigation. Graham needs to be aware of our concerns about those officers, but don't tell him we had our hands on their files. He'd fire both of us, good intentions or not," Ramirez said.

Chatham could sense the emotion in Jose's voice and felt for him. This case had become personal. Chatham would've tried to tell him none of it had been because of his lack of diligence, but it wouldn't have helped. Daniel just hoped they found the bastard soon. He wasn't sure how much longer the two of them could hold it together.

"Breakfast you two," Erin called from the small kitchen. The smell of her delightful cooking was little consolation to Jose, but he sat down in front of his plate and ate as though he had an appetite anyway. His day would be full, and he needed all the strength he could muster.

"What are the plans?" Erin asked.

"We're going to talk to Graham," Jose answered in between bites of bacon.

"Is that a good idea?" Erin asked.

"It's time. He needs to know where this investigation is going. There isn't any reason to hide our concern over these cops from him. We aren't close to any of them. Chatham has to get back to the precinct, or he'll lose his job, no doubt about that. This way, he can investigate most of the officers in the files. I think Graham will keep the names under wraps from the rest of the detectives. He doesn't need to know about the personnel files. We're calling it *gut instinct*. He'll go for it. I'm just dreading the Malone fiasco. I have to come clean about it. Cap will be pissed, though. Thank God, I still have sick days," Ramirez said.

"Lovely," Chatham said, sinking back into his chair. "I'll be there to receive the brunt of it."

"Comes with the territory," Jose said, patting him on the back.

"You guys might need to reconsider that. Should you go to Captain Graham right now?" Erin asked nervously.

"What's not to go to him about, Erin?" Jose asked.

"We have to share something with him. We've been on the case for weeks now."

"I guess you're right. But, I wouldn't tell him about breaking into Malone's office."

"I sure as hell wish I didn't have to, but I don't see any other way to get him to consider the possibility of Malone being our man. It may put me in the lion's den for a minute but, let's face it, we've got a killer out there and he needs to be stopped." Jose said.

"I love you, Jose Ramirez," Erin said, leaning down and kissing him on the mouth.

"And I love you too, Erin Sommers."

"Um, excuse me," Chatham interjected. "Is there something you two want to share with me?"

"No," Jose said bluntly

****

.Jose and Chatham had dropped Erin off at her parents' house for the day, and were on their way to Joe's Deli to meet Captain Graham. Neither of them was looking forward to the meeting, but knew it'd mean the investigation was moving forward, and that couldn't be all bad.

Graham was in the back, waiting impatiently with a fresh soda and half-eaten sandwich. "You're both late," he said in between bites.

"Good to see you too, Cap," Jose said as he slid into the booth. "I'm doing much better, thanks for asking. How about yourself?"

"Why aren't you home in bed? That's the doc's orders. You know the department won't allow you back to work without your *physician's* official release," Captain Graham mumbled.

"What's a *physician*?" Jose asked.

"Smart-ass. How's Erin?" Graham asked.

"She's doing pretty good. Much better in fact."

"So, what's up? You two screw-ups must have something, so spit it out," the Captain demanded.

"Well, our *gut feeling* is it may be a cop. It's pointing that way," Ramirez said.

"How do you figure?" Graham asked, looking up with peaked interest. "I tend to agree, but I'd like to hear how you got there. I mean, it wouldn't take a cop to weasel his way into a young girl's apartment."

"You're right there. But, if Erin's attack had anything to do with it, a cop would know she works with us. And a cop would be able to get into her apartment. Only a cop would know we were taking time off to go to the cabin, and only a

228

cop would talk to a cop, who would talk to a cop. For all we know, a cop is holding a badge at these girls' doors. I don't know how to explain it. I just have a bad feeling, call it vibes," Jose continued.

"Maybe it's campus security," Graham suggested.

Chatham looked over at Jose. That thought hadn't even occurred to him.

"Could be. But most of all, Cap, I think a real possibility here, is Ken Malone," Ramirez stated flatly.

"You really hate that arrogant son-of-a-bitch, don't you?" Graham said.

"Damn right I do. The guy's not playing with a full deck. I'm telling you, he might be our guy," Ramirez continued to insist.

"I don't like him, and I don't necessarily trust him, but just because I wouldn't play poker with him doesn't mean I can get the DA to bring charges against him," Graham said.

"Well, after you hear what I have to say, you might change your mind." Jose took a deep breath and drug out the sordid tale as long as he could. The Captain took it better than Jose had expected, although he'd owe him big, for the remainder of his career.

"He'll be cleaning out anything that could possibly relate to criminal mischief now," Graham barked as he ranted on in an overly abusive tirade. "We'll never get *anything* related to this case. All we can hope for is to keep him from killing again, that is, if he's our man. There's still a chance he's just a sick pervert, but we can't even prove that now."

"So, in other words, he's safe either way," Jose snorted.

"Basically," Graham retorted. "That's unless he screws up again, or we can find enough forensic evidence on the bodies. That'll be tricky since he's had his hands all over them."

"Yeah, that's pretty damn convenient."

"What do you think, Chatham?" Graham asked, turning his attention to the rookie.

"Well, Sir, I'm just following Detective Ramirez's leads, but I have to go along with the theories on the cops. We've found several we'd like to investigate."

"Let me hear 'em," Graham said, as he took another large bite from the remaining half of his turkey club.

"Sir, we have, I think, there is um, let's see, eight here, I believe," Chatham stammered.

"Damn it, son," Graham yelled, causing the other diners to turn around, and Hazel, their waitress, to give him a raised eyebrow. "Just give me the names. You ought to know by now I'm not going to bite you, and for God's sake, we're in a public place, what could I do to you here?"

"Yes, Sir, I mean, nothing, Sir," Chatham said, fumbling with his paperwork. "I understand. We've selected eight officers who we feel could be possible suspects."

"And how exactly did you *select* these officers, Mr. Chatham?"

"Well, Sir…" Chatham started before clamming up.

"Shit, Chatham, hand me the list," Ramirez said, tugging the papers away. "You know he's just trying to be professional with you, Cap. We didn't select anybody. We checked out a few people, know what I mean? Anyway, we came up with a few guys who might fit our bill. As Chatham said, we came up with eight, to be exact. I've got their names and precincts right here. Officers Richman, O'Boyle, Skelton, Wessinger, Martin, Parks, Minnix, and Cates. Chatham wrote you a nice little bio on each one. It should be quite helpful. He's turned out to be a decent partner after all," Ramirez said.

"You two seem to be hitting it off. All I need is another detective working under me who thinks he can do whatever the hell he pleases," Graham grumbled.

Ramirez grinned at Chatham. "That's a compliment, kid."

Chatham nodded, his face still pink with embarrassment.

"What're you two up to today? I'm not naïve enough to think Ramirez is going home to rest."

"We thought we'd look into a couple of these guys," Ramirez answered, pointing to the list in front of Graham. "Might as well start with the top. That'd be Richman and O'Boyle. Both of them are from the 34th Precinct. They were partners at one time, until the department decided to separate them. They were making record arrests but had multiple complaints filed against them. Apparently, the public thought they were a little too rough. It seems the two tended to throw the rulebook out the window in order to get the bad guys. At any rate, the department felt they were worth salvaging, so they split the duo up and put them out on routine patrol. There haven't been any complaints since."

"Doesn't sound like it sends up too big of a red flag to me," Graham said.

"Well, maybe not, but we thought they might be worth looking into," Ramirez added.

"Do you think we could be looking at *two* killers?" Captain Graham asked, raising his eyebrows for a brief second.

"No, I don't. I think one of them may have been the ringleader. Who knows, it's worth a shot," Ramirez answered.

"Well, keep me informed, and Officer Chatham, please grace us with your presence tomorrow morning at 9:00 sharp. It'd mean so much to me," Graham said sarcastically.

Chatham blushed a deeper shade of crimson before agreeing to be there promptly. Captain Graham tossed his check to Ramirez. "Don't say I never gave you anything, Detective. Glad to see you back on the job."

Chapter 37

Officer Richman's house was located in an old community, but the yards were well tended and the houses recently painted and tidy. His home was a small, brick box that appeared to be a two or three bedroom, with most likely one bath.

"He definitely lives within the means of a cop's salary," Chatham said. "Doesn't appear to be living off of any kickback money."

"Don't be so gullible, Chatham," Ramirez snorted. "You should know by now that appearances can be deceiving."

"Yeah, you're right there. But look, I see a tricycle, two different sized bicycles, and a swing set in the back. Would you live in that little house with kids? Come on, man. He has to have at least three, judging by the different sizes of those toys."

"You're right there. Point taken. Hell, I'd have to consider being on the take myself if I were in his situation."

"Look, his wife is coming out," Chatham said in a panic. "I'm pulling off."

The two men watched her as much as possible without being too obvious. She was taking out the trash, with a toddler in tow, and a cell phone cradled between her left shoulder and ear.

"Typical housewife," Jose said as he watched her in the rearview mirror. His mind immediately went back to Erin and he wondered what kind of mother she'd be. She would make a good one, no doubt about it, he thought definitively. Chatham brought him back to the moment.

"Okay, so Officer Richman works day shift. Everything seems on the up and up. Now we need to see what he does at night. Let's head over to O'Boyle's side of town."

"Ten-four," Ramirez said.

Jose's cell phone was ringing. He felt around everywhere for it, finally finding it in the pocket of his jacket.

"Ramirez, here."

"Yeah, it's Graham. Guess who I just got a call from?"

"Oprah?"

"Screw you, Ramirez. Malone wants to see you."

"You're shitting me," Ramirez said.

"He wants you to come by his office."

"Oh, lovely. Did you tell him I was out on injury leave?"

"Yep, sure did. He wouldn't tell me what it's about, only that he needed to speak to you. Said it was urgent. Funny thing, he never mentioned the break in," Graham said.

"Shit. You're going to make me go, aren't you?" Ramirez asked.

"Be there in thirty minutes."

"Let me guess," Chatham said as soon as Jose had disconnected. "That was Captain Graham."

"Are you telepathic? That's amazing. Now if you could just tell me who the hell the killer is, we could go home and call it a day!" Jose bellowed.

"What did he want?" Chatham continued, ignoring the comment.

"Seems like our boy, Malone, wants to see me. I wonder if he's going to try to blackmail me about breaking into his office."

"Well, it probably has something to do with the break-in. What're you going to say?" Chatham asked.

"I don't know yet. Any suggestions?"

"I tried to talk you out of it. I knew something like this was going to happen," Chatham said sternly.

"Oh, shut up," Ramirez said as he reached down to massage his aching thigh. They rode the rest of the way in silence, Jose sucking loudly on two pain pills.

Malone was waiting in the lobby when the two arrived, pacing restlessly back and forth across the polished tile.

"What the hell took you so long, Ramirez?" he asked in a panicked voice, one strangely absent of anger.

"Look, Malone, I got here as soon as I could. This better be important. I'm supposed to be home resting my leg," Ramirez seethed, as the pain continued to radiate.

Chatham had to hand it to Jose. He played a convincing part.

"I need to talk to you. It's important," Malone said nervously.

"No problem," Ramirez said.

Malone looked over at Chatham. "I mean, alone, Ramirez."

"He's my partner now, Malone. He's cool."

"I don't trust anybody," he whispered as he leaned over to Jose. "I want to talk to you and only you."

"Chatham, take a breather, man. There's a lounge down the hall. I'll meet you there in a few minutes," Ramirez said, motioning with his right hand in the direction of the break room.

This seemed to relax Malone. He motioned for Jose to follow him back to his office. Malone shut the door and pointed toward a chair across from his desk. Ramirez sat down, casually stretching out his wounded leg.

"So, what's of such grave importance, Malone, and why so secretive?"

"Look," Malone answered, leaning forward, his eyes bulging in fear. "Something's going on here, and I'm not sure what to make of it. This morning when I came in, my office door was ajar. I wasn't that concerned at first, but then I noticed my desk and files had been broken into."

Jose felt his pulse quicken. "Did you have the department make a report?"

"I would have, but there's something else." Malone slid the bottom drawer out and retrieved the stacked photos of the dead girls, in their poses. "These were in my desk along with the files of the girls killed during this serial killer's spree. As you can see, not only am I embarrassed they were found in my desk, but I'm scared that someone obviously put them here to frame me. As sad as it may seem, you're the only detective I feel I can trust. I don't know who's behind this," Malone said as he wiped his hand across his perspiring forehead.

Jose didn't know how to feel. This could go either way. Malone was definitely a sick individual. He'd caught him buying crack, having sex with a prostitute, and Malone was emotionless as a pimp. Jose didn't trust him, yet, none of those things made him a serial killer. Then again, maybe Malone knew someone had seen the pictures. That'd sure constitute an attempt to cover his ass.

"What do you make of it?" Malone asked, almost in a whimper.

"I don't know. Who'd do this? What would be their motivation?" Ramirez asked.

"You tell me. It's a frame-up. Somebody's trying to frame me for the murders."

Dr. Ken Malone was crying now, as Jose shifted back and forth in his chair, feeling more and more uncomfortable.

"If somebody wanted to frame you, Malone, it seems like they'd have taken the pictures. Why break in and leave them in your desk?"

"I don't know, Ramirez," he said, sobbing openly, and attempting to calm his shaking hands.

Jose rested his chin on his folded hands and shut his eyes. *Damn. What in the hell's going on?* He was beginning to believe Malone and wasn't quite sure why. It didn't make any sense for Malone to leave the pictures in his desk. It was, after all, county property. If he were in a car accident, or became sick for any length of time, then anyone could come in and take over his office until he returned. It was a huge risk to leave anything here. "If someone was trying to frame you, they'd have to make sure the pictures were found. Nobody found them," Jose stated.

"I know. Maybe they were scared away, and I got here before they could formulate a plan."

"Formulate a plan, hell! They posed those bodies for pictures. I'd think they could hide the damn things and make a phone call to frame your ass," Ramirez said, his patience growing thin.

"I don't know what the answer is, Ramirez," Malone sobbed. "I swear to God, man, I didn't do this. I know you don't like me and you think I don't give a shit about those girls that've been murdered. But the truth is, I have to keep my distance from my cases. I moved here from Detroit because my fourteen-year-old son got caught up in the wrong crowd. He wound up on an autopsy table with a .38 slug between his eyes, courtesy of a rival gang." Malone sobbed uncontrollably for a couple of minutes while Jose tried to think of something to say. Malone continued before he could offer any comforting words. "Imagine that. I went to medical school and still couldn't keep my own kid out of a rotten street gang. I moved my wife and younger daughter here, hoping to start over, but it's never that easy, you know? The fact is, my life was probably better when my kid was in a fucking gang. My wife and I haven't held a conversation in years, and my daughter got knocked up by a loser who works at a fast food joint." He wiped his sleeve across his running nose and took a gulp of air. "Now, somebody's trying to frame me for some sick-ass shit like this. I can't take it, man. I just can't take it."

Jose rubbed his eyes and looked up to meet Malone's gaze. The growing lump in his throat was forming from guilt. The prostitute was to fill some type of void in Malone's life, and although it wasn't the answer, Ramirez felt dirty for invading Ken Malone's privacy. How could he expect a medical examiner to feel sorrow for every homicide he covered? Maybe Malone was right. He would've been in a mental institution if he'd approached his job that way. Jose suddenly felt empathy for the man in front of him. If someone had told him he would've ever experienced those feelings for Ken Malone, he'd have called them a liar. But, nonetheless, here he was, feeling bad for him just the same. Jose felt a sting of fear, a strong sting.

"I think we need to get Detective Chatham in here. You can trust him. Right now, we're even considering the possibility of this being a cop. If that's the case, Daniel Chatham is the only one I trust."

Jose walked quickly down the hall and into the lounge. Chatham was eating a bag of Doritos out of the vending machine and sipping on a soda.

"What's going on, man?" Chatham asked.

"I'm not quite sure, but come on back to Malone's office. Someone's trying to frame him for the murders."

Chapter 38

It took the two detectives quite some time to convince
Ken Malone they were on his side. He finally retreated to
his office and allowed them to leave. It'd been an
exhausting day, and it wasn't even 2:30 in the afternoon.

"What're you thinking, Chatham?" Jose asked as soon
as the two got back into the car.

"I'm scared, I hate to say it."

"I know what you're going to say, but don't say it yet,
not in the car. Let's go get Erin and go to your place. Mine
isn't safe."

Jose phoned ahead and got Erin's father, who was none
too happy to hear from him. He wouldn't have let the call
through had Erin not already heard it ring. She was waiting
on the front porch, with her purse in hand, when they
pulled up.

"What's going on, guys?" she asked suspiciously.

"Not much," Jose answered nonchalantly. "We're going back to Chatham's for some lunch. Just a little change from the routine."

"That should be nice," Erin chirped from the backseat of the cruiser.

"Yeah."

"Where'd you go today? How did it go with Graham?" Erin asked.

"We'll talk when we get there. How were your folks?" Jose asked, clearly disinterested in her answer.

Erin looked tired, but she talked the remainder of the way about her family, and how protective her father was becoming, and how chubby her older sister was getting. Chatham and Jose only heard words being spoken as their minds whirled with thoughts of betrayal.

Jose wasn't surprised at the apartment inhabited by his partner. It fit him perfectly. If he was meant to share cases with someone, it was only fitting that they be exact opposites. The old adage *opposites attract* fit well here. Ramirez wouldn't have lasted two days with a dominant personality like his own. The apartment was neat and tidy, the furniture expensive and recently purchased.

"My furniture's the same age as you are, Chatham. You should feel at home in my place."

"Just have a seat, Ramirez. Don't start dogging out my apartment. I'll grab us a soda," Chatham said.

"Hey, I'm not knocking it. I'm glad some of us make more money than others," Ramirez said sarcastically.

"I just manage mine better," Chatham said from the kitchen.

"Okay you two," Erin interjected. "Why are we here? I must be missing something."

The room got solemn as the two men looked at one another.

"Go ahead, partner," Chatham said, looking at Jose. "Tell her what we're thinking."

"I'm ashamed to say it. If we don't say it out loud, then it won't be true."

"Say it, damn it. Say it," Erin said, quickly losing her patience.

"It looks like Malone was framed. Somebody put those pictures there for us to find. They wanted us to think it was Malone," Jose said.

"Why would somebody do that?" Erin asked.

"To make it look like he's been the killer, Erin," Jose said slowly.

"I understand that Jose, but who?" she asked.

"Well, who has known every move we've made? Who knew we were going to Whispering Hollow? Who knew I cared so much about the Everetts? Who knew you were working on this case? Who's a cop? Who could use a badge to get a girl to open an apartment door?" Jose asked, drilling her with question after question.

"Oh Jose, please don't tell me," Erin said sadly.

"Just think about it, Erin. Who else could it be? The Captain is the only one with all that information," Ramirez said.

"I just can't believe it. I *won't* believe it, Jose," Erin said adamantly.

"I don't want to believe it either, but it all fits," he continued.

"Why would he do that? What would be his motive?"

"Serial killers don't have motives, Erin," Chatham said. "They just kill for the pure evil of it."

"I refuse to believe it. Not after all this time. Graham has spent his whole life with this department. There's never been a history of this type of thing. *No*, I refuse to believe it."

"Erin, honey, come on. At least entertain the possibility," Jose said, trying to sway her.

"Okay, I will. But at least entertain the possibility that it *isn't*. How'd it go with Officer Richman?" she asked.

"Textbook cop. Little house, wife and kids, swing set in the backyard."

"Well, keep going down the list," Erin said stubbornly.

Jose ran his fingers through his hair and looked at Chatham, who appeared just as exhausted and frustrated.

"Listen, Erin. We're going to check on O'Boyle's residence. You stay here, and don't open the door for *anybody*, you hear me? Not even Mother Teresa! We'll be back in a few hours. Don't go *anywhere*! Have you got your cell phone?" Jose questioned.

"Yes, I've got it. Call me."

"We will. Try to get some rest."

By the time the men reached the car, Chatham was covered with perspiration.

"We need to ride by Graham's house, Ramirez. We should check on his family," Chatham said sternly.

"I don't think that's such a good idea. Cap would be the first to recognize a departmental car in the area."

"He's got that young daughter and a wife, they can't be safe. I think we need to get them out of there," Chatham insisted.

"Are you nuts? What the hell are you thinking? You can't possibly be suggesting we run in and evacuate the family. Damn, that wouldn't give anything away at all!" Ramirez snorted.

"They could be in danger, Ramirez. Stop fucking around! I'm telling you, we've got to get over there and get them out," Chatham demanded.

"What's the matter with you? You were the one screaming at me for breaking into Malone's office and blowing that investigation. Now you want to run over and grab Graham's family out from under his nose. How many serial killers take out their own families anyway?" Ramirez asked.

"Do you want to take any chances?" Chatham asked frantically.

"Get control of yourself, Chatham. Now, it's you that's taking it personally. Look at yourself. Your shirt is soaked and you're shaking like a leaf. Let's go back inside. You can change into a sweatshirt and have a shot of liquor. I need to grab a pain pill, and we should probably plot out our strategy more proficiently. What do you say?"

"Maybe you're right," Chatham answered, hanging his head in defeat.

"I'll call Erin to let her know we're coming back. I don't want to scare her."

Erin was glad to see them. She'd clearly been crying and hugged them both closely. "I think we all need a stiff drink and some rest. Our minds are racing too fast, and we're making rash decisions," she insisted. "I'm not saying the possibility of Graham's guilt isn't there, but we're running on adrenaline right now. Let's calm down for a few minutes. I'll make a snack, and let's relax. Let me get you a towel, Daniel. Where are they?"

"At the end of the hall in the closet. Thanks."

Erin returned with the towel. "I'm sorry about yelling at you two earlier. I'm not myself lately," she said.

"It's okay, Erin. I need to take your opinion into consideration, too," Jose said. "You always look at more than one angle. Let's talk about it. Maybe he is innocent, but I don't know who else could've known all of that information."

"Let's not think about it right now, okay? Here Chatham, take this blanket," Erin said as she unfolded a flannel throw. "Take off your shirt and tie, and I'll grab you a sweatshirt."

"That'd probably make me feel better. I was trying to impress Graham this morning. That was a joke," Chatham said.

"Yeah, you should've learned to talk before you learned to dress," Jose laughed as he watched his thin partner strip out of his dampened Oxford and undershirt. He stared intently at the small tattoo on his right shoulder blade while his mind struggled to place the symbol. He'd seen it someplace before. Just as Erin walked in with the sweatshirt, Chatham noticed Jose's stare.

"I've seen that symbol somewhere. What does it stand for?" Ramirez asked.

"Oh, some Chinese symbol. Means peace or something. Got it during a frat party in college. Thank God I put it where nobody could see it." He pulled the sweatshirt on and stuffed a piece of cheese in his mouth. "So, where to this afternoon?" Chatham asked casually.

"Um, I don't know. That's bugging me. I swear I've seen that before," Ramirez persisted.

"Do you want to go back by O'Boyle's?" Chatham asked nervously.

Erin picked up her wine and was reaching for a cracker when Jose reached for his gun. She dropped the burgundy Merlot, spilling it onto the couch and across the beige carpet.

"Wh…?" Chatham stammered.

"Don't what me, you son-of-a-bitch!" Jose screamed, his gun shaking slightly in his hands. "It was *you* all along. It was you *and* the Captain."

"What're you talking about, Ramirez?" Chatham asked. "I didn't do anything, man, I swear. I don't know what you're talking about. Put the gun down, we can talk about this," he pleaded.

"Jose, please. What are you doing?" Erin cried.

"It was him, Erin. That tattoo, it's the same symbol as Captain Graham's daughter's necklace. She said it was some Indian symbol for good luck. I hadn't ever seen one before, so I asked her about it. She'd gotten it from her mother. He's got the same one for a tattoo, *go figure*. Chatham knew about the whole investigation. He was there when we got shot at. Funny thing though, he *wasn't* shot, I *was*. He's young and good-looking, handsome enough for young girls to open a door to, huh? And a cop, too. Strange, how does a cop afford a Corvette and an apartment like this? I've been working with a serial killer all along. Son-of-a-bitch! Why didn't you kill me? Why?" Ramirez ranted.

"Ramirez, please. Put the gun down, let me explain. It wasn't me. I didn't do anything," Chatham insisted.

"Hell no, I won't put the gun down! Get down on the floor. Erin, call 911."

"Wait, Erin, *please*! Don't do that. Let me explain. You've got a gun on me, so I can't do anything. Give me a minute to explain. *Please*!"

"Shut up, college boy. You've said all you're going to say," Ramirez said, his voice flat and full of disdain.

"Jose, let him talk. You said you respected my opinion. Give him two minutes."

"Erin…"

"No, Jose. Give him two minutes," Erin demanded.

"Two minutes," Jose spat.

"Can I sit up?" Chatham asked.

"No."

"Yes, Daniel," Erin answered softly. "You can sit up."

"Thank you. Yes, Jose, the tattoo is the same symbol as Alyssa Graham's. It's from an old Indian Proverb, and to make a long story short, it brings good luck. Irene Graham's grandmother was Cherokee Indian," Chatham said.

"So why do you have the same symbol as Alyssa Graham, and *why* did you lie about it?" Ramirez asked coldly.

"Because Irene Graham is my mother."

"What?" Jose asked as if he hadn't heard him.

"It's true. She gave birth to me when she was in college in Rhode Island. My father was ten years older than her and a respected businessman. Irene never told her family, and when I was born, she gave sole custody to my father. He was married, so he and his wife adopted me, and no one ever knew any different. It worked out well, except my mother regretted it terribly. She threatened to go public with it if my father didn't at least let her see me from time to time. He agreed to it, and for the past fifteen years, my mother and I have met secretly, two or three times a year. No one knows about it, but when I wanted to go into law enforcement, my father, who's quite wealthy and powerful, made a few calls on my behalf, and got this job for me. As for the apartment and the car, let's just say, I still get a small allowance. If you don't believe me, all of this can easily be checked out. But, please don't call the department. I don't want to hurt my mother."

Erin had her arms around Daniel, rocking him back and forth. "I believe you, Daniel. I believe you."

"Thank you." He looked up at Jose, who was slowly lowering the gun.

"I didn't do it, man. I wouldn't hurt anybody."

"I know. Why didn't you just tell me?"

"I couldn't. I wasn't sure if I could yet."

"Do you think it could be Cap?" Ramirez asked.

"I hope not. I'm scared for my mother, but I thought about what you said, rarely does a serial killer do anything to his family. We could easily find out if he was in town the weekend we were in the mountains."

"In the meantime, we need to stay on our other leads. If he's our main suspect, we can't be too obvious. You need to make that meeting in the morning," Ramirez said as he sank down onto the sofa.

Chapter 39

Detective Chatham jumped out of his car and ran through the rain to make his meeting on time. His umbrella had been turned inside out, and his hair was soaked as he burst through the double doors and into the precinct.

"Great way to start the day, huh?" one of the other detectives asked smugly.

"Yeah," Chatham answered. "Great." He'd planned on being much earlier, but Erin had insisted on preparing a large breakfast. They'd spent a great portion of the night going through files and trying to come up with other potential suspects. It'd worked. They came up with about six more officers to investigate. All three of them wanted desperately to let Captain Graham off the hook.

The meeting was like so many others. The detectives had nothing to go on, so they spent the hour bragging about their other cases, and placing the blame on Chatham and Ramirez for the unsolved murder cases. It was to be expected. Chatham followed the Captain into his office after it was over.

"Did you find out anything yesterday?" Graham asked.

"Not much. We rode around and checked out a few leads, but it didn't lead to much. Richman checked out."

"What about Malone?" the Captain asked.

"He didn't want to talk to me and Ramirez didn't say much about it."

"Well, let me know."

"Will do," Chatham answered.

The Captain's phone rang. As he answered it, he motioned for the detective to stay seated. His face mirrored shock, then concern, and then deep sorrow.

"I've got Chatham in my office. We'll be right there. Keep everybody out of there." He laid the phone down softly before quietly clearing his throat. "There's been another murder, Officer Richman's wife. He found her this morning when he came by for coffee."

* * * *

The once quiet neighborhood was flooded with cold, red lights and uniformed officers. Plain-clothed detectives stood vigil everywhere, most there to support their fellow officer. It caused a knot to rise in Chatham's throat as he got out of the Captain's car. Neither had spoken a word on the ride over.

"Let us through," the Captain barked, motioning for everyone to part either to one side or the other. Someone had apparently taken the children away because there weren't any signs of them. Daniel was grateful for that. The scene before them was, perhaps, the most horrific so far. The killer wasn't taking any chances that the victim would survive this attack. The small living room was covered in blood.

The victim lay on the tattered sofa with her eyes wide open. The knife still jutted out of her abdomen in an eerie gesture, as if to mock anyone who attempted to solve the case. Officer Richman was sitting at the kitchen table, his uniform covered in blood, where he'd held his wife long after her death. He was close to being in shock as the paramedics tried desperately to sedate him.

"I never thought I'd see this day," Captain Graham said as he motioned toward the door.

Ramirez hobbled in with Ken Malone and his crew. Jose and Chatham's eyes met as Ramirez walked over.

"I can't believe this. You two had already left the precinct when I heard. I called Malone's office and caught a ride over. What do you make of it?" Jose asked.

"Richman found her about an hour ago when he stopped by for a cup of coffee. He did it every morning at the same time," Graham answered.

"Somebody's following us," Jose said. "Somebody knows we had him under surveillance yesterday. What's going on?"

"I want you to go over that list with a fine-tooth comb. See if any of our officers work extra jobs at the mall or the university. I'll handle this. You guys get busy," Graham said.

"Let's go," Jose said to Chatham. "I'll meet you at the car."

Ramirez walked over to Malone, who was surveying the scene. "You all right, man?"

"Yeah. This one's bad, the wound is much deeper. He's showing more anger. She didn't suffer long, which is good, but he's manic now," Malone whispered.

"Here's my cell number, call me when you're finished here."

Back in the car, Jose phoned Erin. "Can you set up Chatham's computer to access the department's database?"

"Yeah, I think so. Where are you guys?"

"We're on our way back. Start hacking into it now if you can. We'll be there in thirty minutes."

* * * *

"Are you two still convinced Captain Graham has something to do with this?" Erin asked as soon as they came through the door.

"I don't know," Chatham answered. "He was genuinely upset about Richman's wife. This whole thing is rather bizarre. We could possibly justify the other killings with motives. But this last murder, there wasn't anyone else who knew about the investigation but us."

"But that would've meant Graham had to kill her this morning, after Richman left for work, and he was at the meeting with Chatham," Jose answered.

"You're right there," Chatham confirmed.

"What do you guys want to pull up on this computer?" Erin asked.

"We want to see where these officers are working their second jobs. The Captain thinks they're working at the mall or maybe even the University. It's worth a shot," Chatham said.

"Good idea. Let me fix something to eat first before we get started."

"Damn, Erin," Jose started. "We just left a murder scene. Why does everything have to revolve around food with you?"

"I don't know, Jose, it just does. I can't work when I'm hungry. Now if you want my help, you'll have to feed me. Daniel, there isn't anything else in the fridge, so I'm ordering from Gellar's. It'll take them at least an hour to deliver, so Jose, you'll get that much work out of me before I take a break," Erin said.

"Gellar's?" Jose snorted. "They don't deliver all the way over here. For heaven's sake Erin, that's on my side of town. That little shop would shrivel up and die if it had to deliver this far."

"Shrivel up and *die*?" Erin laughed. "You must be *kidding*. Just because you have the original Gellar's in your neighborhood doesn't mean there aren't any more in existence. Where have you been the past five years? There are as many Gellar's Grocery Stores as there are Bare Necessity stores."

"*What* did you say?" Jose asked.

"I said that there are as many…"

"I know what you said!" Jose yelled. "Who delivers your groceries?"

"Sweet Zac Gellar. He's the area manager now, traveling from store to store, overseeing operations. He still delivers to some of his old customers to keep up with how the quality of business is going."

"Holy shit, that's our man! I buy my coffee and newspaper from him every morning. Who knows what all I've told him the past few months."

"I can't believe he'd do that, Jose. His wife just had a baby," Erin said.

"There you go," Chatham interjected. "The sweet guy next door, with a family, and a job. Sounds like our guy."

"I say we go to the Captain right now and get a search warrant. It shouldn't be hard to prove that all of those girls shopped at Gellar's."

"You're right. Let's go, partner," Chatham said.

"Erin, don't open the door to *anybody* while we're gone. You've solved another one." Jose said.

"You can thank me later. I guess this means I don't get anything to eat."

"Don't even answer her, Chatham. Let's go."

Chapter 40

Erin sat on Daniel's sofa, shivering at the thought of how many times Zac Gellar had delivered groceries to her apartment, and how trusting she'd been. It gave her cold chills. She was startled to hear three light taps on the door.

Erin reached for her cell phone as she walked over to look through the peephole.

"Who is it?" she asked.

"It's me, Sally. Is that you, Erin?"

"Yes, it is," she answered as she swung open the door. "You won't believe what's happened."

"Are you okay? You look like you've seen a ghost." Sally said.

"Well, in a way, I have. Have you ever heard of Gellar's Grocery Stores?"

"Yes, who hasn't?" Sally answered,

"Well, their son is our killer. He's the one we've been looking for all this time."

"Erin, what are you talking about?"

"The *killer* Sally, the *serial killer*. He's their deliveryman. He's been using that to get into these girls' apartments."

"Oh, give me a damn break, Erin," Sally laughed. "You should be smart enough to come up with something better than that. We came up with all of those crooked cops, remember?"

"What?" Erin asked, confused by Sally's tone of voice. It suddenly dawned on her and she struggled against panic. "How did you know where to find me? How do you know where Daniel lives?"

"Don't act innocent with me, Erin Sommers. You snooty little bitches think you're better than a deliveryman, don't you? It's easy to pick on the little guy."

"Sally, what're you talking about? I've always liked Zac. I didn't want to believe it was him," Erin said.

"I told him he should've killed you that night. He knew Jose was smart enough to figure it out, and Zac thought if he beat you up, Jose would be too upset to stay on the case. He was wrong, and I told him so," Sally sneered.

"What are you talking about?" Erin pleaded.

"Don't be so naïve. You make me sick. You've always had everything given to you, haven't you, Erin? You've always been pretty and smart. You always got the good-looking guys, didn't you? Well, you aren't lucking out this time." Sally opened her coat, revealing a large butcher knife. "I haven't ever used one of these but decided to today. In case you were wondering, it was me who shot Jose. Not a bad shot, huh? Zac really likes him, and didn't want me to kill him, so I just wounded him. It wouldn't have bothered me to kill him," Sally said flatly.

"Why? Why are you doing this?" Erin asked.

"It's simple, really. You see, there were three of us. Me, my sister Angela, Zac's wife, and my brother Henry. Henry fell in love with a girl in college, and they were going to get married. She was a pretty girl, but decided she wanted to marry somebody with a little more money, and broke his heart. Then she started lying about him, telling people he was stalking her, and shit like that. She even went so far as to say he raped her. It drove Henry crazy, until one day he killed himself."

"I'm sorry about that, Sally, but maybe Henry did do it. Maybe she was telling the truth," Erin said.

"No! No! No! No way would he do that. You're a *liar*!" Sally screamed.

"Why are you killing people? Why would you hurt innocent people, Sally?"

"It's *your* fault. Its women like you, and all those pretty girls, who think they can go through life and get what they want and not be punished. It's people like you who took our brother from us."

"Why did you bring Zac into it? He would've never hurt anybody."

"Amazing what love will make you do, isn't it? I bet if you begged him hard enough, Jose would kill for you."

"Never," Erin said firmly.

"He would if you gave him an ultimatum," Sally said.

"It's all been a game. A game to lure everyone in that you could, hasn't it, Sally? You used the three of us to get close to the investigation."

"It was pretty damn smart of me to get Zac to kill Chrissy Ozette's roommate, wasn't it? She's been in and out of Lobale so many times I've lost count. I knew it'd lead you guys straight to us and give me an inside scoop into the investigation. I never counted on a good-looking young cop though. That was an added bonus. I'm a little disappointed you all figured it out so quickly. Kind of a shame, actually," she sighed heavily.

Erin shook her head in disbelief as she watched Sally move closer with the grace and ease of a hunter. "Sally, I didn't take your brother. I wouldn't hurt you, I promise. Now put the knife down. We don't want anybody else to get hurt."

"One cut, that's all it takes. You won't suffer long, trust me, don't worry."

"Stop, Sally!" Erin screamed.

Sally lunged just as Erin reached for Jose's back up weapon.

* * * *

Jose's cell phone rang as he left the DA's office with the search warrant.

"Yeah, Ramirez."

"Jose…come quick…I've just killed Zac's accomplice."

Chapter 41

Jose turned to Chatham and reached for his friend's shoulder to steady himself.

"That was Erin. She's killed Zac's accomplice in your apartment."

"What are you talking about? Who? What?" Chatham stammered.

"Help me to the car. I feel like I'm gonna pass out. We've got to get to her."

"Shouldn't we radio any units in the area? Somebody could get to her before we do," Chatham stated.

"I…I don't know. I don't know how the whole thing went down. We may need to get there before anyone else," Ramirez said.

"You know we can't disrupt a crime scene or change the scenario of what happened. We have to think of her safety first," Chatham insisted.

"Get on the radio then, and for God's sake, let's get to her as quickly as we can."

Erin stood there shaking violently, the gun still grasped tightly between her hands. As if acting with a mind of their own, her arms lowered themselves as the gun landed with a thud on the hardwood floor, bouncing a couple of times, before coming to rest at Sally's feet. Her first thought was of the many horror flicks she'd watched over the years, and how the victim always heaved a sigh of relief too soon, confident the killer was surely dead. Erin wouldn't allow herself to be fooled so easily. Inching herself closer to the body, she looked at the enormous bloodstain on Sally's pale-yellow blouse. It'd clearly been a straight shot to the heart. She hadn't even let out a sound when she hit the floor. Erin pointed her toe and nudged Sally's leg with the tip of her sneaker. No response. She poked a little more aggressively, still nothing. She strained her eyes to see if the bloody chest was rising and falling in some form of rhythmic breathing, but couldn't detect any. *She's got to be dead*, Erin thought. *She's lost a tremendous amount of blood.*

Erin was still studying the status of the corpse when she heard the banging at the door. She jumped at first, frightened by the panicked, incessant knocking, then felt a wave of relief wash over her. She had no idea of how much time had lapsed since she'd shot Sally. It was as if time had remained in some freeze-frame sensation of slow-motion movements. "Oh, thank God," she said aloud, as she unlocked the dead bolt and flung open the door. The relief was instantly replaced with a cold, frenzied fear.

"Step back inside and don't make a sound," Zac ordered. "By now you know what I'm capable of. I never wanted to hurt you, but I can't make any promises now. You're a liability."

The shock of not finding Jose and Daniel at the door had literally taken her breath away, and any attempts to answer failed her. She stepped backward into the living room. Her first thought was of how Zac would react to the dead body of his sister-in-law lying on the floor. Erin had expected him to be angry, even emotional, but he appeared to be neither.

"Is she dead?" he asked quickly.

"As far as I can tell, yes," she replied as calmly as her voice would allow. "I didn't mean to kill her. She was going to stab me, I had no choice."

Zac seemed to dismiss her explanation and grabbed her tightly by her forearm, causing her to yelp.

"You're coming with me. Don't ask any questions. Act natural if we pass anyone. Not only do I have a gun, but I won't hesitate to use it, on you or anyone else."

Erin walked quickly beside him, trying to keep up with his brisk pace. She knew what this meant. She was being held hostage, a bargaining chip, if you will. If nothing else, it was buying her some time to get out of the predicament. It could go either way, but the positive side was she was still alive and didn't have a Henckels blade protruding from her belly. Things could definitely be worse. Zac avoided the elevator and led her swiftly down the concrete stairwell. She went from praying silently that someone would open the door on one of the landings, to praying that they wouldn't. She didn't want to be responsible for the death of another innocent person. Erin remained silent as they made their way out of a back-exit door and into a narrow alleyway. She was looking for the small, white delivery truck, but didn't see it. Instead, he pushed her into a black SUV, walked hastily to the other side and jumped into the driver's seat.

"Zac, you know you won't get away with this," Erin said calmly. "Jose will hunt you to the ends of the earth."

"Don't you think I know that? That's why I tried to keep you two out of this. You should've let it go. If I'd killed you both, like Sally wanted, I wouldn't be in this predicament now," Zac said nervously.

"Zac, you're a good man, why on earth are you part of this?" Erin asked.

"It's none of your business. Don't say anything else, I have to think. Angela is going to be beside herself when she finds out about Sally. It won't be good, with her just having the baby and all."

"Zac…" Erin started, attempting to talk some sense into him.

"Quiet, I mean it! It'd be a hell of a lot easier for me to just kill you right now. Don't make me do it."

Erin wanted to continue, but she didn't. Zac was getting agitated, and she knew he wouldn't be capable of dealing with so many emotions. He cranked the vehicle and pulled slowly, and inconspicuously, into traffic. They were headed north, away from town, and she wondered how Jose would ever find them. Unsure of how much time had really passed between the shot fired at Sally and when Zac had knocked on the door, she had no idea how much of a head start they'd get before anyone picked up their trail. Erin closed her eyes and tried to assemble her thoughts. *Where were they headed? What would happen next? Would she get a chance to escape?*

"Son-of-a-bitch!" Zac screamed as he slammed his hands on the steering wheel. "Why'd you have to get involved in this?"

"Zac," Erin said in a soothing voice, "you can stop at any time. You know you won't get away with it. As soon as they find Sally's body and discover I'm missing, everyone will be after you...the State Police, the FBI, not to mention Jose. Turn yourself in. We know you didn't want to do it. It was all Sally and Angela." Clearly, she'd been making headway until she mentioned his wife.

"I won't let Angela take the blame, and I won't let them take me alive!" Zac screamed.

Again, she closed her eyes in an attempt to regroup. They rode in silence for what seemed like miles. The only sound was the motor and Zac's heavy, nervous breathing. Erin glanced at her watch. It was just after noon, and she was certain Jose had discovered her missing by now. He'd be frantic, but he and Chatham would soon be on their trail. *Where was Zac taking her?*

Chapter 42

Jose had to wait for the elevator because of his wounded leg, but Chatham bounded up the stairs to his apartment. He could hear the sirens in the background, but no one had beaten them to the scene. Jose shifted from one foot to the other as he pushed the elevator's button again, in hopes it'd arrive quicker.

Chatham reached the third floor, flung open the door leading into the hallway, and ran to his apartment. His stomach sunk when he saw the open door leading to the bloody scene and Sally's corpse, but more disturbing was the absence of Erin Sommers. With his weapon already pulled from its holster, he made his way quickly through the apartment calling her name. There wasn't a response, and nothing suggested a struggle had ensued.

"Erin, Erin!" Jose screamed as soon as he entered the apartment. "Chatham, what the hell's going on here?"

"Someone must've taken her," Daniel responded, careful to keep the panic from his voice. "She wouldn't have left without telling us. There's no sign of her in the apartment." He took a minute to steady his friend by firmly grasping his shoulder. "Look, Jose, it's a damn good sign she isn't laying here with a knife in her gut. She's got to be alive. Whoever took her will use her as bait to try to lure us in. We've got this."

"It's Zac, it's got to be him. Let's get the hell out of here. As soon as the cavalry arrives, we'll be stuck here explaining this whole thing. We can't afford to lose that much time." He curled his muscular arm around Chatham's neck. "Help me down the stairs. We'll meet up with somebody if we take the elevator."

"Cap's gonna shit bricks," Chatham said, quickly making his way down the stairs. "I'll have to call him from the car, we don't need a BOLO out on us."

"We'll figure it out in the car," Ramirez said as he tried to steady his breathing.

"We don't even know where we're headed. He could be taking her anywhere!"

For the first time, Chatham's thoughts went to Sally's limp body lying on his apartment floor. "Sally must've walked in the middle of it all," he said, his voice cracking with emotion.

"I'm sorry," Jose said. He felt guilty for not taking more time to console his partner, but all he could think about now was finding Erin.

Daniel brushed a tear from his eye before it rolled down his cheek. "I didn't even take the time to cover her up. What kind of animal am I?"

* * * *

Erin pressed the palms of her hands firmly against the top of her thighs to thwart their shaking. Opening her eyes, she knew she had to remember the route they were taking. If she did get an opportunity to escape, she'd need to know her location. The city landscape came and went, followed by desert, before the mountains began to come into view. Zac was starting to calm down, his breathing wasn't as labored. Glancing out of the corner of her eye, she could see the perspiration beading on his forehead. He was keeping a steady beat with his fingers on the steering wheel.

"Zac," Erin began. "Where are you taking me?'

"Just stay quiet. I've got to get us out of here," Zac answered nervously.

"Jose will know about my abduction by now. I'm sure Angela has heard about Sally. Things are going south quick. You can always let me out of the car, you know?" Erin suggested calmly.

"I've got to get to Angela and the baby. If my plan works, they'll be at the cabin waiting for us now."

"What cabin, Zac?"

"This is where it gets tricky. We're headed to Jose's cabin. He'll never think of finding us there. In fact, I'm sure it's the last place he'd ever return to."

"But, why?" Erin asked.

"It's simple. We have to finish what we started."

Chapter 43

Captain Graham and the other detectives remained at Daniel Chatham's apartment scouring it for any clues that'd give them some answers to the crazy turn of events. They were all frustrated at being outwitted by a delivery boy, of all people.

"We need to figure out how this dead corpse is related to these murders," Captain Graham growled at the nearest investigator. Detective Brooks, a short, scrawny man in his fifties, was placing Jose's weapon in an evidence bag. "Looks like Ms. Sommers was one hell of a shot," he grinned, holding up the gun for the captain's inspection.

"Well, according to Chatham, Erin told Ramirez she'd shot the accomplice. She clearly meant business. The dead girl's a nurse at the mental institution, but beyond that, we have no way of knowing how she could be tied to the

Gellar boy," Graham said, motioning toward Sally's
bloodied body.

"Man, Captain," Detective Brooks corrected him.

"Huh?"

"Everyone keeps calling him a *kid*. He's a grown man. I
still can't believe he could be involved in this."

"Boy, man, who gives a fuck?" Graham snapped.
"Where the hell is Detective Porter?"

"Porter's over there, Sir," Brooks answered, pointing
toward the bedroom before placing the evidence bag in a
box with some other items.

Graham mumbled a few choice words under his breath
as he made his way back to Chatham's bedroom. Detective
Porter had his flashlight out and was shining it in the
corners of the closet.

"What the hell are you looking for?" Graham asked
impatiently. "It's painfully obvious nothing more than a
shooting went on here."

"Just checking out every possibility, Cap," the
investigator answered, turning his attention to his superior.
Detective Porter was a thirty-year veteran of the police
force and a fine man. He was tall, probably close to six-

four, and terribly thin. If one didn't know him, they might be tempted to think he was either sickly or favored the bottle a little, but neither was the case. Over the years, his hair had turned a dull color of gray, and thinned to nothing more than a few long wisps that he was determined to brush into some sort of outdated comb-over. His oversized glasses were always clinging desperately to the edge of his nose. If Captain Graham had any complaints about him, it'd be that he overanalyzed the hell out of everything, and searched for clues that more than likely didn't exist.

"I need you to come with me, Porter," Graham said. "Let's head to Gellar's Grocery and get some more details."

"I thought you sent Detective Hodges over there with some uniformed patrolmen," Porter said, pushing his glasses up on his nose and turning off his flashlight.

"I did," Graham answered, his patience clearly wearing thin. "But they were looking for any info on Zac and his whereabouts. The parents couldn't give Hodges any information, or so they said. I'm looking for a connection between the dead Ms. Sally Spriggs and our boy Zac. I need you to drive me over."

"Let's do it, Cap," Porter answered, as he followed Graham out to the cruiser.

It was a fifteen-minute ride and another few minutes to find a parking space on the street.

"Damn," Graham said. "How can they do any business without a parking lot? Stupidest shit I've ever seen."

"It's a neighborhood grocery, Sir. Most folks just walk over," Porter answered.

"I'd never send my wife out to struggle home with our groceries," Graham snapped.

"Hence the home delivery," Porter continued. "It's made them a mint."

"And gotten our boy into the apartments to murder innocent young girls. I just never have been a fan of delivery. I don't even like for a stranger to deliver my pizza. This is a crazy world we live in."

"You've got a point there," Porter agreed, once again pushing up his large spectacles. Captain Graham wanted to snap at him and tell him to invest in some new ones, but decided against it. He'd just be taking out his bad mood on Porter, and it wouldn't be fair.

Mr. and Mrs. Gellar were sitting in the back of the store in their small, cramped office. Mrs. Gellar was crying and holding a roll of paper towels in her lap that she was utilizing as tissue. Detective Hodges was seated just inside the room with his pen poised over a clipboard, frustration written all over his face. He glanced up and seemed relieved to see the Captain and Porter.

"They can't give me anything, Cap," Hodges said, standing up to greet his supervisor.

"Step out here with us for a minute," Graham said to him before turning to the Gellars. "Please bear with us for a minute, and I'll be right back with you." Mr. Gellar nodded in agreement while Mrs. Gellar buried her face in the towel and continued to sob, her beefy shoulders heaving up and down.

"So," Graham asked quietly, "what've we got?"

"Not much of anything," Hodges answered. "I have to say, I believe 'em, Cap. They seem as shocked as anybody that their son's involved in this. They don't know where he is and haven't had any contact with his wife, Angela. Apparently, none of them are ever out of contact for any length of time. They talk numerous times a day, via cell phones, about their numerous stores and deliveries. They appear to be good folks."

"Yeah, so did their murdering, piece-of-shit son," Graham seethed.

"I think I've gotten all I can out of 'em," Hodges continued. "We might want to consider getting the mother some medical attention. She's close to going into shock."

"Hell," Graham grumbled, "let me get in there and see if there's anything else I can get from them before it comes to that. Porter will take me back to the precinct when we're done here. Thanks for your help, Hodges."

"No problem, Cap," Hodges answered, relieved to exit the situation.

Captain Graham motioned for Porter to stand back as he made his way into the office. If the Gellars knew anything about their son's other life, they were putting on an Oscar-worthy performance.

They appeared to be hardworking, honest people, and although they'd made quite a success of their business, still appeared to live meagerly. Mr. Gellar wore a stoic, confused expression on his face and Mrs.

Gellar, as Hodges had said, was pretty damn close to going into shock. Graham knew he was on borrowed time if he expected to get any information out of them.

"I'm so sorry to intrude at a time like this," he said soothingly, "but it's imperative we get any information we can. Time is of the essence."

"We told the detective everything we know," Mr. Gellar said quietly. "We had no idea our son was capable of such a thing. In fact, we still don't believe it."

"I'm sure this is difficult for you, Mr. Gellar," Graham continued, aware that any harsh words would shut the pair down completely. "Do you know of a Sally Spriggs?" Captain Graham asked.

Mrs. Gellar looked up to meet Graham's eyes. "Yes, Detective, we do," she answered, wiping the rough paper towel across her running nose. "She's Angela's sister. Angela is our daughter-in-law. Is Sally okay?"

Captain Graham made every attempt to hide his surprise. "Apparently…" Graham started, then paused briefly to get his thoughts together. "Apparently, Mrs. Gellar, Sally was your son's accomplice."

The Gellars both gasped, and Captain Graham could see Mr. Gellar reaching for his heart. "Please, Mr. Gellar, take a seat," he instructed him quickly. Leaning out the door, Graham made eye contact with Porter. "Get an ambulance, ASAP. We may have a heart attack on our hands."

Chapter 44

"What?" Ramirez screamed into his cell phone. "You've got to be *shitting* me!" he ranted.

Chatham was behind the wheel, speeding to Ken Malone's office, and not even sure why.

"What's going on, Ramirez?" he asked in between expletives. Ramirez waved him off with his left hand and continued to listen to the person on the other end of the line. "I can't believe this," he stammered. "We'll be in touch, Cap," Ramirez said. "Right now, we have to figure out where the hell he's taken Erin."

Jose laid his cell phone on the seat and vigorously ran his fingers through his hair. *This was going to be tough to share with Chatham.*

"Are you going to tell me what that was all about?"

"Well, it appears we've been *had* by more than one person," Jose said, struggling to find a gentle way to break the news to his partner.

"What're you trying to say? Spit it out, Ramirez. In case you aren't aware, we're fighting against the clock here!" Chatham said angrily.

"Okay, Chatham, you aren't going to like this, but Sally was Zac Gellar's accomplice." *There. He'd said it.*

All of the color drained instantly from Daniel's face and his hands started to shake.

"How…how can that be?" Chatham stammered. "I don't understand. I don't believe it, it has to be a mistake," he rambled on. "She's so smart, so caring…"

"That's what she wanted us to believe," Ramirez added. "According to the Gellars, she's Angela's sister."

"Who's Angela?"

"Zac's wife. Believe it or not, she just had a baby," Jose said.

"Well, I'll be a son-of-a-bitch!" Chatham said, his surprise quickly turning to anger. "Sally told me she could stay with her sister, remember that? She said she'd just had a baby."

"Well, at least we know *that* was the truth. Sally was feeding us a lot of shit, but we need to remember *everything* she said. Some of it may've had some truth to it. She's probably our only way of finding Erin," Jose said.

"Sally can't help us now, Ramirez. She's dead. I know, I saw it myself."

"Oh, she's dead, all right," Jose said, "but she can still help us. We have to remember anything she told us about herself."

"We're two blocks from Malone's office," Chatham said. "I don't know why I'm headed there, but we have to go somewhere to get our plan together. His office computer can get us into the department's central database."

****

Five minutes later, Chatham and Ramirez were in Ken Malone's office.

What a strange turn of events, Jose thought. The one man I was convinced was the serial killer is now the one I'm trusting to find the woman I love. Jesus, talk about irony!

"What's up, guys?" Malone asked as he reached for his equipment bag, and jacket.

"Zac's got Erin," Jose said, startled by the sound of his own panicked voice.

"What? Who the hell's Zac? I'm already late for a crime scene. Tell me about it in the car."

"We don't have that kind of time," Chatham said. "The crime scene you're headed to is at my apartment. Things have taken an ugly twist. Erin Sommers killed the young lady you're going to see. Sally Spriggs was an accomplice to the serial killer."

"Looks like I've been left out of the loop. Who's the guy?"

"Zac Gellar," Jose said rapidly, his voice still wavering. "He delivered groceries to the victims. Listen, we don't have time to spare. We need to figure out where he took Erin. I know you have to get to the shooting, but we need some help."

"I'm not sure how much help I can be," Malone interjected, "but I'll do whatever I can."

"We're trying to stay under the radar," Chatham said. "If we go to the crime scene, we'll be immersed in paperwork and pounded with questions. Right now, we need a place to assemble our thoughts. Could we stay here and use your computer?"

"Sure, no problem," Malone answered. He turned and motioned toward a large chalkboard. "Feel free to use anything I've got. I shouldn't be more than an hour or so." He paused long enough to scribble the password to his computer before closing his office door behind him.

Chatham and Ramirez sat silent for a few minutes after Malone left, each deep in their own thoughts. Jose spoke first. "We should find out all we can about Ms. Spriggs. I haven't known her long, but I've known Zac for years. I practically watched him grow up. I just can't come to terms with the fact he's involved in this. And who's ever heard of a serial killer in cahoots with his sister-in-law? Have you ever read about that in any of your textbooks?"

"Can't say I have," Chatham said, rubbing his temples in a circular motion. "She was smart, no doubt about that. Our meeting couldn't have been a coincidence. Damn, I'm gullible!"

"Now's not the time to beat ourselves up," Ramirez said. "We're losing precious time, and Erin's life could be in danger. Let's start with what we know, or think we know, about Sally Spriggs. One thing for sure, she was a nurse at Lobale Mental Institute. I say we start there. What was the doctor's name she worked for?"

"Um," Chatham stammered, closing his eyes to search his memory. "Easton, I'm pretty sure it was Dr. Easton. He's Chrissy Ozette's doctor and not very fond of me, to put it mildly. He ordered me out during my last visit and told me not to return. I don't think he'll give us much without a warrant and being as time is so crucial, it may be a dead-end."

"We'll have to pay him a visit, no doubt about it, but let's see what we can find on the department's database and on social media. That'll give us a start," Jose said, sitting down behind Malone's desk and entering his password. Chatham paced back and forth as he listened to Ramirez run his fingers across the keyboard.

"Okay," Jose said, leaning closer to read the information on the screen. "Looks like we have her here. Sally Alicia Spriggs, age twenty-five, resides at 1820 Evergreen Circle, Apt. G-2, in Sierra Hills. Known associates include Angela Spriggs Gellar, Henry Spriggs, Harriett Spriggs, and Harry

Spriggs. They must be her siblings and parents, that'd be my guess. We can go back and pull them up individually if we need to. She doesn't appear to have a criminal history, she has two unpaid parking tickets past due over sixty days and is a registered nurse. That last fact alone gives us a lot of information."

"What do you mean?" Chatham asked.

"Well, being a registered nurse is pretty serious stuff. For starters, the Washington State Police, and the FBI, run a fingerprint-based background check. The state also looks into any preexisting medical conditions, past or current use of chemical substances, and any civil issues she may have had. Clearly, she beat the system. We weren't the only ones fooled by her kind, innocent demeanor."

"Okay, she was a psychopath. Now what? We still need a motive, and a way to find Erin."

"Zac has to have her," Jose said, shaking his head in disbelief. "Angela and the baby have to be with them too. According to Graham, the Gellars haven't been able to get in touch with her."

"Maybe that's a good sign," Chatham said. "Surely he wouldn't hurt Erin with his wife and baby there."

"Ha!" Jose sneered. "Even after Sally pulled the wool over our eyes, you're still being naïve."

"Look, Ramirez," Chatham said, pausing to make intentional eye contact with his partner. "Zac clearly doesn't want to hurt her. If he did, he would have killed her in my apartment. It would've made things a hell of a lot easier for him to just take his family and run. Bringing a hostage along takes it to another level."

"But a hostage can come in handy," Jose added. "They can be used as a bargaining chip if things go wrong."

"Yeah, you have a point there," Chatham added. "However, you and Zac were almost like friends. He's undoubtedly aware you'll do whatever it takes to get her back. Personally, I think our boy has a conscience."

"*What?* Have you lost your damn mind?" Jose screamed, slamming his fist down on Malone's desk.

"Just think about it for a minute," Chatham said calmly. "Zac has clearly kept you alive in the midst of this whole ordeal. He knows everything about you, down to where you're traveling, what you're investigating, and your working relationship with Erin, and *The Seattle Times*. It'd only make sense to take you and Erin out of the equation.

Zac Gellar tried to scare you off the case, but he's let you live. He showed up at my apartment to save Erin's life, and had no choice but to kidnap her."

Jose's expression began to soften and he contemplated what Chatham was saying. Perhaps there was some truth to it. "Maybe you're right," he conceded. "But we're still at square one, and we need to find Erin as soon as possible. Who knows what'll happen if Zac gets cornered. He might be forced to choose between Erin and his freedom. We've got to find them before that happens."

"Okay," Chatham said, "but right now we need a motive."

Chapter 45

Zac had made several calls to his wife, Angela, and was beginning to calm down a bit as they traveled down the highway in route to Jose's cabin. His hands continued to tremble, but his breathing had slowed to a normal rate. Erin still didn't attempt any conversation. He was clearly overwhelmed with their situation and wouldn't respond to reason. Her primary concern was tracking their course and committing any landmarks to her memory. Erin didn't know what she was in for, but clearly escape would be at the forefront of her plans.

The highway soon gave way to mountain views, and she struggled to remember how long they'd been gone from Chatham's apartment. She had no idea what time of day it was or how much time had lapsed during their drive. Her mind was still racing with the day's events and how quickly, and unexpectedly, everything had unfolded.

Erin's stomach had begun to growl, not from hunger, but because she hadn't eaten all day, and her body was showing its displeasure. Her mind started to reel and the thought of getting Zac to stop, even at a convenience store, might lead to the two of them showing up on surveillance tape. Better yet, someone might recognize them when the news communicated their stories later in the day. He was probably smarter than that, but it was worth a try.

"Zac," Erin asked softly. "I haven't eaten all day and I need to use the restroom. Do you think we could stop for a pack of crackers and a soda? I really need to pee."

For a minute, Erin thought he hadn't heard her, but then Zac turned to face her. "We're making good time. I want to get further away from the city. I'll stop in about twenty minutes." That was more than Erin had hoped for, so she sat silently for the next several miles, memorizing the scenery.

It was well over thirty minutes before Zac decided to pull into a gas station. He reached for Erin's forearm and squeezed it forcefully. "Don't try anything stupid in here," he said as he looked her in the eye. "I have a gun, and you won't be the only one hurt."

Erin thought of responding, but instead shook her head in agreement. Zac gave her arm one final squeeze, making her cringe with pain. The effort told her all she needed to know, he wasn't fooling around. Stepping out of the SUV brought some much-needed relief, and she stretched her limbs and back. A bathroom break would help, too.

They walked into the small, unkempt convenience store looking like two anxious fugitives on the run. The young girl behind the counter had a cell phone to her ear and her nose in the latest edition of *The National Inquirer*. She didn't look up to offer them any form of greeting.

The restrooms were in the far left corner, out of view of the front door, and the disinterested employee. Erin made her way to the back, aware that Zac was watching her every move. Opening the door to the restroom, she immediately scanned the filthy space for a window, or back exit. No such luck. Any other time she would've forgone utilizing such repulsive facilities, but she wasn't sure when the opportunity would present itself again. Erin turned on the water and briefly lathered her hands with the cheap soap before rinsing them off. If only she had her purse, she would've been able to scribble an SOS on the wall, but Zac hadn't given her an opportunity to grab anything when he'd abducted her from the apartment. Erin prolonged the bathroom break as long as she could before coming out. Zac was standing about five feet from the women's room, clearly anxious to get back to the car. He was holding a bag of chips, a couple of candy bars, and two sodas.

"Hurry up," he whispered, carefully maintaining eye contact with Erin. "Remember what I said. Don't try anything funny. It won't end well."

Erin shook her head in agreement and followed him to the register. She prayed silently the young girl would look up from her magazine and notice their appearance, in case someone was to come along and question her later.

"Will that be it?" she asked, barely glancing up at them, instead concentrating on the items she was scanning.

"Yeah," Zac said in a raspy voice.

Erin kept her stare fixated on the young girl, but she never looked up to meet her gaze, instead rummaging through her purse for a cigarette. Zac took advantage of the employee's momentary distraction and led Erin to the car by her elbow. Neither of them spoke as he cranked the SUV. Just as Erin was about to ask about their location,

Zac's phone rang. Judging from his end of the conversation, it was Angela. She'd made it to the cabin. This brought obvious relief, and his demeanor had completely transformed by the end of their brief conversation.

"Did your wife and baby make it to Jose's cabin?" Erin asked innocently.

"Yes," Zac sighed. "Thank God, they're safe."

Inching out slowly, as if on to thin ice, Erin continued, "Are we almost there, Zac?"

"It won't be long," he answered almost kindly. "I never wanted you and Jose to be involved in this," he continued. "I did everything I could to keep you both out of it."

"I still don't understand," Erin said. "Why you? I understand Sally's pain over the loss of her brother, and the false allegations against him, but why you? Zac, you're a good man, and you come from a good, strong family. I just don't understand."

"There's a little more to it than that, Erin. It's crazy what one will do for love. And now I have a son," Zac answered, his voice faltering. "I had to do what I had to do."

"But Sally's gone, Zac. It can end now. You don't want anything to happen to Angela or the baby."

His fingers started tapping rapidly on the steering wheel, and his breathing quickened. It was Erin's clue to be silent for now. Her thoughts immediately turned to the situation she was soon to enter. She was unsure of how Angela would react to Sally's death and if she too was a psycho like her sister had been.

Chapter 46

Sally Spriggs did have an active Facebook account, but that was clearly the extent of it. There weren't any friends on her page, and her profile picture was a silhouetted image of a female. It'd been established back when Facebook first began and must've been utilized to simply creep on other people's pages, much like Jose and Daniel were attempting to do now. There wasn't any evidence of any tweets or an Instagram account ever existing. Social media wasn't going to help them in this case.

"Did we really expect her to have any friends?" Chatham asked. "Who the hell would hang out with her?"

"Um, we did, dumb-ass," Jose said sarcastically. "Let's pull up the family members on the database. Then we'll head over to Lobale. I can't imagine that doctor not helping, especially with this turn of events."

Daniel let out a sigh, knowing the visit was inevitable. Then his thoughts turned to Chrissy Ozette. "Sally set us up the whole time, Ramirez."

"Clearly," he answered as his fingers tapped across the keys of Malone's computer.

"No, I mean she used us by killing Bridgette, Chrissy Ozette's roommate. Chrissy had a history of being admitted to Lobale. Sally knew we'd come to question that poor girl and she'd wiggle her way into the investigation. That's the sickest thing I've ever heard."

"Sick, but pretty damn clever, you have to admit. We may be dealing with a psycho, but we're not dealing with an idiot. What we need now is motive."

"Have you found *anything* on the database?" Chatham asked impatiently.

"I'm looking at Angela Spriggs Gellar now. Clean as a whistle. Married Zac two years ago, current age twenty-three, no criminal record, not even a speeding ticket, and no known work history. Her driver's license is current, and her name's registered, along with Zac's, on a 2012 dark blue Dodge Caravan, insurance is current as well. We need to put out a BOLO on that now."

"I'll call Captain Graham," Chatham answered. "Hopefully it won't be a long conversation." Daniel dug in his front pocket then opened his hand, displaying several coins resting in his palm. "Want a soda? I'm going to walk to the break room while I make this call."

"Yeah, sounds good. Hurry back." Jose continued to read what little information he could find on Angela Gellar. How strange, he thought. She and Sally were the target ages for Facebook, Twitter, and all the other bullshit young people are involved with now. Did they not have any friends or current drama to share with others? Jose was shaking his head in confusion when Chatham returned with their drinks.

"Anything?"

"Nope. They must be one weird family. They're close to you in age. Do you know of anybody that isn't on Facebook?"

"Yep, me. But, I have to admit it's because I'm in law enforcement."

"But don't most girls love this stuff?" Jose asked.

"From what I understand, it's quite the platform to air your dirty laundry and turn one friend against the other. Isn't that what females live for?"

"Apparently these two didn't want any of their dirty laundry out there."

"Then why create an account at all?" Jose asked.

"Well, they can see who else is on Facebook and get basic information."

"Forgive my ignorance on this, but what kind of information?"

"People list things such as where they work and their relationship status," Chatham answered.

"You've *got* to be shitting me," Jose snorted. "And everyone can see that?"

"Pretty much. They can see basic stuff anyway, but to go onto someone's page, you have to be accepted as a friend."

Jose shook his head in disgust. "So, what if you aren't accepted?" he asked sarcastically.

"Then you can't see daily posts. However, some people don't limit their posts to friends. They may not understand how to put the filters on their page, or they may not care. In that case, someone creeping on their Facebook page might get any info they want, including any pictures placed on their site."

"It's official," Jose sighed. "I'm an old man. It's a miracle we don't have more crime than we do."

"I agree with you there."

"What did Cap say?"

"He's sending out the BOLO on the Dodge as we speak. He's not happy that we aren't at the precinct. He's demanding we get over there now," Chatham answered.

"I'm sure he is," Ramirez answered. "We've got to go to Gellar's Grocery and talk to Zac's parents. We need to find out everything we can about Angela. We aren't getting shit here."

"What about her folks? I'm sure they'd know more than the Gellars. And do you really think they have the store open right now?"

Jose rubbed his eyes and pushed his chair away from the desk. "You're right. I'm not thinking straight."

"Find anything yet?" Ken Malone asked as he strode into his office.

"Nope," Jose answered. "We don't have anything. That was a quick crime-scene visit."

"There wasn't much to linger over," Malone answered. "Your girl put a clean one straight through her heart. Death was instantaneous. I'll have to do an autopsy, of course, but this isn't my first rodeo. The detectives were going over the place with a fine-tooth comb, but I didn't see anything out of the ordinary. Looks like she came in, pulled out a knife on Ms. Sommers, and she gave her what she had coming."

"Thank God," Ramirez sighed. "I just hope Erin's okay."

"By the way," Malone interjected. "How the hell can you afford such a nice place, Chatham? Are you a bookie on the side or what?"

"The kid's got a trust fund," Jose answered crisply. "He's clean."

"Hey," Malone said. "No offense intended, Kid."

Daniel waved him off with his right hand and asked, "Was it the same knife as the others, Henckels, I mean?"

"Yep. It's headed over here with the body. They're probably pulling the van in the bay now. The deceased was a looker. What's the story there?"

"It was all a set up from the beginning," Chatham said, sitting down in one of Malone's office chairs before continuing. "She was a nurse at Lobale where one of our witnesses was sent after her roommate was murdered. It was an easy way to get the inside scoop on our investigation. She's the killer's sister-in-law."

"Damn. What a tangled web," Malone said. "Sounds like a family affair. You don't hear of that very often."

"You aren't kidding," Jose said. "I'm going to pull up her folks and her brother, and get their addresses. We've got to hit the road."

"Keep me updated," Malone said. "I'll do anything I can from here."

"I appreciate it," Jose said, taking time to look Ken Malone in the eye. "You don't know how much. I'll be in touch. Let me see here," he continued as he turned back to the computer, "my bet's on Harriett Spriggs being the mother. If we want to find Zac and Angela, our best bet is to find mama."

Chapter 47

Despite her current situation, Erin couldn't help but appreciate the beauty around her. Washington was a gorgeous state. There was certainly a place for everyone, ranging from city life, to desert, to mountain ranges. Jose had told her about this part of his life but had never taken her here. Perhaps since their lives had taken a romantic turn, he'd have thought of bringing her here, but it'd be tainted now.

Clearly, they were getting closer to the cabin because Zac put in another call to his wife. "Hey, Babe, we're almost there. Do you have everything we need? Does the baby have enough diapers?" He sat in silence as he listened to Angela's response. "I'm sure he doesn't leave the electricity on when he's not there. I'll turn it on, don't panic. Everything's going to be okay."

The cell phone! Erin thought, almost shrieking with excitement. She hadn't thought of it before. Jose would certainly subpoena the records, and it'd lead him directly to her. *Oh, thank God,* she sighed. *It's only a matter of time.*

They made several turns, and with the area becoming more and more rugged, Erin was beginning to lose her bearings. There were no longer any landmarks, just one tree after another, and one dirt road after the next. *This is where it could get real tricky,* Erin thought.

Then she saw a building up ahead. It had to be the Everett's Supply Store because it looked just like Jose had described it. It was an old building, clearly on its last leg of life. The front porch was sagging in the middle, and it seemed as though the whole place was leaning to one side. An old, wood-paneled station wagon sat out front and Erin could see lights on inside. *This has to be a good sign,* she thought. *They will surely notice someone occupying Jose's cabin, that's if they ever go in that direction.*

Erin felt as though she knew the Everetts, although they'd never had a chance to meet. Her heart went out to them after recent events had dragged them into such a diabolical situation. But thank goodness, they hadn't been at the supply store on the morning Zac had come. He'd surely have murdered them too.

The two-lane road soon merged into one, and they passed a few small cabins along the way. The big SUV was not taking the ruts in the roadway very well. Zac and Erin bounced back and forth, shoulders bumping one another, until finally she heard Zac sigh heavily. He turned the vehicle into the next drive, which led up to a small, simple cabin. There was a blue minivan in the driveway. Erin was certain it was Angela's, there hadn't been any discussion of anyone else meeting them there. The front door opened and a young woman carrying a baby wrapped in a blanket walked out onto the porch. She wasn't as attractive as Sally had been, but instead was quite plain. Her mousy brown hair was pulled into a ponytail, and she wore large, unbecoming glasses.

Angela had on what appeared to be a maternity dress and white tennis shoes. Erin immediately felt empathy for the girl. She, like Zac, had been manipulated. But, that was neither here nor there now. Far too much damage had been done.

"Get out of the car," Zac said hastily. "Don't be stupid."

Erin shook her head and opened the car door. Relief washed over Zac's face as he walked quickly to his wife and child. Erin stood at a distance, giving them time to reunite. She knew now was not the time to make a break for it. Her escape would take planning and she needed to be patient until the time was right. These two were not the masterminds of this whole crime spree. They'd been led by a narcissistic sociopath and were simply pawns in her game. Just what her game had been was yet to be determined, but she'd get to the bottom of it, of that she was certain.

Chapter 48

"Damn," Ramirez said, looking up from Malone's computer. "Looks like Harriett Spriggs lives two hours away in Fairfield. It's an apartment, and there isn't a landline listed."

"I'll put a call in to Fairfield PD," Chatham said quickly. "They can pick her up and bring her to us."

"Oh, hell no," Ramirez said. "I don't want anyone touching this case but me. Erin's life is on the line."

"Are you kidding me?" Chatham all but screamed. "We don't have two hours to make a drive to east bumble, and who's to say she'll even be there."

"The kid's got a point," Malone interjected. "Time's not on your side."

"First of all, I'm not a *kid*, damn it!"

"Okay, okay," Jose said, for the first time feeling defeated. "Quit wearing your feelings on your sleeve,

Chatham. Maybe you're both right. Sit down, you're making me nervous." Ramirez looked up and waved his hands at the two men, motioning to the chairs in front of the desk. They took a seat and looked up at him.

"Let's stop going about this randomly. We've got to establish a plan of action, or we'll just continue to chase our tails." Jose picked up the few pieces of paper he'd been scribbling notes on and walked toward the chalkboard. With chalk in hand, he started to write. "Let's start with the Spriggs family. We have Sally, who lived nearby and worked at Lobale. No criminal record, but clearly involved. I've known the Gellars for years, and if there was some kind of controversy in their family, or business, I feel certain I'd have known about it. It has to come from the Spriggs family."

"Why do you say that, Ramirez?" Chatham asked. "Just because you bought your morning coffee there doesn't make you part of the family."

Malone opened his mouth to speak, but Jose cut him off. "Call it *gut instinct*, Chatham. I know good, decent people when I see them. Besides that, if their business has grown as big as Erin said it has, it didn't get that way by bad business."

"Look at Vegas," Chatham added. "The mob built that empire, and the last time I looked it was a pretty big business."

Ramirez was exasperated but spoke patiently to Chatham. "I know what you're saying, and there's a lot of truth to it, but I've been a cop for a long time. There are a million reasons to doubt the Gellars, hell maybe even comparing them to the mob, but nothing beats gut instinct. We can sit in front of this computer for days and probably get some pertinent information from it, but nothing beats human intelligence."

"Point taken," Chatham said. "What've we got on Harriett Spriggs?"

Malone got up, moved behind his desk, and sat in front of the computer. "Not much more than an address really," he said, looking over at Ramirez then back at the screen. "Age sixty, no criminal history."

"Harriett has to be the mother," Jose said, rubbing a handkerchief across his forehead. "Has to be. Chatham, get

Graham on it. She's got to be notified about the death anyway. I want to talk to her ASAP."

Chatham stepped out into the hall to make the call. Jose turned to Malone. "We need some more info on Sally Spriggs. She worked for a Dr. Easton at Lobale Institute. Apparently, our boy Chatham didn't make a great first impression, and I'm afraid the doc won't give us much information without a subpoena."

"So, you need me to ask for a favor from one doctor to another?" Malone asked.

"Well, if you're offering," Jose said.

Malone let out a chuckle. "All right, I'll see what I can do. But, I have to tell you, Ramirez, we may not get much. If she was a whack job, they wouldn't have kept her there."

"I have to give it to her, she's damn good. We all thought she was the greatest thing since sliced bread."

"Sliced bread is overrated," Malone jeered.

Jose joined in the laugh, but it didn't last long. The door swung open, hitting against the wall. Captain Graham stood in the doorway with Chatham cowering behind him.

"What the fuck is going on here?" Captain Graham shouted, his face beet red and his fists clenched. "There appears to be a party I wasn't invited to!"

Ramirez and Malone were instantly on their feet. "It's not what it looks like, Cap," Jose said.

"It sure as hell better not be," Graham shouted, his voice reverberating down the hallway. "Have you lost your damned mind, Ramirez? For Christ's sake, we have a murder investigation of historical proportions, and you're writing on a chalkboard at the ME's office."

"I felt like we could make more headway away from the office," Jose said calmly. "They have Erin, Cap. I've got to find her!"

"No, what you have to do is get your defiant ass back to the precinct and work with the rest of the detectives on this case."

"I'm on sick leave, Sir," Jose added, grasping at straws.

"Then get your *sick ass* back to the precinct, now!"

Jose looked back at Malone with a pleading glance, hoping he'd contact Dr. Easton as soon as possible.

Chapter 49

Captain Graham had Chatham in his cruiser while Ramirez followed behind. Unaware of the pain in his thigh, his mind was racing with the possibilities of where Zac could've possibly taken Erin. The BOLO was out on Angela's van, and he'd get someone on a subpoena for cell phone records. Beyond that, he'd just have to dig up all he could on the Spriggs and Gellars. The answers had to be there.

Jose made his way into the roll call room where the other detectives had folders spread across every available surface.

"Glad you could make it, Ramirez," one of them yelled from the back.

Jose didn't answer but glanced down quickly at the documents on the desk nearby. Before he could dig in,

Captain Graham motioned for him and Chatham to follow him to his office.

The antiquated metal blinds were pulled tightly shut, something Jose had never seen the Captain do before. It made a chill go down his spine.

"After you," Graham said as he motioned for them to enter.

The office was a small space, but Jose noticed right away the extra chairs lined along the walls. He didn't know who'd be joining them, but hoped they weren't claustrophobic. They were going to be crammed in like sardines.

"Sit down," Graham said. "I'll be back in a minute."

Chatham and Ramirez shared a glance, but beyond that, made no conversation. The Captain was in charge of the investigation now. They'd taken things too far this time, and frankly, Jose feared they'd both be put on suspension. He glanced down at his watch and noted it'd been well over seven hours since he'd gotten the initial call from Erin. He didn't know where Zac was holding her, but for some reason, wasn't afraid he'd kill her. Any rational person would think Jose was crazy, but he felt Sally was the driving force behind the murders. Maybe the investigation would prove him wrong, but for the time being, he didn't think Zac would harm her.

The two detectives could hear Captain Graham immersed in conversation, followed by footsteps leading to the office. They sat up straight in the metal folding chairs and for the first time in hours, Jose wished he had a pain pill.

The office door opened and the Gellars walked in. Jose's heart instantly ached for the elderly couple. They'd aged ten years since learning of their son's part in the murders. He stood to greet them, and although their eyes were glazed over from tears and fatigue, he saw recognition there.

"Jose," Mrs. Gellar said, her voice cracking before the sobbing began. "I just didn't know…"

"Shh, shh," Jose said as he helped her sit down. "It's going to be okay, shh, shh."

Chatham fumbled around for something for Mrs. Gellar to wipe her tears and nose, but came up with nothing. Captain Graham pulled a handkerchief out of his sports coat and took a seat behind his desk. The others followed suit and sat down.

"Thank you both for coming," Graham said kindly, as though they had a choice in the matter.

"I've been thinking about this," Mr. Gellar said firmly. "What makes you think this was our son? Just what proof do you have?"

Jose sat stunned for a minute, but remained speechless. He could feel his face and ears burning. The simple fact was, they didn't have any proof at all that it was Zac Gellar. He'd jumped to that realization when he discovered Zac delivered all over the city. Beyond that, they didn't have any forensic evidence, and Erin's call, although confirming Zac's accomplice, didn't really give them enough for any warrants.

"It'll take time to match any forensic evidence, Mr. Gellar," Graham said. "Your son either made or monitored grocery deliveries for each of the murdered girls, I have no doubt we can confirm that."

"That doesn't mean anything. Our deliveries are quite extensive, Detective," Mr. Gellar rebutted. "Our business has grown a great deal over the past few years."

"I understand that," Captain Graham continued, his voice even and in control. "However, we did receive a call from Erin Sommers prior to her disappearance. She told Detective Ramirez she'd just killed Zac's accomplice. That accomplice proved to be Sally Spriggs, his sister-in-law. At the present time, three people are unaccounted for, Zac and Angela Gellar, and Erin Sommers. Have you been able to contact your son or his wife since noon today?"

It was Mr. Gellar's turn to search for the right words. "Not exactly."

"Not exactly? What does that mean?"

"It means no. I haven't been able to contact either of them."

"It's my understanding from Detective Hodges that's a rare occurrence. It sounds as though you have constant contact with your son during the work day." Mr. Gellar's face reflected a glimpse of defeat, but he was quickly able to regroup. "Maybe Sally was involved in this mess, I don't know, but I don't believe my son was and certainly not sweet, innocent Angela. She just had a baby for Christ's sake."

Graham looked down at his intertwined fingers and realized this was going nowhere. He turned his gaze to Jose and raised his eyebrows.

Ramirez took the hint. "Mr. Gellar," Jose began, "I'm so sorry about all of this. I, too, hope that Zac's not part of it. Right now, time is not on our side, and we desperately need to find him, his wife, and Ms. Sommers." Jose was well aware he needed to stay on the Gellar's good side. He measured his words carefully before continuing. "I don't mean to alarm you, but they could all three be in danger."

"Alarm me?" Mr. Gellar almost shouted. "You've got to be kidding. We just left the hospital where my wife was given Valium and treated for high blood pressure. I think we're already alarmed, Jose!"

The use of his first name made it personal. These were fine people, and he hated to hurt them. "Forgive me, Mr. Gellar. I'm on edge too. I've known Zac since he was a child. I'm not wording things appropriately here, but the fact is, we don't have much time. I'm sure you feel something isn't right. It's unusual for you to be out of touch with him. Have you tried to reach him on his cell phone?"

Mr. Gellar released a heavy, defeated sigh. "Yes, Jose, I have. I can't count the times the wife and I have phoned Zac and Angela. We drove over to their place before coming here and both their phones were left on the kitchen table."

It was Jose's turn to sigh heavily. He'd been banking on the cell phones pinging off some towers to give them a location. Unfortunately, that wouldn't be the case now. Maybe Zac was shrewder than they'd given him credit for and was using a disposable phone. This was a hard blow to the investigation, and it left Jose speechless.

Chatham cleared his throat and sat up straight in the old metal chair. "Mr. Gellar," he began compassionately. "Can you think of any place Zac and Angela may have gone? Do you have any vacation property or relatives nearby?"

Mr. Gellar shook his head from side to side. "I've racked my brain, son. I can't think of anywhere those two would go."

"Do they have a favorite vacation spot?" Chatham continued without hesitation. "Do they have any friends who live out of town?"

"We're a very close family, Detective…"

"Detective Chatham. Daniel Chatham."

"We didn't ever vacation. We've been too busy building our business."

This comment brought loud, heaving sobs from Mrs. Gellar. "I'm sorry, Honey," her husband said softly, lightly patting her broad shoulder. "I suppose I've been concentrating on all the wrong things."

Chatham leaned forward, continuing in a calm, soft-spoken tone. "What do you know about your daughter-in-law's family, Mr. Gellar?"

The Gellars looked at one another, then Mr. Gellar wiped his brow with a trembling hand. "Not a great deal. Angela's mother was, well, um…"

"Let's not worry about how we word things right now," Chatham said. "We simply need the facts, Sir. We aren't going to judge anyone."

"Harriett, Angela's mother, is not a very motivated person."

"Oh, for heaven's sake, Harold," Mrs. Gellar groaned. "We need to tell it like it is." She blew her nose loudly before continuing. "That woman's good for nothing. She lives in a subsidized apartment, drinks liquor, and watches talk shows all day. She was never kind to our sweet Angela, just breaks my heart."

"Do you have any contact with her?" Chatham asked.

"We've met her a few times but haven't had any desire to get close to her. She had a son, Henry was his name. From what I understand, he caused her a lot of problems. He committed suicide a few years back before Angela and Zac married."

Chatham and Jose exchanged glances. "Do you know any details about the suicide?"

"No, and I didn't want to know any. All Harriett seemed to care about was that unruly son and her pretty daughter, Sally."

"What do you know about Sally?"

"She was a good-looking girl and quite smart too. Made a big deal about being a college graduate, which didn't sit too well with me. Sally knew Angela hadn't completed high school and seemed to enjoy rubbing her nose in the fact she was a nurse. It upset us terribly to see how she ran over Angela."

"Ran over her? What do you mean?" Chatham asked.

"Oh, I don't know exactly. It seemed like, by putting Angela down, she felt better about herself. Angela is a plain girl. She's never been concerned about makeup, expensive clothes, or jewelry. She loves our Zac and all she's ever wanted was a family."

"What do you know about her father?"

"Nothing. We asked Angela about him once, early on, when Zac first started bringing her around. She started to tear up, and Zac immediately told us not to ever bring him up again. We never did."

Jose reached over to touch Mrs. Gellar's arm. "Was his name Harry?"

"Yes, I believe it was, but don't quote me on that. Like I said, we never spoke of him, but that does sound familiar.

"Did Angela visit her mother very often?" Jose asked.

"She lived over two hours away, so Angela didn't visit regularly, but I do know that she talked to her on the phone," Mrs. Gellar added with disgust.

Chapter 50

Medical Examiner Ken Malone decided to put off the autopsy of Sally Spriggs and take a trip to Lobale Institute. He thought of calling first, but quickly changed his mind. Perhaps catching the doctor off guard would acquire him more information. If all that Chatham and Ramirez had shared with him was true, this Spriggs woman was one hell of a chameleon.

Malone considered for a moment the chance Dr. Easton wouldn't see him, but quickly dismissed the idea altogether. Doctors, like cops, shared a certain bond with one another. He snickered for a moment as he compared his duties to that of a psychiatrist. The two men had chosen entirely different fields, but still had a great deal in common.

Placing the Lexus in park, the ME made a mental comparison of the morgue and the mental institution.

There were far more similarities than differences. Hospitals had recently made vast improvements in architecture and interior design in attempts to make them feel homey and welcoming. Obviously, Lobale hadn't gotten the memo. It gave off a cold, unnerving vibe, just as his building did. Taking an extra minute to adjust his tie and pull on his suit jacket, Malone headed toward the building. For some strange reason, he felt a growing knot in his gut, which was a rarity for him. Very few situations made him uneasy, perhaps due to the fact that he performed autopsies for a living. Ken Malone hadn't always felt comfortable with his vocation, but years of experience and maturity had taken care of that. Some situations were more gruesome or traumatic than others, but he could always count on one thing to remain constant, all of his patients were deceased. The only attitudes and idiosyncrasies he had to deal with were among the living, the detectives, the office staff, and the ever-present powers that be who felt the need to bring politics into his workplace.

Malone opened the double-glass doors, taking notice they were free of fingerprints. Maybe he could get the name of the janitorial crew from the doctor if nothing else. The lobby was absent of any foot traffic, so he made his way to what appeared to be the only information desk in sight. Peering over the counter, Malone could see a half-eaten sandwich, a few chips, and an open soda. He looked around for a buzzer, but when he couldn't find one, he decided to wait. Patience was not one of his virtues, and his weight shifted from one foot to the next as he tapped his watch face with his index finger.

"Oh, pardon me," a young girl said. "Our receptionist is out this week and I'm trying to do my job and hers, too. My name's Emily, how can I help you?"

The young lady appeared to be in her mid-twenties with short, cropped hair, and electric blue eyes. Her personality was vibrant and energetic, and Malone was instantly impressed with her.

"Well, Miss Emily," Malone answered, "it appears I've interrupted your lunch. My apologies."

"Oh, not a problem. We normally wouldn't eat at our workstations, but today's an exception." She quickly gathered up the remains of her midday meal and tucked them into a drawer.

"I'm Dr. Ken Malone. I was wondering if I might speak to Dr. Easton."

"Why sure, let me dial his extension. Could I tell him what this is in reference to?"

The question caught Malone off guard. He wasn't even sure if the facility was aware that one of their employees had been killed. This visit might prove to be more difficult than anticipated.

"Actually, I'm here to discuss an employee."

Emily looked up at him and furrowed her brows. The phone's receiver was at her ear, and her finger was poised over the numbers. "An employee?" she asked. "Perhaps you'd rather speak to someone in Human Resources."

For a moment, Dr. Malone's face reflected exasperation. "You know what, Emily? I suppose I'll need to speak to both the doctor and human resources."

"I'm sure we can set something up for you, but I feel certain it won't happen today. Dr. Easton is doing his rounds and interviews are currently being conducted for new positions in the laundry. I'm sure you understand. We're a rather large facility."

It was Malone's turn to be courteous. "I fully understand, but this isn't your usual request for information. Time is of the essence, and frankly, lives could be at stake."

Emily's blue eyes grew large and she placed the phone back on its receiver. "I-I-don't-think I understand."

"Emily, if I explain all of this to you, I'll only have to explain it over again to your superiors. I think once I speak with them, they'll understand your intrusion on their time."

She opened her mouth to speak but decided against it. This doctor looked serious and perhaps making the call would be the best idea. "Just a moment," Emily said, reaching for the phone once again.

"Dr. Easton's office," a woman's voice answered.

"Yes, Shirley, this is Emily. I'm filling in up front this week." Malone sighed heavily, demonstrating his impatience. "There is a Doctor…"

"Malone, Dr. Ken Malone."

"There's is a Dr. Ken Malone here to see Dr. Easton. It appears to be an urgent matter, one he'd rather discuss only with Dr. Easton."

Malone could hear a rebuttal from the other end of the line but couldn't make out what was being said. He gave Emily a piercing stare, but she refused to make eye contact with him. The conversation finally ended, and she placed the receiver back on the hook. She looked more than a little uncomfortable.

"As I said before, Dr. Easton is doing rounds. It'll be a few minutes before he's available. You're welcome to sit in the lounge area over there," she said, waving her small, manicured hand in the direction of a few waiting chairs.

"Thank you, Emily. I'm sorry if I put you in an uncomfortable situation. I'm sure you will understand later."

She was obviously rattled, and a nervous smile was her only response. Malone didn't offer any further comment, but quietly made his way to the orange chairs.

Yet another institutional color that should be abolished, he thought. Expecting a long, drawn-out wait, Malone was surprised when Dr. Easton arrived within minutes.

"Dr. Easton," he said, reaching out his hand to meet Malone's. "I understand you're here to see me on an urgent matter."

"Yes, Doctor, I am. I appreciate you seeing me so quickly. Is there somewhere we could talk?"

"Certainly. We can talk in my office," he answered, motioning for Malone to follow him. They wound their way down several corridors before stepping into a large, surprisingly well-decorated office with a view of the surrounding property.

"Please, make yourself comfortable," Dr. Easton said as he sat down in the chair behind his desk. "I must say, you've piqued my curiosity. What seems to be so pressing?"

Malone felt an uncomfortable knot in his stomach again. "I understand you employ a nurse by the name of Sally Spriggs?"

"Yes, I do. She's a very good nurse, although she's taken several days off lately. Is there a problem?"

"Frankly, I'm a little surprised I beat the cops here," Malone said. "It's all happened so quickly…"

"*Cops?* What on earth are you talking about?" he asked, alarm apparent on his face.

"I don't know how to put this delicately."

"Just say it, Doctor. How bad can it be?"

"Dr. Easton, Ms. Spriggs has been shot. She's dead."

This clearly hit the doctor from out of left field, his mouth flew open to speak, but the words wouldn't form.

"I'm sure this is a shock to you."

"To say the least. Was it a robbery, carjacking, what happened?"

Malone sat back in his chair and intertwined his fingers. "I'm sure you've heard of the recent murders of the young girls in the area?"

"I certainly have. It's in all of the papers and on the news every night. Was she one of the serial killer's victims?"

Oh, wow, he is clueless, Malone thought. He isn't going to believe this one.

He cleared his throat before continuing, "Actually, Dr. Easton, it appears Nurse Sally Spriggs *was* the serial killer."

Dr. Easton reacted as if Malone had punched him unexpectedly. He bent over the desk and gasped for air.

"Hey, are you all right?"

Easton held up his hand as if to hold Malone at bay while he composed himself. After several minutes, he had most of his composure back, but his face remained crimson.

"I'm afraid I don't understand what you're saying, and honestly, I don't understand why you're here. It'd be far more appropriate for the proper authorities to deliver this information. What type of practice do you have, Dr. Malone?"

It was time once again for Malone to be uncomfortable. "Actually, I'm the Medical Examiner on this case," he mumbled. *Captain Graham is going to go for my jugular on this one,* Malone thought. *How did I let Ramirez and Chatham get me involved in this?*

"Medical Examiner? Please, fill me in."

Malone took in a deep breath and exhaled it slowly, in an attempt to prolong the inevitable.

"If Ms. Spriggs is dead, what's so urgent?"

"It appears she had an accomplice who has abducted a local journalist. Her life could be hanging in the balance as we speak."

"So, let me get this straight," Dr. Easton said sarcastically. "You not only do autopsies, but investigations as well."

Ken Malone threw his arms up in defeat, stood up, and paced frantically across the tiled floor. "Let me be honest with you," Malone said. "I'm way out of my league here and I'll probably be suspended, if not fired outright. The kidnapped woman is a friend of one of the lead investigators. He's frantic, to say the least."

"So, he thought sending a doctor here might get more information from me than a detective would."

"Well, to be honest, yes. You and I both know this whole ordeal could drag out for days, especially if you require law enforcement to get subpoenas. That's precious time we don't have. So, I'm asking you, from one doctor to another, to help us out here."

Dr. Easton's face softened. "The roommate to one of the serial killer's victims is my patient. She'll struggle with this event for the remainder of her life. I don't see a need for anyone else to suffer, Dr. Malone. You do understand there are certain protocols for the release of information, but I'll tell you what I can. That is, if we can keep this off the record."

Keep this off the record? That was more than Malone could hope for. "You're damn right we can keep it off the record," he said, sitting back down in the chair across from

Dr. Easton. "Other than being a good nurse, what more can you tell me about Sally?"

"She worked directly under me and was, or portrayed herself to be, a compassionate and capable nurse. She was prompt, professional, and never missed work. That is, until these past few days. It was unlike her to take time off, especially without prior approval. Sally called the nurses' station and said something had come up and she'd need a few days off. I found that odd, but because of her previous work history, I didn't feel the need to question it further. We all have emergencies that come up from time to time."

"I understand your reasoning," Malone said. "However, she was utilizing that time off to worm her way into the investigation and to stay one step ahead of the authorities. The sad truth is, Sally had your patient's roommate killed because she knew the girl had a mental health history that'd lead her straight to Lobale. A path that would inevitably get Ms. Spriggs on the inside of the investigation."

"Oh, good Lord," Dr. Easton sighed. "And I'm a psychiatrist, you would've thought…"

"Don't beat yourself up," Malone interjected. "She was a cunning girl, and you weren't the only one taken by her.

Besides her work history, what more can you tell me about her?"

Dr. Easton leaned back in his desk chair and rubbed his chin. "I really don't know much, Doctor. We certainly never associated outside of the workplace. I interviewed her myself prior to her employment. She had the proper credentials, was well spoken, seemed eager to work, and I hired her on the spot."

"Proper credentials? Let's start there. Do you suppose she falsified any of her work history or education?"

"She really didn't have any work history to speak of if I recall correctly. We can request her file from human resources. She'd just passed her state RN exam, and I felt comfortable taking a chance on her. Until today, I assumed I'd made an excellent choice. It would be virtually impossible to falsify a state document."

Embarrassment instantly flashed across the psychiatrist's face as soon as the words exited his mouth. "I suppose you're going to tell me nothing is impossible."

"No, I would imagine it'd be impossible, or certainly extremely difficult, to register herself on the state board database."

"That would be HR's responsibility. Checking out her references, education, and test results, that is."

"I realize you're a busy man, Dr. Easton," Ken Malone said. "I'm sure you have rounds to do, and I have an autopsy I should be conducting as we speak. Do you suppose we could get her employment file pulled sometime today?"

"I'll put a call in immediately. I can't imagine how I could possibly work today," the doctor answered, holding up his hands to demonstrate their shakiness. "They should be able to pull it fairly quick. Why don't you start your autopsy, and as soon as I get the information in hand, I'll give you a call. Do you want me to meet you somewhere with it?"

Ken Malone was astonished. This was working out far greater than he'd expected. "You don't know how much I appreciate this," he said, reaching his hand across the desk to meet Dr. Easton's. "Here's my card, my cell is listed at the bottom. Call me as soon as you have anything."

"What exactly are we looking for, Doctor?"

"Motive, her accomplice, and Erin Sommers."

Chapter 51

The morning sun came early, but Ramirez, Chatham, and the Captain were unaware of their exhaustion. The night hours hadn't yielded any answers, so they'd sent for the Gellars one more time, in hopes of finding a lead.

The questioning led to nothing more than further frustration and fatigue. Captain Graham felt no need to prolong their interrogation any further. They were still exemplifying symptoms of shock and clearly didn't have any more information to share. He asked Detective Hodges to drive them home and see to it they'd be readily available should there be a quick turn of events.

"Damn, I feel for them," Jose said as soon as the two were out of earshot. "I'm telling you, Cap, they're fine people. This has to be coming from Sally's family. That's where we'll find our motive."

Graham leaned back in his office chair and stretched his long arms as far as he could. Weariness was evident on his face as he sighed heavily. "Well," he started, "they say the apple doesn't fall far from the tree. My money is on the parents. Let's start with them. Fairfield PD located the mother at her residence. Unfortunately, she's still drunk from last night so they're filling her with coffee. They've assured me they'll head this way as soon as they can sober her up."

"Have they told her about Sally's death?" Chatham asked.

"Not yet. The Fairfield Chief is a pretty amenable guy. He believes telling her now, while she's inebriated, wouldn't serve much of a purpose. Besides, he agreed with me that if we tell her here, the shock of it all may get us more information."

"That makes sense," Jose interjected. "I wouldn't have expected such cooperation from a small police department. Too bad he doesn't work for us."

Graham didn't comment. Instead, he gazed out of his small excuse for a window. "So, what have we got on the father, Harry, is it?"

"Yes, Sir," Chatham spoke up. "We were about to pull him up when you located us at Malone's office."

"Located? Ha! I *found* your asses. You two are as predictable as an old drunk. You don't exactly have many friends, and with Sommers missing, that left Ken Malone. I still don't understand that one."

"Let's just say Malone turned out to be an asset," Jose chimed in. "Let's pull up the dad. The Gellars seem to think he's deceased."

Graham pointed at Chatham and then at the computer on his desk. "Look him up, Kid. I hate those damned computers."

Daniel quickly slid into the tattered chair and ran his thin fingers hastily across the keys. "This is interesting," he said, leaning closer to the computer as if his eyesight were failing.

"Hmmm. Interesting."

"What is it, Chatham?" Ramirez asked impatiently.

Daniel held up a finger as if to bide some time. "We should've seen this one coming. Interesting."

"Okay, damn it," Captain Graham said, turning from the window and eyeing Chatham with a discerning look. "What is it?"

"Seems like old dad is locked away at Clallam Bay. His classification lists him in Maximum Security in the IMU."

"Intensive Management Units aren't for choir boys," Graham said, his interest growing. "What's his charge?"

Chatham leaned even closer to the screen. "Get this, he was recently convicted of two rapes and has apparently served eight years on a prior aggravated sexual battery charge. Sounds like it runs in the family, Cap. You were right. The apple doesn't fall far from the tree."

"We've got to pay him a visit, and quick," Jose said.

"That's almost four hours away," Graham said. "Our best bet is to get on the phone with the Superintendent. Last I heard Donovan Simpson was running that place. Not an easy job, I might add. They only house maximum-security inmates. Never a dull moment, or so I hear."

"You know him?" Jose asked.

"Yeah, we've been to a few conferences together. We don't exactly exchange Christmas cards, but he knows who I am."

"What the hell are you waiting for?" Ramirez asked impatiently. "Get him on the horn, let's find out who visits him, where he committed these rapes, and if he has any property Angela would've known about and taken Erin to."

"Pull up the number for Clallam Bay Corrections Center, Chatham," Graham said. "Simpson's a nice enough guy. I'm sure he'll be willing to help."

Several exasperating transfers later, Superintendent Donovan Simpson answered his office phone. "Well, well, well," he said, laughing heartily into the phone. "To what do I owe the pleasure, Graham? I bet I haven't talked to you in five years. I assumed your old ass had retired by now."

The Captain wasn't in any mood for pleasantries but chose to entertain him just the same. "Hell no, I haven't retired. Sure would like to though. It's past time the department put me out to pasture."

"I know what you mean," Simpson concurred. "I'm ready to grab my hat and go too. Seems like this old world just keeps getting crazier. Every time I think I've seen it all, some idiot tops it. I've been following Sierra Hills on the news. Sounds like you've got a real serious problem on your hands."

"That's putting it lightly. Listen, Simpson, I could use your help. Seems one of your prisoners is the father of one of our suspects."

"Really? You've got a suspect in the serial killings?"

Graham hesitated to confirm any details, but decided he needed all the assistance he could get. "It's unconfirmed, and certainly hasn't been shared with the media. We're still early in the investigation."

"You know you don't have to worry about me contacting anyone with information," Simpson quickly added. "I'm sure you're working against the clock, so what can I do for you?"

Graham heaved a large sigh of relief. *Thank God I don't have to waste valuable time going into details,* he thought. "Are you familiar with an inmate by the name of Harry Spriggs? He's about sixty years old."

"We house a little under nine hundred inmates here, but I know Spriggs well. He's in our Intensive Management Unit and has been since he arrived. As you know, most sex offenders prefer to be out of the general population, but personally, I don't think he'd give a damn. He's a sick, dangerous man. Sounds like he had a sick son, too."

"Actually," Graham started, then wondered why he was offering the information. "It's his daughter. She was quite the evil manipulator. Finally met her match though and was killed early yesterday."

"We haven't received that information. I'm surprised no one has contacted us so we could let Spriggs know."

"Fairfield PD is bringing the mother up our way in the next couple of hours. She isn't aware of it either, and we haven't leaked anything to the press. I'd hold off on sharing the death with Mr. Spriggs for now. I'm unsure of which turn this investigation may take next, so I'd rather him be kept in the dark for the time being."

"No problem here," Simpson said. "It's not like he'll be attending the funeral."

"What do you know about him?" Graham asked, turning back to the investigation. "I mean, just off the top of your head. I'm sure one inmate jacket runs into the next, but we're short on leads."

"Let's see," Simpson started. "He came in about three years ago and started off with a bang, as I recall. Spriggs caught both an inmate and staff assault charge on the same day. I don't believe that's ever happened here. He's been a pain in the ass for the officers ever since. We control his behavior by keeping him on lockdown as much as the state will allow. I'm not sure if that's of much help to you, but I don't have his file here in front of me. I could get back to you within the hour. What type of things are you looking for?"

"I'd like to know who's been on his visitation list, anyone that may've put money on his books, and his last known address. That'd be a good start."

"I'll have my secretary pull his file, and I'll meet with his counselor. I don't know what we'll find as far as home addresses. From what I remember, the State of Washington has been housing him on and off for most of his life."

Chapter 52

Early morning sunlight filtered through the thin curtains, causing Erin Sommers to awaken. Even after all that'd transpired the day before, it took her a few moments to realize where she was. She'd slept for several hours, and as the bedroom came into view, panic quickly swept over her. She remembered Zac tying her wrists to the headboard. She rotated her hands clockwise in an attempt to free herself.

"You're wasting your time. Zac's very good at tying knots."

"Angela?" Erin asked. "Is that you?"

Angela walked around the corner with the baby in her arms. Her eyes reflected a sleepless, tear-filled night. "We never wanted you to be involved in this," she said, her voice soft and kind. "I can fix you some breakfast if you're hungry."

Erin sat up as much as she could and faced Angela, looking at her more closely than she had the night before. She wasn't exactly an unattractive girl, but there was something very nondescript about her, something almost forgettable, like a person passing you on the sidewalk that you failed to notice. She was wearing a long flannel nightgown, which Erin associated with an older person, a grandmother perhaps. She couldn't see the baby because he was wrapped tightly in a crocheted afghan.

"How's your baby?" Erin asked carefully.

"He's fine, he slept all night," she said proudly.

"What's his name?"

"Trace," she answered as her expression swiftly changed to regret. She hadn't intended on providing any information on the child.

"He's a very good baby," Erin said. "I haven't heard him cry once."

Angela held him a little closer as if to protect him from their current situation.

Note to self, Erin thought. The baby is off limits.

"Are you hungry?"

"Yes. Can you untie me?"

"Zac will have to do that, he told me not to. He's outside surveying the perimeter. He should be back in a few minutes. I'll start breakfast."

Erin lay on the bed, trying to make sense of all that'd come to light in the past twenty-four hours. First, there was the initial shock of Zac being their killer and then realizing Sally had been involved too. She closed her eyes as she relived the conversation with Sally and the fatal shot that'd dropped her instantly to the floor. Her mind kept going back to the tip of her sneaker, as she nudged Sally to ensure she was deceased. Unbelievably, she felt no sense of regret or guilt. It'd been a cut and dry case of self-defense, and she was *alive*. For that, Erin was grateful. Now, she had to figure out how to escape and get to the Everetts Supply Store for help. They'd surely notice soon that someone was inhabiting Jose's cabin, and she feared they'd come to inquire about it. That wouldn't end well. Before she could start formulating her plan of action, she heard the front door open, and Zac talking with Angela. From the tone of the conversation, he seemed to be satisfied with the way things were going. For the first time since her abduction, Erin felt the sensation of hunger.

The sound of rattling dishes and the smell of sizzling bacon came from the kitchen, as Erin waited impatiently for Zac to untie her. She desperately wanted to wash her face and use the restroom. The faint thumping of his boots became louder as he rounded the corner and entered her room.

"I'm going to untie you," he said, narrowing his eyes in a threatening gaze. "Angela has laid out a towel for you to shower and a clean sweat suit. It may not be your size, but it'll serve its purpose. I'm sure I don't have to tell you not to try anything crazy. Just because it's a new day doesn't mean anything's changed."

Erin nodded in agreement, grateful for the opportunity to have her hands free for the first time in hours. He loosened the knots and slid the ropes off, leaving them attached to the headboard. That could only mean she'd be bound nightly. She rubbed both wrists lightly and opened and closed her fingers as she felt the blood flowing back to them. Zac motioned for her to follow him as he ambled down the short narrow hallway, and pointed to the left, indicating where she'd find the bathroom.

"In case you're thinking of being smart, I've taken the liberty of nailing the window shut."

Erin shut the bathroom door, thankful for the opportunity to shower and get out of the dirty clothes that represented a day of unbelievable hell. She stood under the hot water, allowing it to wet her hair and run over her face. The last thing on her mind had been that she was in need of a shower, but it was welcoming now.

Afraid that Zac may cut her time short, she wet the washcloth and lathered it with Dial soap. She scrubbed her body until she was certain she'd washed away yesterday's grime, then rinsed off and shut off the water. She glanced around and hadn't been able to locate any shampoo, but it didn't matter. Erin felt like a new woman.

The panties and sweat suit were rather large but would suffice. She put on her own bra from the day before, and made a mental note to rinse it out in the shower later that night if there wasn't a washer and dryer. She slipped her feet back in her sandals and followed the scent of bacon and eggs to the kitchen.

Angela was rocking the baby while Zac paced around the small kitchen. There was a full plate at the table with a glass of orange juice beside it.

"That's yours," Angela said. "It's still warm."

"Thanks so much, I'm so hungry," Erin said, sliding onto the chair. She scanned the table briefly for a napkin, and when she didn't find one, she picked up her fork and began to eat. Every bite seemed to refuel her energy, making her optimistic for the first time.

She watched Angela as she mixed the baby's formula and began feeding him his bottle. Erin was able to see his face now and the bright shock of red hair like his father's. He was a beautiful baby, and she'd yet to hear him cry.

His skin was as white and smooth as porcelain, his cheeks displaying just a dash of pink. He appeared to be a happy and healthy baby, and she couldn't help but wonder what would happen to him when this whole ordeal was over.

"Zac told me that you shot Sally," Angela said softly, allowing her eyes to meet Erin's.

Erin felt herself gasp, unable to control it. As her hands started to tremble, she heard her fork hit the table, unaware her fingers had even released it.

"Don't be nervous," Angela assured her. "She was there to kill you. You did the only thing you could. Sally was, well, she was not like us."

"I…I'm afraid I don't understand," Erin said cautiously.

"She believed the best way to handle all of the horrible things that've happened to our family was to punish people. To punish them before they could punish us."

"I'm still not following you," Erin continued. "Who's hurt your family?"

"That's enough, Angela!" Zac interrupted. "There'll be no more of this. Our concern is Trace now. Sally said he'd be the next one. We have to protect him."

Erin sat up straight and tried desperately to compose herself. There was some twisted story here that Sally had utilized to frighten them. Jesus, they were so vulnerable and naïve.

"Zac," Erin started. "Don't you see? Sally was the one to be frightened of. Trace is a beautiful, healthy boy. No one wants to harm him."

"Don't you *dare* say his name! You don't know him. You don't know anything about him. He *has* to be protected."

"Sally has gotten you brainwashed. I'm not quite sure about what yet, but you've got it all wrong. It's not too late. You have the power to turn this whole thing around. We know she manipulated you both, and now she's dead. Let this whole nightmare die with her, Zac. I promise Jose and I will do everything we can to help. For Christ's sake, don't go down with the ship!"

Zac slammed his fist down on the counter, startling both Erin and Angela, and causing the baby to cry for the first time since their arrival.

"I don't want to hear any more. I'm going outside to think. And I don't want you two talking. Do you understand me?"

"Yes, I understand," Erin answered, aware she'd said all she'd be allowed to. Hopefully, it had given him some food for thought anyway.

"I'm going to tie you back to the bed. I'll let you out for lunch."

Zac didn't tie the knots as tightly this time, leaving her some room to move, but not enough to get loose. He didn't offer any conversation as he left the room.

The baby's cries were silenced now, and Erin strained to hear any conversation. The words were muffled, but she could make out Zac's last sentence before shutting the front door behind him. "I'm sorry, Angela, but we're going to have to do away with our hostage."

Chapter 53

"Well, Superintendent Simpson was helpful," Graham said as he placed his office phone back on the receiver. "Seems old Harry is a piece of work. He's spent most of his life in and out of the system, and is a thorn in their side, to put it mildly. Simpson's going to pull his file and get back with me, apparently within the hour. Can't ask for much more than that."

"I want to see him, Cap," Jose said flatly. "I want to be the one to tell him that his sick, twisted daughter is dead with a slug in her heart."

"I think you're taking this a little too far, Ramirez. I know you're concerned about the Sommers girl, but we'll find her. We have to work smart."

"*Concerned?* Are you fucking kidding me? Do you know what they may do to her? This is *personal!*"

"Well, make it not personal, and I mean immediately, or I'll take you off this case quicker than you can spit. Do you understand? We don't have the time or energy for renegades. We're close, don't fuck it up."

Jose's face turned a deep red, but he knew when to shut up. There were times he could push the Captain, but this wasn't one of them.

"I have to say I agree with Ramirez," Chatham said, looking up from the computer screen for the first time. "We need to be face-to-face with Mr. Spriggs when he learns of his daughter's death, just as we're going to do with the mother. There's something about the element of surprise to get Intel we might not get otherwise."

"I agree with that theory too, Chatham, but he's four hours away. That's four hours we can't spare."

"It's not four hours away by chopper," Chatham said. "I bet the WSP would jump at the chance to fly us down there."

"You've got to be kidding," Graham chuckled. "They have over six hundred officers. They don't have time for the Sierra Hills's PD."

"I think he's onto something, Cap," Jose piped up. "The State Police can't possibly have anything of this magnitude. Just stroke their egos and get our asses to Clallam Bay. Who gives a rat's ass if they get the credit?"

Graham stood and walked over to the window again, pondering the possibility of Ramirez and Chatham actually interviewing this prick face-to-face. It could work, but it could also backfire. Either way, he knew he had to take the chance.

"I'm not thrilled with the idea, but I'll get Major Kensington on the phone. He'll have to coordinate this with the WSP and Clallam Bay. I'd be way out of line to try to coordinate something on that scale by myself."

A light tap on the door was followed by Detective Porter stepping through the doorway. His glasses were making another desperate attempt to cling to the tip of his nose, and Jose's first thought was how in the hell he stayed so wiry thin. Every time he saw the man, he had something from the vending machines in his hand. This time wasn't an exception, and Ramirez looked on as he took a bite of a heavily iced honey bun.

"What is it, Porter?" Graham barked impatiently. "We're dealing with some important stuff right now."

He finished chewing the bite of pastry in his mouth then his big Adam's apple wiggled up and down as he swallowed. It made Chatham shiver.

"Sorry, Cap," he said with a lazy grin. "Chief Abbott's here from Fairfield. He's asking for you."

"I can't do it all, Fellas," Graham said to Jose and Chatham, waving them in the direction of the door. "Handle this one while I put in that call to Major Kensington." He thought of telling them how important this interview would be, but thought better of it. Thankfully, these were detectives he didn't have to babysit.

The two men followed Porter's scant frame into the lobby where they found the Chief and a very unkempt, hung-over Harriett Spriggs.

"Chief Abbott," Ramirez said as he extended his hand. "Very nice to meet you. I can't thank you enough."

"Pleasure's all mine," he answered. "We colleagues in blue have to look out for each other."

Jose looked at the man in front of him. He wasn't at all what he'd expected. In fact, he'd imagined a fat, jovial man who ran a small-town police department similar to Mayberry. Instead, the man before him was tall and muscular, with thick salt and pepper hair, and a starched uniform. He exuded professionalism, and for a moment, Ramirez had a pang of guilt.

"At any rate, you're a busy man, and that was quite the drive for you. We don't have many other agencies that'd cooperate with us to that extent."

"As I said, I'm happy to do it."

Jose motioned for him to step into the hallway with him and pointed Chatham in the direction of some metal chairs to lead Mrs. Spriggs to.

Once they were out of earshot, Ramirez questioned the Chief. "Has she sobered up?"

"Yeah, she's much better. We got some black coffee and a sausage biscuit down her. She slept the whole way here."

"Does she suspect anything?"

"No, I don't think so. She's mad as an old wet hen though. She didn't appreciate being taken out of that filth she lives in," he said, shaking his head in disgust.

"She's awfully thin. Does she do any drugs that you're aware of?"

"From the looks of her place, just alcohol. Cheap vodka. I couldn't count all the empty bottles strewn throughout the apartment."

"Damn, what a miserable life. Listen, we appreciate your time. We can take it from here. I'll get one of our officers to take her back home when we've finished questioning her."

"I don't mind waiting around. There's no reason to tie up one of your guys when I've got to go back that way anyhow."

"All right then. How'd you end up in Fairfield?"

"I retired from the State Police two years ago. I'm divorced and didn't have anything to do with my time, the city needed a Chief, and so I figured what the hell."

"I suppose you can't find a safer job than Fairfield, huh?"

This brought a hearty laugh from Abbott as he smiled in agreement. "Nothing ever happens there. Gets a little mind numbing so I jumped at the chance to get out of town for a few hours."

"Hey, do you have any connections with the department that schedules WSP's choppers? We're trying to get one from here to Clallam Bay later this afternoon. Mrs. Spriggs' husband is there and we want to interview him. I'm sure you understand our time constraints. We have a hostage situation going on."

A broad grin spread across his face. "As a matter-of-fact, I do have a few connections."

"Would you mind speaking with our Captain? I'm sure he'd welcome the help."

"I'd love to."

Jose instructed Daniel to take Harriett into one of the vacant interview rooms and walked Chief Abbott to Graham's office. *Just maybe things are coming together,* he thought.

Harriett Spriggs sat defiantly at the laminated table in the cool, nondescript room. She was, at the least, disinterested and angry about being driven two hours to a police department she knew nothing about.

Daniel Chatham studied the woman in front of him. If he wasn't already aware that she was sixty years old, he would've sworn she was eighty. She was rail thin, her hair a dull shade of light brown mixed with gray.

She didn't have any makeup on, and there didn't appear to be any remnants from the night before. Her skin and eyes were tinged with yellow, suggesting jaundice, or even worse, Cirrhosis. She held an unlit cigarette between her index and middle fingers and had thick glasses perched on top of her head.

Ramirez came into the room and took a seat across the table from her and next to Chatham. Harriett Spriggs looked at him with disgust.

"Are either of you idiots gonna tell me why the hell I was drug here from the comfort of my own home? The last time I checked, this was the United States, not communist Russia."

"Actually, Russia freed itself from communism in 1991," Chatham said nonchalantly.

"Impressive," Jose said as he reached over and patted his friend on the back.

"Just a bunch of smart-asses!" Harriett sneered. "I don't have time for this shit."

"Oh, I'm sorry," Jose interrupted. "Are we infringing on your vodka time? It is five o'clock somewhere, I suppose."

"Get me an attorney. I don't have to take this shit."

Jose kneed Chatham under the table, signaling for him to take the lead.

"Mrs. Spriggs," Daniel began. "What can you tell me about your husband?"

"That's what this is all about? I don't know anything. He's locked up and has been most of our marriage. Sorry piece of shit left me with all the bills and raising our young-uns. Hasn't ever done nothin' for me."

"What has he done that's had him incarcerated for so long?"

"You aren't fooling me, you know exactly what all he's done. You're the cops, and you can find out all that. He never was a faithful man, never."

"So, he's locked up because he was *unfaithful?*"

"Girls these days think they can lead a man on, tease him with their skimpy clothes, then get pissed when he's interested in 'em. They get what they deserve in my opinion." She lifted the cigarette and asked for a light.

"Public building, Ma'am," Jose said. "No smoking allowed."

"I ain't no lawyer, but I do know you can't keep me here against my will unless you arrest me. So, I suggest you light this cigarette, or I'm outta here."

Jose knew they'd have to let her smoke if they expected to keep her in the building, so he pulled a lighter from his front pocket. She leaned forward and inhaled deeply as she lit her smoke.

"You had the Chief drive me all the way from Fairfield just to question me about my old man?"

"Actually, we're here to deliver some bad news to you," Daniel said softly. "Is Sally Spriggs your daughter?"

The mention of Sally's name instantly got her attention, and her eyes opened wide with panic. "What's the matter with my Sally? I know she ain't in any trouble, she's a good girl."

For a brief moment, Detective Chatham pitied her. Once he shared the news of Sally's death, Harriett Spriggs would never be the same. He wanted desperately to hand the conversation over to Ramirez, but knew it'd be the easy way out, and he couldn't fold now.

"Mrs. Spriggs, I'm afraid your daughter's dead."

The two detectives knew the mother wasn't going to handle the news well, but certainly weren't prepared for the reaction that followed. Her facial expressions went blank for a brief moment, then before either man could react, Harriett Spriggs leaped across the table and wrapped her hands around Chatham's neck.

Chatham was gasping for air as Ramirez tried desperately to pry her old, thin hands from his throat. He hated to hurt the woman, but if she didn't release his partner soon, it'd come to that. He wasn't making any headway with her hands, so he grabbed her tightly around the waist, pulling with all his might. Jose and Harriett both ended up on the floor while Chatham gagged and clawed at his red neck.

"You crazy bitch!" Chatham spat in between coughing spells. "What the hell is wrong with you?"

"You're a liar!" Mrs. Spriggs screamed. "A fucking, low-down liar! I won't listen to you. I want out of here!"

By this time, everyone in the precinct had heard the commotion. Captain Graham and Chief Abbott both came rushing through the door and tried their best to calm her.

This only seemed to further fuel the fire and Harriett began flailing her arms and grabbing at anyone within her reach. It was then that Captain Graham did something no one in the police department had ever seen him do, he remained calm. Instead of fighting her, he simply put his arms around her in a firm embrace and spoke softly to her.

"Mrs. Spriggs, it's going to be okay. Shh, shh," he continued as he rubbed her unkempt hair. "Sit down and let me get you something to drink. We'll talk about this, okay?"

Her body instantly relaxed, then went limp from the sheer exhaustion and surprise of it all. Graham eased her down onto the nearest chair and squatted beside her.

"Chatham," he said in the same soft voice. "We need a wet rag and a cold soda. Can you get those for me please, quickly?"

"Yes, Sir, I'm on it."

Jose watched as Graham pulled a pressed, white handkerchief out of his pocket and handed it to Harriett. She gently dabbed her eyes and wiped her nose. Her breathing was slowing to a normal rate, and the tears were beginning to dry.

371

"I don't understand. She can't be dead. She's a beautiful, healthy girl. How can she be gone? This has to be some kind of mistake. I want to see her. I want to see her now!" she demanded, her voice starting to rise again.

"Mrs. Spriggs," Graham continued, gently placing his hand on her forearm. "We'll let you see her soon, I promise. She's been transported, and we'll get you to her as soon as possible. We have a few questions for you first. We need your help."

"What?" she asked, her voice barely above a whisper. "How can I help you? Please, tell me what happened to my baby. I have to know what happened to her."

Jose realized the Captain was struggling with how he was going to break the cause of Sally's death to her. He seemed grateful for the momentary distraction of Chatham returning with the soda and rag.

"Here," Graham said. "Have a sip of soda and put this cool rag on your face. We'll answer all of your questions, one by one." He rose and sat in the chair next to her while her shaking hands lifted the drink to and from her mouth.

"I'm sorry to tell you that your daughter was shot yesterday."

The four men paused for it to register with her, then waited for her to go back into the hysterics they'd witnessed earlier. She inhaled a big breath of surprise and covered her face with the rag.

"Who on earth would shoot her? Was it a robbery? She had a good job, you know. She was a nurse, a real one, not just one of those people that clean bedpans."

"Yes, we're aware she was a nurse, and according to her boss, a very good one."

His use of the term *was* seemed to start the tears flowing again.

"I can't say that I know how you feel, I can only imagine how tough this has to be. I need you to be strong for me right now, okay?"

She answered with a nod of her head, hiding her face behind the rag again.

"Do you know Zac Gellar, Mrs. Spriggs?"

Moving the rag away from her face, her expression mirrored confusion. "Why, yes. He's married to my daughter Angela. Don't tell me he killed my Sally."

"No, Ma'am, he didn't. We have reason to believe he's the serial killer we've been chasing." Graham paused to let it sink in and watched for her reaction. He got nothing, just an honest look of confusion.

"No way, not that kid. He's a damn wuss, wouldn't hurt a fly."

"Apparently, he had us all fooled. We have a witness who confirms Sally was his accomplice." Again, a few seconds passed as everyone in the room held their breath.

Harriett Spriggs looked Graham in the eye. "Your witness is a liar. I want to see my daughter now."

"As I promised you earlier, I'll take you to her in a few minutes. Please, just answer a few questions. We need to get to the bottom of this, and if you believe these two are innocent, we're going to need your help."

She folded the wet rag, placed it on the table, and took a long sip of the soda.

"Fire away, ask me anything you want to," Harriett Spriggs said as she sat up straight in the metal chair and looked Graham in the eye.

Chapter 54

Dr. Ken Malone got back to his office, gladly took off his suit and tie and donned his medical scrubs. He'd never felt comfortable in anything buttoned to his throat, so he only wore a tie when absolutely necessary. Thankfully for him, that left only a few occasions, such as meetings with his bosses and times he was required to testify in court.

He buzzed his secretary and asked her to have Jeffrey, his morgue attendant, prepare the area for Sally Spriggs' autopsy. Malone had expected to perform the procedure much earlier, but wasn't anticipating his meeting with Easton to take so long.

He reached for his mug and stopped by the coffee maker on the way down the hall, taking a minute to savor a few sips of the strong hot brew. Sleep hadn't come easy the night before, and his body felt it now.

As always, Jeffrey was busying himself with laying out the variety of instruments for Sally's autopsy. Malone noticed his attire had been carefully laid out for him, so he set his coffee cup down and started dressing. First the scrub suit, then the surgical gown, shoe covers, and finally the surgical mask that he pushed up on the top of his head for now. He'd put on the required two pair of surgical gloves when he was ready to begin.

Jeffrey wheeled the gurney in with Sally's body, and Malone walked toward her, putting on his gloves as he made his way over. His assistant was a fairly young man, probably in his early thirties, and extremely thorough and professional. Malone often thought Jeffrey could perform any autopsy himself. He'd encouraged him more than once to continue his education, but it seemed to fall on deaf ears. Today's efforts were no exception as Malone's young charge unzipped the body bag and began the gamut of X-rays performed on the body before removing it from the plastic. He slapped the pictures on the lighted wall for Malone to peruse while he transferred the body to the aluminum table for the external and internal exam.

"Looks like we'll find the slug there in the chest cavity," Malone said as he looked over the X-rays. "I figured that since the detectives couldn't locate it at the scene. It appears to match the weapon. Open and shut case, just as I figured."

He made his way over to the body and shook his head at the scene. Sally Spriggs had been a beautiful young lady, and he understood how she could've fooled so many people. "The picture of innocence," Malone said aloud. "Who would've ever thought?"

Jeffrey didn't respond to the comments. He never did. Always the consummate professional, he busied himself with taking photos and supplying his boss with whatever instrument was required. As suspected, a slug through the heart was the cause of death. Otherwise, Sally Spriggs was the picture of health.

"Well, I'll be damned," Malone said. "Didn't see this coming."

Jeffrey was drawing blood for the toxicology reports but turned and moved over to where the doctor was working. "What ya got, Doc?"

"Seems like our little murderer was pregnant. My educated guess is twelve weeks, making the fetal age about ten weeks." Even in his professional mode, this always saddened Malone. He reached down and removed the fetus, deciding to use the moment to educate Jeffrey. They didn't often see this type of thing, thank goodness. "The skin is still very translucent, but the eyelids are already covering the eyes. Toenails and fingernails are apparent and soft. Fetus is 2.5 inches long."

Jeffrey turned away, having never said a word, and documented the condition and length of the small embryo.

"Just a damn shame," Malone said softly. "But then again, what would that poor child have endured had it been born to an evil mother like that?"

Chapter 55

Harriett Spriggs had sobered up and built up an emotional wall to the death of her daughter. Her main agenda now seemed to be proving her daughter's innocence.

"Mrs. Spriggs," Chatham asked, still a little skeptical she may jump up and attack him again. "Do you know of any reason why your daughter may have plotted to murder these young women?"

"Absolutely not. She would never have done such a thing."

"Could you tell us a little about her? Who were her friends? Where did she spend her spare time?"

"She worked," Mrs. Spriggs stated flatly. "She worked and went home. Before that, she studied all the time. All she ever wanted was to be a nurse."

Chatham glanced over at Ramirez as he remembered her telling them she'd simply chosen nursing because she'd failed at everything else.

"Tell us about her roommate," Jose chimed in. "I remember her telling us she'd committed suicide in college."

This subject clearly hit Harriett from left field, and her shock didn't go unnoticed. "How do you know about that?" she demanded.

"Is this a touchy subject?" Ramirez continued to probe. "That seems to be Sally's reason for going to work at Lobale, to help those that'd been abused and sexually assaulted."

"That's a crock of shit!" Mrs. Spriggs shouted. "That girl was a liar!"

Chatham felt the hairs on his neck standing up, but he knew they were onto something and had to get to the bottom of it. They'd have to tread lightly on this one. "I'm sorry," he quickly interjected. "We must've gotten the story wrong from her employer," he fibbed. Now was not a good time to let her know they knew Sally. She wouldn't take it well. "What was her college roommate's name? Maybe we could look into the situation and quickly clear this up."

"You don't need to look into it. She's a liar, simple as that."

"What exactly did she lie about?"

"My poor Henry. She lied about Henry," she said, her hands instantly flying to her mouth as she gasped.

"Is Henry your son?" Jose asked.

"This ain't got nuthin' to do with Henry. I said I'd talk to you about Sally, that's it."

"Okay, we'll get back to Sally. Can you give us her roommate's name? Maybe *she* framed your daughter," he suggested.

"She didn't frame nobody, she's dead. Killed herself cause she couldn't deal with the guilt of lying about my boy."

"What was her name?"

"Carson, Carson Jennings, or something like that. I said I ain't talking about it no more."

Jose could see Chatham scribbling the name on his pad and knew they were onto something, although he couldn't put his fingers on it yet.

"Did your daughter have any good friends?"

"No, I already told ya. Just work."

"How was her relationship with Zac Gellar?"

"Relationship? She hardly had any contact with her sister, much less her husband."

"So, she wasn't very close to Angela?"

"Not at all," Harriett said as she rolled her eyes. "That Angela's one weird cookie."

Jose looked up at the three other officers in the room, then back at Mrs. Spriggs again. "But, isn't Angela your daughter too?"

"Yep. Never acted like the rest of the family though. She was a homely girl, always has been. Never cared about how she looked like Sally did. Never had any friends until she met Zac. He's just about as homely as she is, maybe that's why they hit it off."

Jose couldn't believe his ears. *How could a mother feel this way about her own child?* "Did Angela ever give you any trouble?"

"Nope. Hardly even knew she was around. Sally would get mad at her for not trying to go to college, but Angela didn't care. She got with that family of Zac's, and that's all she cared about. That and having a baby. We were all kinda embarrassed of her."

Ramirez felt sick to his stomach. He wanted to ask this cruel mother what would ever make her think she was better than Angela. "From what we understand, she and her husband were hard, honest workers. Have you seen your grandchild?"

"Nope, ain't had time."

"Been too busy drinking?" Jose asked before he could stop himself.

"That's it," she said, standing to her feet. "I'm done with all of you. I demand to see my daughter now."

"Chatham," Captain Graham said. "You and Ramirez take her down to Malone's office. We need an official ID on the body anyway. Chief Abbott, you can follow them over if you want to, then you can carry Mrs. Spriggs home from there. We won't be needing her assistance anymore."

Chapter 56

Dr. Easton drank two cups of coffee and took an aspirin to ease his throbbing head. The news of Sally Spriggs' death had both shocked and troubled, him. He'd been quite fond of the young nurse and still refused to wrap his head around the fact that she could've been involved in something so sinister. He'd always prided himself on his judgment of character, but he had clearly failed on this one.

He rubbed his temples and took another sip of coffee before opening the personnel file Human Resources had hand-delivered to him. It reflected all that Sally had shared with him in her employment interview, her transcripts from South Seattle Community College, and Washington State University, along with her RN certificate from the State. Obviously, any documents *could* be altered, but these didn't appear to have been. Her grades hadn't started off well but had gotten increasingly better through the years. The doctor made a notation of her current address on his notepad and struggled to place the apartment complex, but wasn't sure where it was located. Pressing the intercom button on his phone, he asked Emily to come to his office.

"Hi, Dr. Easton," Emily chirped as she poked her head into his office. "What can I do for you?"

"Emily, thanks for coming right over. Do you have a few minutes?"

"Sure, I'm covering the front today, but Jarrod's watching it for me to take a break."

Dr. Easton motioned with his right hand for her to take a seat. "Please, make yourself comfortable. This may seem a little strange, but what do you know about Sally Spriggs?"

"Sally? Well, not much. None of us knew her very well. She was very, um, how should I put this, *guarded*."

"I knew her to be a very competent nurse and I suppose that's all I look for in an employee. I never noticed her being guarded."

"You knew her to be?"

"Pardon me?"

"You said *knew* her, as in the past tense. Has something happened to her? That doctor who visited earlier said he needed to talk to you about an urgent matter."

Dr. Easton stammered around for the right words. He'd assured the Medical Examiner that he wouldn't share the story. "I'm afraid that something has happened to her," he said. "But, I'd appreciate it if you'd keep it under your hat for the time being. There's an ongoing investigation of some kind."

Emily's face reflected the same expression his had worn just a few hours earlier. "I don't understand."

"I don't either, Emily. I'll let you know when I get more details. Right now, I'm just trying to see if anyone here was close to her."

"I can't think of anyone, Dr. Easton. I wish I could help."

"Thanks, Emily. That'll be all, and again, please don't share this with anyone."

She closed the door quietly behind herself, leaving the doctor to wonder if she, too, was not who she appeared to be. Disappointed he hadn't discovered anything that could be of assistance to the investigation, he closed the employment folder, then decided to open it once again. Someone had to be listed on her emergency contact form.

Chapter 57

Chatham and Ramirez were grateful to have a few minutes alone in the cruiser without the evil and self-centered Harriett Spriggs. She'd gladly decided to ride to the morgue with Chief Abbott, whom she believed to be more supportive than the two tyrannical Sierra Hills detectives.

"Can you believe that woman?" Chatham asked.

"Yep, pretty big bitch, huh?" Jose quickly added. "What kind of mother talks about her child like that? I don't know how Angela's involved in this, but she has to be warped from being raised by *that* woman. What a shame."

"I can only imagine the abuse Angela suffered under Sally," Chatham said sadly. "Oh, to be the ugly duckling."

"What would you know about being the ugly duckling?" Ramirez asked sarcastically. "Give me a break."

"I think we may have a lead with the roommate. Mrs. Spriggs was visibly upset when we mentioned her."

"Yeah," Jose said, opening his memo pad. "Carson Jennings is her name. We've got to check that out. Something in the milk isn't clean there. We need to find out more about the brother, too."

"I bet you dollars to doughnuts that he's a sex offender just like his dad. We need to pull his record. I have a strong feeling the roommate wasn't lying about him raping her."

"But why kill herself?"

"We don't know that she did," Chatham said. "She may be alive and well for all we know. Malone should have the autopsy records if she did commit suicide. I bet he has Henry Spriggs' as well. We may be getting closer to answers than we think."

* * * *

Ramirez got out of the undercover car and hobbled into the morgue alongside Chatham. The throbbing in his leg was always present now, and he was learning to live with it. Harriett Spriggs had pulled her rat's nest of a hairdo into some form of a ponytail and was leaning heavily on Chief Abbott's right shoulder.

"I just don't believe something has happened to my beautiful Sally," she mumbled over and over again. "It just can't be true."

Jose tapped the bell at the information desk and waited on Malone to come out to meet them. He walked up in a couple of minutes, looking like he hadn't slept in a week.

Dr. Malone nodded at each of the men before speaking to Harriett Spriggs.

"I understand you're Sally's mother," he said kindly as he reached out his hand to meet hers. This was a side of him the two detectives hadn't ever seen before.

"Yes, I am," she answered before breaking into hysterical sobs. "That can't be my baby in there. It just can't."

Malone pulled up a chair and sat next to her, taking her hand into his own. "Mrs. Spriggs," he said gently. "This is never easy, but I'm going to tell you what it'll be like. We can do this one of two ways, either you can view a photograph of her that's been taken here, or I can take you to a viewing area where you can see her through a window.

390

This isn't going to be a gruesome scene. She looks very much the same as she did before this accident. There isn't any blood or damage to her body. She'll be covered with a sheet up to her neck. Sally looks very much as though she's sleeping."

Mrs. Spriggs sat silent for what seemed an eternity, then turned and looked the doctor in the eye. "Can I be in the room with her? Can I hold her hand?"

"We can do that," he answered, but was quick to counter. "You might want to spend time with her after she's been prepared by the funeral home. We don't recommend it here."

"I want to see her. I want to hold her hand, just give me that."

"No problem, give me a minute and I'll send my assistant Jeffrey out to get you. Will someone be coming back with you?" he asked, looking hopefully at the Detectives then at the Police Chief.

"I'll go back with you, Mrs. Spriggs," Chief Abbott spoke up. "That is, if you want me to."

She nodded her head in agreement and covered her face with her hands.

"Very well then," Malone said, then stood to exit the entryway. "Jeffrey will be out shortly."

As promised, it wasn't long before Jeffrey came for the two of them. Ramirez and Chatham both heaved a collective sigh of relief that they'd be left behind in the waiting area.

Chief Abbott rested his hand on Harriett's back as they followed their guide down the thin hallway and into a small room with a gurney. Sally's body lay under the fluorescent white sheet and the anticipation was almost too much for all of them. Malone came in and shut the door quietly behind him.

"As I told you before, Mrs. Spriggs, Sally looks very much like she's sleeping. It's important that you try to maintain calm for us. I'm going to pull the sheet back now," he said, steadily unveiling the beautiful, yet sinister, young woman who lay beneath.

Much to everyone's surprise, Harriett didn't make a sound. She stood dumbfounded for a few seconds before reaching out and lightly touching her daughter's face. She stroked her full blonde hair, then asked to hold her hand. Jeffrey pulled the sheet back, just enough to reveal her small hand, and her mother held it tightly before patting it several times. It was a tender and heart-wrenching moment that Jeffrey and Malone had unfortunately witnessed many times before.

"That's my Sally," Harriett answered quietly. "That's her all right. What will happen to her now?"

"Her autopsy is complete," Malone answered. "Is there a funeral home you'd prefer? I can have my secretary phone them to transport her."

"I ain't got no money for a funeral," she said flatly, the tender emotion now turned to stone. "You can't get blood from a turnip."

Dr. Ken Malone never missed a beat. "I understand your daughter was a nurse. I'm sure she had some form of life insurance. We can check on that for you and see what can be done to assist with a funeral. Can you leave a number up front for us to reach you?"

"Yeah, sure," she stammered. "You gonna take me home now, Chief?"

The two detectives were standing in the lobby when Abbott and Harriett walked out.

"Can you think of anywhere Angela could be hiding, Mrs. Spriggs?" Ramirez asked.

"Screw you," she answered. "Screw *all* of ya."

Ken Malone was sitting in his office waiting on Ramirez and Chatham. It'd been an eventful day and it was still early.

"So, what did you make of that crazy mother?" Jose asked as he entered the office.

"I've seen it all by now," Malone answered. "Nothing surprises me anymore."

"How did the autopsy go?"

"Just as I suspected. Your girl made a clean shot to the heart. We found the slug in the chest cavity. I'm sure it'll match your weapon. She was an otherwise healthy girl, but there was one surprise."

"Yeah, what was that?"

"Little Miss Sally was twelve weeks pregnant."

"What?" Chatham stammered. "You can't be serious. How do you know that?"

Malone rolled his eyes. "We found the fetus, Chatham."

"How did that happen?"

"It usually happens when one partakes in sexual intercourse."

"Do you believe this, Ramirez?"

"Chatham, what are you so upset about?" Jose asked. "It's not like you two were an item. Damn."

"She never mentioned dating anybody."

"She never mentioned being an accomplice to a series of murders either."

The three men sat silent for a few minutes before Ramirez spoke again. "This could take us in another direction. The baby had to have a daddy. That means she did have some form of a social life. We've got to get into her apartment."

"Hold that thought," Daniel said as he answered his cell phone. "That was Cap. The helicopter will pick us up at the ball field adjacent to the precinct in an hour. We've got to head back."

"Wait a minute," Jose said, opening the memo pad the two detectives shared. "We need some info on a Carson Jennings, Malone. She supposedly committed suicide. She was Sally's roommate in college so they would've been around the same age. Probably happened three to four years ago. You autopsy every suicide, don't you?"

"Every suicide is autopsied, but you have to remember, our office doesn't autopsy everybody in the state. If she wasn't in this county, then another agency took over. What college was it?"

"Damn," Ramirez said. "What colleges did we pull up when we looked her up in the database, Chatham?"

"Hand me that pad," Daniel said, thumbing through pages of notes.

"You mean to tell me that the two of you *share* a notepad? Jesus, I can round another one up for you if the police department's budget is that tight. You're the two detectives on the biggest case this city has ever seen, and you *share* a pad. I've never seen anything like it."

"Hey, it works for us," Jose said without even looking up. "We need any info we can get on the girl ASAP. We also need some info on Henry Spriggs, who, according to the Gellars, also committed suicide a few years back. Warped family, what can I say?"

"I take it you don't have any information on his whereabouts at the time of his suicide either?" Malone asked sarcastically.

Jose wrote the names down on the next available page and tore it out for him. "Have I told you how much we appreciate you, Doc? We've got to meet this chopper. I'll call you if we get any more info, you do the same."

"I think I liked it better when we despised each other," Malone groaned.

Chapter 58

Erin laid quietly in the bed, straining her ears for any sounds of conversation. Zac had stormed out of the cabin and she hadn't heard him return. The ropes had her bound securely to the bed, and escape didn't seem imminent. Her only other option was to talk to Angela, who appeared to be the most vulnerable, and the least upset, over Sally's death.

She waited a few more minutes; the only audible sounds were her own labored breaths. The last thing Erin wanted to do was put Angela in any more danger. Zac was, or had been, a good man, but she wasn't sure how far he'd take things now. He was at the point of no return, and there was no way of knowing what his limits were.

"Angela, Angela," Erin whispered hoarsely. "Can you hear me?" She waited quietly for a few seconds, then decided to call a little louder. "Angela? Please come here. I want to talk to you."

"I'm here," she whispered as she stuck her head around the doorframe. "You have to be quiet. Zac would be furious with me for talking to you."

"I'll speak softly," Erin promised her. "Where did he go?"

"I'm not sure. He could be back at any moment."

"Is he going to hurt anyone else?"

"I don't know," Angela said, tears starting to slide down her pale cheeks.

"Could you untie me?"

"No, and don't ever ask me again. Zac would forbid it."

Erin could sense things taking a bad turn, and could've kicked herself for the brazen request. "I'm sorry. The last thing I want to do is cause problems with the two of you. I just don't want anyone else to get hurt, Zac included."

Angela quickly brushed the tears from her cheeks. "I have to get back to the baby. I can't get caught talking to you."

"I just want to help," Erin said in a desperate attempt to keep the conversation going. "Why did Sally get you involved in this?"

"We had to protect Trace. As soon as we learned he was a male, there was no other choice."

"I don't understand. Protect him from what?"

"The family curse."

"Family curse? Angela, curses don't exist. Is there some kind of medical problem that's hereditary in your family?"

"No. No, there isn't," she said calmly.

"Sally told me about your brother Henry. I'm really sorry he killed himself."

Angela didn't comment, but her gaze fell immediately to the floor. Erin decided to continue. "I don't know why his fiancé would do that to him."

"Fiancé? Henry was never engaged."

"But...?" Erin wasn't sure where to go from here. *Should she share what Sally had said to her?* "Sally told me Henry was engaged and his girlfriend decided to marry someone with more money. She reported that Henry stalked and raped her."

"Henry was never engaged to Sally's roommate."

"What happened, Angela? Please, talk to me."

She slowly pulled her glasses from her face and rubbed her eyes vigorously. "Henry was a bully, plain and simple, just like my father. He wanted every beautiful woman he could get, even if they didn't want him. I think he raped Sally's roommate." Angela put her glasses back on and looked Erin in the eye. "The poor girl killed herself. She couldn't live with it."

"I'm terribly confused now," Erin answered, attempting to sit up in the bed, but the ropes forbid it. "So, if you think Henry raped her, why are you and Zac killing all of these young girls? They're innocent victims, Angela."

"Sally had Zac convinced it's a family curse."

"Please, explain it to me. How is it a family curse?"

"Sally worshipped the ground Henry walked on. He was the oldest and quite handsome, just like our father. But, they were both arrogant and chased young women to a fault. Sally thought the two of them could do no wrong. She told Zac that with us having a son, he'd be framed by all the women of the world, just like the other males in our family. The two of them thought they could rid the world of beautiful, young girls before they started ruining men's lives."

"Angela…" Erin started, but failed to find the words. "You're a sensible woman. How could you have gone along with this? Especially if you knew your brother raped that young girl."

Her voice cracked for the first time, but she continued. "Zac was so proud to be a father. He was thrilled beyond belief to have a son. Sally was determined to take his joy. She polluted his mind."

"But, you, Angela. Why?"

"The truth is, I'm afraid Trace will turn out the same way. It's his destiny."

"His destiny is to become a rapist? Are you serious?"

"It's in our genes. My father, my brother, he won't be able to escape it."

"Angela, I'm no psychiatrist, but I did do a series on rapists a couple of years back. It's a learned behavior, not an inherited one. Trace doesn't have to end up like the two of them."

"I don't want to lose my husband. He's a good man. At least he was until Sally got a hold of him."

"Please, let me help you," Erin pleaded. "I don't want any of you to get hurt. This can all be blamed on Sally. We can build the evidence. She confessed to me!"

The two women heard a car door slam and Angela bolted to the bathroom where she immediately flushed the toilet, just as Zac came in the door. There were a few muffled sounds, but Erin could hear her talking.

"Zac, I've spilled the baby's formula. I'm going to have to go get some more."

"I don't know where to get any," he answered, "and the baby can't stay here with me. I'm afraid I won't be able to take care of him. He's too young to be out at a store. He'll catch all kinds of germs."

"I saw a Walmart a few miles back. I'll take him to my grandmother. He'll be getting fussy real soon without any food."

"Be careful. You shouldn't be out either."

"I'll hurry back. What about that girl?" she asked innocently.

"She's become too much of a liability. She's gotta go."

"Let me think about it while I go to the store," Angela added without missing a beat. "We need a good plan of how to get rid of her. Don't do anything in haste. Wait until I get back. I'll help you."

"I can't make any promises," Zac added. "We've got to make a move soon. I know Jose, he'll be on our trail."

"Oh God," Erin prayed. "I hope you know what you're doing, Angela."

Chapter 59

Jose and Chatham made it to the ball field before the chopper arrived and waited with Captain Graham and Major Kensington for its arrival.

"We're running out of time, Cap," Ramirez said. "I'm really worried about Erin. Zac has to be feeling like a caged animal by now."

"We'll be doing everything we can from this end," Graham answered. "You two get in and out of that prison as quickly as possible. We need you here, but that should go without saying. That worthless piece of shit isn't going to have any information for you, mark my words."

The conversation was abruptly ended as the helicopter came into view. "They'll give you guys an hour with your prisoner. Make the most of it. I now owe the WSP my firstborn. Don't make me regret it," Kensington said.

"We won't," Chatham screamed over the roar of the blades as he and his partner ran, heads bowed, to jump through the open door.

The sound was too loud to allow dialogue, leaving the detectives alone with their thoughts. Luckily, the ride was a relatively short one, and before they knew it, the helicopter was lowering itself onto the compound of Clallam Bay. The chopper's blades slowed then stopped, making the silence that followed a welcome one. Jose swallowed hard in hopes of clearing his ears.

"Okay, Fellas," the pilot said, "you're at your requested destination. You've got an hour to handle your business before this train leaves the station."

"Thanks, man," Chatham said. "We won't be late."

Several correctional officers were headed their way, shotguns in hand. "You must be from Sierra Hills," the largest of the men said.

"Detective Ramirez," Jose said. "We appreciate the assistance."

"Anytime, I'm Officer Neal. We're happy to help. Follow me and I'll take you to Superintendent Simpson's office. He's waiting for you."

The detectives jogged alongside the others at a steady pace, making their way across the complex. As the main entrance came into view, the others veered to the right and disappeared in the distance. Neal slowed to a walk and led them through the large, double doors that opened to the prison's main lobby. He waved at a young man sitting at a desk beside a large metal detector.

"What's up, Milton?"

"Not much, how about you?"

"I'm headed to Simpson's office with these two detectives. They're on a tight schedule so let's get them through as soon as we can."

"No problem. Name's Howard Milton," he said as he nodded his head by way of a greeting. "I'll need your driver's licenses if you don't mind."

Both men opened their wallets, handing them over quickly.

"I take it you don't have any weapons on you?" he asked.

"Nope," Chatham answered. "We were told to leave everything on the chopper."

"Most people think it's odd we can't carry weapons in here," Officer Milton said. "The truth is, it wouldn't do us much good. There's always going to be more prisoners than ammo, know what I mean?"

"Yep," Ramirez said, clearly uninterested in the policies and procedures of the prison. His mind was on Harry Spriggs and how he could help them get Erin home safe and sound.

Milton logged the driver's license info on a form, then placed them in a drawer for safekeeping. "We'll have these ready for you when you come out. If anything goes down, we'll know you're back there."

"That's comforting," Jose said flatly.

He waved them through the metal detector in a single file line, the only thing going off was Chatham's expensive belt buckle. Two sally ports later, they were at the Superintendent's office.

An attractive secretary sat behind a polished desk and smiled kindly as they entered. "You must be the detectives that Superintendent Simpson has been expecting," she said. "Please follow me, he's ready for you."

They walked into the office to find Simpson busy on the phone. He motioned for them to take a seat across from him as he finished his conversation.

"Nice to meet you, Gentleman," he said as he stood from behind the desk. "I haven't talked to that Captain of yours in years. Damn fine fellow."

"We can't thank you enough for your assistance, Sir," Chatham said. "This has been an extremely difficult case, but we believe we're closing in on it now."

"Damn glad to hear it. I understand you're in a rush, so let's walk on back. I have Spriggs waiting for you in a room designated for attorney's visits. He's cuffed and shackled, of course, and Officer Neal here will be with you the whole time. Unfortunately, I have prior arrangements, so I won't be staying with you. Another meeting about the damn food in this place. Go figure. That's all these men think about."

"No problem," Jose answered. "We won't be here long. He'll either help us or he won't."

"Not to burst your bubble," Simpson said, "but I don't expect the son-of-a-bitch to do anything but toy with you. I wish you luck though."

The men rapidly made their way through the cavernous hallways and sally ports to a room far from the prison blocks. A guard waited outside and another on the inside. Each exchanged pleasantries with their boss then Simpson was gone. Officer Neal excused the man from the room, leaving just himself, Jose, Chatham, and Harry Spriggs, who offered little more than a smug smile for his visitors.

Jose took a minute to familiarize himself with the inmate before them. Surprisingly, he was quite a handsome man, and in good shape for his age. He looked at least ten years younger than he was, and taut muscles bulged from under his state-issued T-shirt. Thick, dark brows were a contrast to his bright blue eyes, and his dark hair showed no signs of graying. The only sign of his years behind bars was the prison tattoos covering his brawny arms.

The distraction of being face-to-face with Harry took Jose's mind off of Erin for an instant, but his anger over her abduction swiftly returned. "Well, well, Mr. Spriggs," he said coldly. "Have I got some news for you."

Chatham held his breath. There was just no way of predicting how Ramirez would handle this interview, and his insides were churning.

"Unless you're here to tell me I'm getting out of this hellhole, I couldn't give a rat's ass what you got to tell me," he sneered, revealing teeth that hadn't been well cared for through the years.

"Oh, I'm certainly not the bearer of good news, and you're far from being released," Jose said, laughing a little too long and too loud for Chatham's taste.

"Officer, take me back to my cell," Spriggs demanded. "I don't give a shit what this man has to tell me."

"You may want to wait around for this," Neal suggested.

Spriggs looked up and met Jose's eyes. "What the hell do you want with me?"

"I want to know some of the places your daughters would hide if they were in trouble."

This brought a long, boisterous laugh from Spriggs. "Hide? Why the hell would either of them hide? You've got the wrong inmate, man."

"You're Sally and Angela's father, right?"

Harry brought his cuffed hands down hard on the table, startling the others. "What's this about?"

"There's a hostage situation. Lives are at stake. Where would your daughters hide?"

"There ain't no reason for them to hide anywhere! Sally's a nurse. She's a damn, smart girl. She don't have to hide from nobody."

"Why would you assume we're talking about Sally?"

"That other one ain't never even said two words, what would she know about hiding?"

"The other one? Are you referring to Angela?"

"Yep. Ain't very smart. Wouldn't figure her to have enough sense to get into anything."

"But, on the other hand, Sally would be your bet."

"I don't play games!" Spriggs yelled. "Whatever it is you're trying to say, just say it."

"Your murdering daughter is dead," Jose said through his teeth. "How's that for games, you good for nothin' piece of shit? Shot clean through her cold heart."

All of the color drained from Harry Spriggs' face as Chatham instinctively took a few steps back while his hands went up to his throat. He didn't want another replay of what happened with Sally's mother. Clearly, he and Ramirez should've prepared more for this interview.

"You're lying."

"And why would the State Police fly me here to lie to you?"

Spriggs looked up at Officer Neal, his eyes pleading. "These assholes are lying to me, ain't they? There ain't no way my Sally is dead."

The officer swallowed hard before confirming their story. "You know Simpson wouldn't allow anyone to come in here and lie to you about something like this."

The room remained silent for what seemed like hours before Spriggs spoke again. "What happened? Who'd kill such a good girl?"

The last thing Ramirez wanted to do was to soothe this felon's heart, and Chatham could sense it, so he took the reins. "Look, man, it appears she was involved in some murders we had back in Sierra Hills. It was her, Angela, and Angela's husband, Zac. Angela and Zac have left the area and taken a hostage. Her life's in danger. We need your help."

The three men were expecting nothing less than for Spriggs to spit in their faces, but he sat back and let the information sink in. "I can't believe Sally would do any of that. And besides, she didn't have nothin' to do with that sister of hers."

"What is it with Angela?" Jose quickly interjected. "Why is everyone so cruel to her?"

"I ain't got nothin' against the girl. She's just weird, not like my kids."

"What does that mean?" Chatham asked.

"It means she *ain't* my kid."

"I'm afraid I don't understand. She carries your last name."

"I know. That crazy mother of hers just told her she was mine like the other two. I was locked down at the time. You could prove that in a minute."

"So, who's her father?"

"I don't know and don't think her mother does either. I wasn't mad, hell, you can't expect a woman to be faithful when you're locked up."

"Well, that's interesting," Ramirez said. "That'd explain why she was so different."

"Yeah, *weird*."

"No, I mean *normal*. She just wanted to be a wife and mother. She was manipulated."

"I don't know a thing about any of that. I just know my Sally was beautiful, she was my heart. Smart, too."

"Yeah, beauty is skin deep, my friend. Tell me about Henry."

Spriggs leaned back in his chair and grinned, bearing his cavity-filled teeth again. "He was a good-looking kid, too. Quite the ladies' man."

"So we hear," Jose said snidely. "Rumor has it, he followed in your footsteps."

"What's that supposed to mean?" Spriggs said, his posture becoming erect.

Chatham quickly answered, "He was accused of rape by a friend of Sally's, according to your wife."

"Ah, that's a lie. Hell, any girl would've wanted a chance to be with my boy."

It was Jose's turn to take offense. "Damn, you and your wife sure are wrapped up in looks. So, humor me. What did Henry have that every young woman would want? Maybe he was a looker, I don't know, but what else did he have going for himself? What was his occupation for starters?"

"He did a little of this, a little of that. He made ends meet."

"So, if he had it so good, why the hell did he kill himself?"

Spriggs was on his feet in an instant. "Get me out of here! I'm done."

Officer Neal stepped toward him and waved Jose and Chatham back. "That's about all for today, Fellas. Sorry about that."

"Ramirez, step out for a sec," Chatham said, all but pushing his partner out of the room. When he had gone, and the door was shut, Chatham spoke quietly, but firmly. "Listen, Man, I apologize for my partner, he's a little on edge. I know you're going through a lot of emotions right now, but please, can you think of anywhere that Angela and her husband may have gone?"

Harry Spriggs plopped back down in the metal chair and wiped his face with his shirtsleeve. Perspiration had formed on his face, and his hair was soaking wet. His face was flushed, and he gasped for breath. "Screw you, man. I'm having a heart attack."

Chapter 60

"Well, you did one hell of a job," Chatham said snidely as the three men made their way back to the helicopter. "You gave the one man who could help us find Erin a heart attack. Graham was right, you're too close to this investigation."

Ramirez didn't respond. He'd blown any chances they had now and couldn't blame anyone but himself.

The chopper took off and landed back on the same ball field. The two detectives got back into their cruiser and neither spoke. The trip had been a terrible waste of valuable time, and time was something they had very little of.

"I don't even know where to go from here, Chatham. I've racked my brain. I don't know where else to look for her. The Gellars won't let us in Zac and Angela's place

417

without a warrant, which could take days, and we don't have any other leads."

Jose's cell phone rang and he pulled it from his back pants pocket. "Yeah?"

"It's Malone. Where are you guys?"

"Just got back from Clallam Bay, headed to the precinct."

"Stop by here first. I have some info for you."

"What have you got, Malone?" Chatham asked as he entered the ME's office.

"Got some interesting facts back from Carson Jennings's autopsy, a few red flags, if you will."

"Give it to us quickly. We've wasted enough time today," he said sarcastically, motioning his head in Jose's direction.

"Her death was ruled a suicide, but it was clearly a quick decision that could've benefited from some further investigation."

"Okay, break it down for us."

"For starters, she had a lethal dose of chloral hydrate in her system."

"What's that, exactly?"

"It's prescribed for short-term treatment of insomnia, and often used as a sedative before dental treatment. However, chloral hydrate has been utilized in some high-profile deaths. For starters, it was one of the ingredients in the Kool-Aid ingested in the Jonestown Massacre. Do you know about that, Chatham? It was a little before your time."

"Yes, I'm familiar with it. Thought it was cyanide though."

"Cyanide was used, along with valium and chloral hydrate. Chloral hydrate was also found in Marilyn Monroe's and Anna Nicole Smith's toxicology reports."

"Okay, so what makes it so strange? I wouldn't necessarily consider it a red flag if someone wanted to overdose."

"For starters, it's a very quick acting sedative. In therapeutic doses, it's effective for about twenty minutes. This high of a dose would've instantly sedated her."

"Okay, again, she overdosed and killed herself. I'm not following."

"Both of her wrists were slit."

"Okay, maybe she wanted to make sure she died."

"I would've assumed that too, but look at these photos of her injuries. They emailed them to me."

Chatham and Ramirez walked behind the desk to see the wounds.

"Those are pretty damn deep," Jose commented. "She wasn't taking any chances."

"Exactly," Malone said. "I've seen several deaths by young people slitting their wrists, and I've never seen any wounds that went this deep. In fact, I can't imagine a female being able to do it to herself. Besides, look closely at the two wrists side by side. The cuts are identical, which is difficult to do using different hands. The angles are the same, whereas using a left hand, for example, the wound would go from the right side of the wrist to the left side. That doesn't appear to be the case here."

"Interesting," Chatham said. "So, what you're saying is that someone else did this to her. She was sedated, then someone made it appear to be a suicide."

"That's exactly what I'm saying!"

"Well, if someone had done their job a few years ago, none of this would've happened. This is clearly some of Sally Spriggs' work. My guess is she was pissed at the roommate for exposing the rape. What is it with this Henry guy? Why did Sally and her parents worship him?"

"I pulled up his autopsy as well, although it wasn't easy. I've exhausted any future favors from the other ME's in the state. I'm not very popular right now."

"What did you find out?" Jose asked, consciously ignoring Malone's silent request for a pat on the back.

"You guys aren't going to believe this one. You might want to take a seat."

"Jesus, Malone. Spit it out. I'm exhausted, and I'm gonna have a heart attack myself if I don't get a lead on Erin soon."

"Henry Spriggs died from internal bleeding. He was found with a Henckels blade stuck deep in his gut!"

Chapter 61

Erin held her breath, fearing the worst. She could hear Zac as he paced back and forth across the kitchen floor. She was on borrowed time, and he could be plotting her death. If she was ever going to escape, the time was now. The knots were tied looser than before around her wrists, but they left little room to slip her hands through.

She closed her eyes as Zac could be heard making his way to her room. Struggling to keep her breathing calm and labored, Erin pretended to be in a deep sleep. Apparently, it'd worked. She could sense him looking at her, then heard him walk away and the water for the shower start. It was now or never, and she had little time to make it happen.

Taking a death breath, she made a mental note of her surroundings. The windows were nailed shut, and she was obviously tied too tightly to slip her hands through the knots. Her only other option would be to pry the antique bed's spindles from the headboard. She had considered it before, but feared it'd make too much noise. Erin pulled slowly on one at first, then jerked as violently as she could without causing too much of a racket. The spindle holding her left hand in place wasn't going to give, so she quickly changed to her right. Just when she was ready to break into sobs, she felt it give way. Sliding the rope down and freeing her hand, she swiftly untied the other.

The sounds of the water running still came from the bathroom, so Erin jumped up, grabbed her sandals, and made her way to the front door. Amazingly, it was unlocked. She opened it and ran with all she had. *Oh, for heaven's sake,* she thought. *Of all the days to pick sandals over sneakers!*

Making it to the small dirt road, she turned left toward the Everett's Supply Store. They'd be her only hope. She jogged as quickly as she could, knowing she'd have to make it the two or so half miles without completely giving out. The luxury of running along the roadway would soon have to be avoided because Zac would soon be getting out of the shower and would realize she'd escaped.

The brush beside the road was thick and would offer some cover, but the terrain was much more rugged than the road. Erin knew she needed to enter the woods. As she made her way off of the road, her heel got caught and she stumbled, falling hard on her knees before landing abruptly on her stomach. It knocked the breath out of her, and she spent several unnecessary minutes trying to get her composure back. She thought of ditching the sandals altogether, but reconsidered. She wouldn't make it far without them. Remembering a scene from a movie, she tugged at the heels until they broke off, leaving her with a strangely shaped sole that at least covered the bottom of her feet.

The branches and briars that cut at her face did little to discourage her. It felt like hours before she could make out the old building in the distance. "Please Lord, let me get there before Zac does. He'll surely kill the old couple this time."

She made her way closer to the road, listening for the sound of a vehicle coming before exiting the tree line.

Erin considered knocking on the door, but instead burst through it, allowing herself the luxury of sobbing uncontrollably. An older gentleman in overalls met her as she came bounding in and reached out to stabilize her.

"Oh my goodness, child," he said calmly. "What's happened to you?"

Erin was bent over, her arms wrapped around her waist, struggling to breathe. "Please, please. You have to help me."

"Come with me, dear, my wife's in the back. I'll get you some water."

She followed Mr. Everett through a curtained-off doorway in the back of the store. Her sobs weren't as intense now, so she allowed herself a moment of calmness.

"This is my wife," he said. "Honey, I'm going to get this young lady some water."

Mrs. Everett looked up and said, "Don't mind me, dear, I'm just rocking my grandson."

Erin's mouth fell open as she saw the shock of red hair on Trace's head.

Chapter 62

"Okay," Jose started, after taking a few seconds to let the initial shock of Henry's manner of death settle in. "The question here is whether it was suicide or a murder."

"My educated guess would certainly be murder," Malone answered. "Technically, he could've done it to himself, but from what you've told me, he was an extremely narcissistic person. First of all, I can't imagine a self-centered person taking their own life. And secondly, he wouldn't allow himself to suffer. As I've discussed with you two about the young girls' deaths, a deep cut to the liver, if left untreated, means imminent death. However, it's a slow and excruciating way to die. It also sounds like there are a number of people who wouldn't have minded killing him."

"Maybe Carson Jennings, the roommate, killed him and Sally killed her in retribution," Chatham said. "That would make perfect sense."

"Sally continued using the Henckels knives as a signature, a kind of a way of keeping Henry's sick legacy alive," Jose added. "She was a twisted woman. I understand how this all played out now, but I still don't get how Zac got involved and why?"

"That'd be the sixty-four-thousand-dollar question," Chatham said.

The ringing of Malone's cell phone interrupted the men.

"Yeah, Malone here."

"Yes, how are you, Dr. Easton?" Malone asked, looking up at Chatham to make sure the name registered with him. He nodded his recognition.

"Yes, we pulled up her education and state certification on the database here. Hmm. So, nothing unusual huh? No infractions of any kind at the University? That's interesting."

A few moments of silence followed. "Well, Dr. Easton, I appreciate your efforts. I'm sorry you didn't find out any more for us. Yes, yes, I understand. No, nothing is too insignificant." Another few seconds of silence on Malone's end. "Hmm, that's interesting and may be much more of a lead that you initially thought. Let me get off the phone here and share this with the investigators. I'll be back in touch. And, thanks so much again. I owe you one."

"What is it?" Ramirez said before Malone had even disconnected the call.

"Maybe you should sit down," Malone suggested for the second time of the day. "This is big, really big."

"You better tell us, Malone," Chatham said, reaching over to hold his partner at bay. "We've wasted several days, and we can't waste a second more."

"Dr. Easton didn't come across much more than we did as he reviewed Sally's personnel file. He'd all but given up when he decided to go back and check her emergency contact information."

"Who was it?" Jose screamed.

"She listed her grandparents from Whispering Hollow. Mabel and Josiah Everett."

Ramirez took Malone's words like a hard blow to the chest and fell back against the wall and onto a chair. "No, it can't be. It can't be."

"You know what this means," Chatham said, not taking any time to coddle his coworker and friend. "Zac has Erin at the cabin. We've got to get there now."

"It's two hours away," Jose said. "Let's get the chopper again."

"There isn't time to work out the logistics. I'll drive, you call Captain Graham and fill him in. He can get local and state authorities there before we can spit. Thanks, Malone. You're one hell of a guy."

Chapter 63

Erin tried to move her feet, but they remained stationary as though they were weighed down by cement.

"Don't worry, child," Mrs. Everett said. "We aren't going to hurt you. Angela? Angela, come on out."

"I'm sorry," Angela said as she came through a back doorway. "I was praying you'd escape. I had no choice but to risk leaving you there. I hope you understand."

"But, the Everetts," Erin stammered. "They're Jose's friends."

"Yep, coincidence really. They're my mother's parents, and outside of the Gellars, the only people who've ever been kind to me. Zac knew Jose long before he met me, but never knew he had a cabin right down from the store until he followed him here with his partner. He never wanted to hurt him."

Erin looked at the Everetts. "You're nice people, why are you involved in this?"

"They aren't," Angela said. "They didn't know anything about it until I got here a few minutes ago. They did know we were afraid for Trace, even before he was born. Neither of them had much to do with my siblings. They could sense they were bad seeds, just like our father."

"It can be over now, Angela. We can contact the authorities and stop this whole thing before Zac gets hurt. You haven't done anything. You can go free and raise your son."

"I have done something, Erin. I started this whole thing. I murdered my brother."

"What?"

"I couldn't help it. He was the devil, always hurting others, never cared about anyone but himself and Sally. He raped that poor girl in college. He tormented and threatened her until finally talking my sister into faking her suicide. The two of them were unstoppable, and I knew it'd only get worse. I did what I had to do. I stabbed him in the stomach with a knife that I had stolen from a restaurant where I was working. You should've seen his face. He couldn't believe it. Little, meek Angela had actually stood up to him. The knife went in deep, but he didn't die right away. I was so frightened that I couldn't remove it and stab him again, so I ran. I ran so hard that I still remember how badly my lungs burned. No one ever suspected me. After all, I was invisible."

"Did you tell your grandparents?"

The Everetts both nodded they'd long been aware of the murder.

"The way I figure it," Mr. Everett said softly, "is that Angela saved a lot of innocent folks from being hurt. We've never told a soul, not even her mama."

Erin shook her head, trying the digest the information she'd just been given. "But why all these new deaths? I don't understand."

"It's all been Sally. She decided to use the expensive Henckels knives to kill all of the women as a way of paying homage to Henry. She felt that each death, somehow, brought back a piece of him."

"But if you knew it was wrong, why'd you go along with it?"

"I didn't, but I couldn't stop Zac. Sally had him convinced that Trace would end up being framed by beautiful women and his life would end up just like Henry's. I'm not sure why he went along with Sally. I begged him, I pleaded with him. He's just not the same man I fell in love with."

"Yes, I'm still the man you fell in love with," Zac said from across the room. None of them had seen or heard him enter the supply house.

"Zac," Angela said, tears welling instantly in her eyes. "Oh, Zac, please, let's end this. I love you so much."

"I love you too, Angela. I never wanted to be a part of any of this, but Sally made me. She knew you'd killed Henry and she threatened to turn you in if I didn't go along with her. She said she had proof, and you'd spend the rest of your life in prison, away from me and our new baby. I couldn't take the chance."

Angela ran to Zac and collapsed into his arms. "I'm sorry, Zac. I'm so sorry."

The conversation was muted by the sound of the cavalry coming to rescue Erin.

Within seconds, the building was filled with law enforcement, and Zac and Angela were cuffed and placed in the back of two separate black Suburbans. EMTs wrapped Erin in a blanket and led her to an awaiting ambulance. *It was finally over.*

Epilogue

Erin, Jose, Malone, and Captain Graham sat in Chatham's den having a long overdue and well-deserved drink.

"I have to hand it you guys," Graham said. "You did one hell of a job."

"I recall you had a little to do with it, too," Ramirez said. "It seems like a lifetime ago when this all started. Remember the day the brass sent this green kid down to your office to help us?"

"I remember you could've spit fire," Graham laughed.

"Okay, enough of that," Chatham said.

"I have to hand it to you, Chatham," Jose said sincerely. "You turned out to be one hell of a cop and not a bad partner, either."

"I never thought I'd hear you say that. Makes me want to cry."

"Smart-ass. He's just a smart-ass, Cap."

"What do you think will happen to Zac and Angela?" Erin asked sadly. "What a horrible situation."

"We've been working with the DA. Zac will most likely spend a few years in a psychiatric hospital, but he'll be out before his son is grown. Angela will likely remain a free woman and will live with the Gellars. Because of all the publicity, they've decided to sell the business. They'll make enough to live well for the rest of their lives. I'm assuming they'll move away, where no one has heard of the story. Not the ideal situation, but could be a lot worse."

"Did anyone ever figure out where they were purchasing all of those knives?" Chatham asked. "That's really bugging me. I was sure we'd find a trail."

"Nope, we'll probably never find out. Zac said Sally delivered them to him, but as you know, we never found any receipts in her apartment."

"The irony of it all," Erin said, "was poor Angela was worried about her son inheriting the rapist characteristics, and Harry wasn't even her father."

"Yeah," Graham answered. "She was too good of a person to be grouped with that crazy bunch. Henry did follow in his father's footsteps, but not because of any screwed-up family genes. I'm grateful that my son Chad has never witnessed me being disrespectful to women. I may not have taught him a lot, but I did teach him to respect the opposite sex."

"Isn't it about time for Chad to graduate?" Ramirez asked.

"Yep, sure is. Irene and I are headed out to U.N.C. in two weeks to see him walk across the stage. She's proud as punch. I'm just grateful not to have to pay that tuition anymore. Maybe he'll be able to support himself on a teacher's salary."

That got a laugh from the group.

* * * *

Chad Graham walked across the lush green grass of the college campus without a care in the world. It'd been a combination of good and bad times, but his college career was coming to an end. He stopped and took a school newspaper from a freshman that was handing them out to students as they left the rehearsal for graduation. Unfolding it as he walked, he scanned the latest headline printed in bold letters:

"Campus Rapist Remains At Large."

He folded the paper back, grinned, and tossed it into the nearest trash receptacle. "You guys won't have that problem for long," he thought. Prince James' All-Girls Academy will be posting the same headline soon.

Chad's parents were on their way to the college, driving across the country to see him receive his diploma. He'd be glad to see them, but he had a few things to take care of first. He walked nonchalantly into his small dorm room and slid the shredder over next to his desk. He'd start with the Henckels receipts, then the letters from Sally, and finally, the congratulations card she'd sent to him about her pregnancy. *Yep, that should take care of everything.*

Other Works by Kim Carter

Sweet Dreams, Baby Belle

Murder Among The Tombstones

When Dawn Never Comes

No Second Chances

Deadly Odds

About the Author

Kim Carter is an author of contemporary mystery, suspense, and thrillers. She has won the 2017 Readers' Choice Award for Murder Among The Tombstones. This is the first book in her Clara and Iris Mystery series. Her other titles include: When Dawn Never Comes, Deadly Odds, No Second Chances, And The Forecast Called For Rain, and Sweet Dreams, Baby Belle.

Kim has been writing mysteries for some time and has a large reader fan base that she enjoys interacting and engaging with. One of her favorite things about writing mysteries is the research and traveling she does to bring her novels to life. Her research has taken her to places such as morgues, death row, and midnight cemetery visits.

Kim and her husband have raised three successful grown children. They now spend their time in Atlanta with their three retired greyhounds.

She is a college graduate of Saint Leo University, has a Bachelor Degree of Arts in Sociology, and now has become a career writer and author. Between reading and traveling, she will continue to write mysteries.

Get In Touch With Kim Carter:

Website: https://www.kimcarterauthor.com/

Made in the USA
Columbia, SC
25 March 2022

58157995R00269